IT'S NEWS
TO ME

Also by R. G. Belsky

The Clare Carlson Mysteries
Yesterday's News
Below the Fold
The Last Scoop
Beyond the Headlines

The Gil Malloy Series
Blonde Ice
Shooting for the Stars
The Midnight Hour
The Kennedy Connection

Other Novels
Loverboy
Playing Dead

Writing as Dana Perry
The Silent Victim
The Golden Girl
Her Ocean Grave
Silent Island

IT'S NEWS TO ME

A CLARE CARLSON MYSTERY

R. G. BELSKY

OCEANVIEW PUBLISHING
SARASOTA, FLORIDA

ISBN 978-1-60809-580-3

Published in the United States of America by Oceanview Publishing

Sarasota, Florida

www.oceanviewpub.com

10 9 8 7 6 5 4 3 2

PRINTED IN THE UNITED STATES OF AMERICA

As always, for Laura Morgan

"*Time shall unfold what plaited cunning hides.*"
—WILLIAM SHAKESPEARE
KING LEAR

"*I'm kind of a big deal. People know me.*"
—RON BURGUNDY
ANCHORMAN

IT'S NEWS
TO ME

PROLOGUE

She felt like someone was watching her.

Following her.

It was a strange sensation, and she was having it more and more recently. Right now, she tried to dismiss it as just paranoia or nerves from being alone on the darkened New York City street.

She hadn't lived in New York for a long time, but she felt comfortable in her ability to watch out for herself and stay safe here. She was a survivor. Always had been. She didn't scare easily.

Still, she began walking faster, toward the lights on the campus ahead of her. Her college and her dorm and all her friends were there. Yes, as soon as she reached those beckoning lights, everything would be all right.

Behind her, she thought she heard a noise.

She whirled around, but no one was there.

It wasn't until she turned back toward her destination again that she discovered her mistake.

Because, as she soon found out, the danger wasn't behind her.

It was right in front of her.

When the first blow hit her, she screamed and tried to run—but it was too late.

"Why?" she thought to herself a few minutes later as the life drained out of her. "Why are you doing this?"

It was the last thought Riley Hunt would ever have . . .

OPENING CREDITS

THE RULES ACCORDING TO CLARE

I LOVE TO tell the "Didn't She Used to Be Kathleen Sullivan" story to the young reporters who work for me at Channel 10 News. It goes like this:

Back in the 1980s, Kathleen Sullivan was the hottest thing in the TV news business. She hosted the nighttime updates from the Winter Olympics in Switzerland for ABC Sports, and she wore tight sweaters that everyone was talking about. The ratings went through the roof every time she wore one of those sweaters on air.

Then, after the Olympics, ABC brought her back and she substituted for Joan Lunden on *Good Morning America* for a few months while Joan was having a baby. More blockbuster ratings. Everyone in the media business wanted her now. Everyone wanted Kathleen Sullivan and her sweaters.

CBS News signed her for really big money—and with all sorts of publicity—to host the *CBS Morning Show*. Kathleen Sullivan sure seemed to be on her way to the top of the media world.

But then a few years later, after the ratings fell, she got fired by CBS and dropped out of sight for a while.

Later, she tried making a comeback on cable and doing commercials and radio and stuff like that.

I saw her at a broadcasting party once after all this had happened. Not many people recognized her anymore. But one guy finally did. He looked at her now, then turned to me and said, "Hey, didn't she used to be Kathleen Sullivan?"

Do you see the point I'm trying to make to young journalists here?

No, not that it's a good idea for women to wear tight sweaters on the air in the wintertime.

My point is that—in television news—you're only as good as today's show.

The other story that I tell them is a classic one that I've heard in the journalism business for years. I'm not totally sure if its apocryphal or not, but that doesn't really matter. Because the message is still a true one.

The story goes like this:

A reporter for a newspaper wins the Pulitzer Prize for an exclusive, blockbuster investigative story he writes, and so the newspaper throws him a big party afterward in the newsroom to celebrate.

Champagne corks are popped, toasts are offered, and everyone at the newspaper praises the reporter as the greatest thing to come along in journalism since Woodward and Bernstein with Watergate. It is the moment every reporter dreams about with a story. The ultimate triumph of a journalistic lifetime.

Then—amidst all the champagne and the toasts and the adoration—the reporter's editor pulls him aside and asks him: "So, what have you got for me tomorrow?"

Yep, the message here I'm trying to send to the young reporters who work for me is a pretty clear and a pretty obvious one.

It doesn't matter how big the last story was, you always have to do it again.

Nobody cares about yesterday's news.

Not in newspapers.

And even more so in the fast-paced world of television news where I work today.

That's an important rule every journalist always needs to remember.

Even me . . .

PART I

THE COLD OPEN

CHAPTER 1

I MET BRENDAN Kaiser, the owner of my TV station, Channel 10, and about a zillion other properties, for lunch on a sunny spring day at a restaurant called Tri-Bar in Lower Manhattan.

Tri-Bar is what's known in New York as a celebrity restaurant. In other words, whenever you read the gossip columns, there'll be an item about how "so and so said such and such over dinner last night at Tri-Bar . . ."

Robert De Niro sometimes ate there. So did Jimmy Fallon and Alec Baldwin and Julia Roberts when she was in town.

I'd been to trendy hot spots like this a few times to see if I could spot someone famous. Mostly all I ever saw were a lot of other people like me hoping to see if they could recognize anyone. The closest I ever came to a celebrity was when I ran into Sally Struthers once in the ladies' room of a restaurant on the Upper East Side. It had been a long time since Sally was a big star on *All in the Family*. My last memory of her had been doing those late-night infomercials about world hunger, and she sure didn't look much like Gloria Bunker anymore. I decided not to ask for her autograph.

There was some kind of a maître d' standing at the entrance to Tri-Bar. He wore a black tuxedo-like outfit, highly shined shoes, and white gloves. I had on a pair of tan Calvin Klein jeans, a chocolate-colored silk blouse, and beige sandals. I thought my outfit was pretty swell, but he looked me over coolly.

"Is there something I can do for you, ma'am?"

"I'm looking for Brendan Kaiser. My name is Clare Carlson."

"And?"

"I'm the news editor of Channel 10 News."

He still didn't seem too impressed.

Maybe he didn't like my color coordination.

"And what might your business be with Mr. Kaiser?"

"Well, I might be here to pick up his dry cleaning, but I'm not. How about I discuss my business with him?"

He scowled and picked up a phone to check with someone inside.

The truth was I wasn't sure why Brendan Kaiser wanted to meet me here. I'd had a few dealings with him in the past on big stories in my job as the news director for Channel 10—but he'd never invited me to lunch. Maybe he was going to give me a raise. Maybe he was going to tell me I'd been named Employee of the Month. All I knew is that when the big boss asks you to go to lunch with him, you go to lunch.

The maître d' still looked unhappy when he got off the phone, but he eventually directed me to a table inside. Brendan Kaiser was already there. Kaiser was in his 50s, with thick gray hair. Not a bad-looking guy, but he did have a bit of a paunch. I noticed it when he stood up to greet me. Probably from eating too many lunches at a place like Tri-Bar.

"Thank you for coming on such short notice, Clare," he said. His office had just arranged the meeting with me a few hours earlier. "I hope I didn't interfere with any other lunch plans you had for today."

"Well, until I got your call, my lunch plan had been to go for a Big Mac at McDonald's. That special sauce they put on it is to die for."

He smiled.

We made small talk for a few minutes, and then a waiter came over and took our orders. Kaiser was having some kind of duck dish with orange sauce and shoestring potatoes. I went for the tortellini with a salad. According to the menu I'd scanned, this meal was going to cost a lot of money. What the hell—he was paying, not me. Whatever happened next, maybe I'd at least get a good meal out of it.

"So do you want to tell me what this whole lunch deal between me and you is all about?" I said after a bit more conversation.

"You do get to the point, don't you?"

"I'm a journalist. I used to be a newspaper reporter. I like to get to the lead of the story as quickly as I can."

He nodded.

"The reason I asked to see you like this was to discuss a situation we need to deal with, Clare."

"What kind of situation?"

"A situation involving Channel 10 News."

"I didn't know we had a situation."

I took a drink of some iced tea I'd ordered with my meal. I wished now it was something stronger.

"Look, I think that everyone at Channel 10 News is doing a really terrific job," Kaiser said.

"Glad to hear it."

"Especially you as news director."

"Glad to hear that too."

"And you're a star, besides being the news director. You've broken some big stories for us, gotten a lot of publicity and notice in the media world. The Charles Hollister murder case. The serial killer you helped catch. I appreciate that from you, Clare. I appreciate all of your success and all your hard work. I really do."

"But?"

"Excuse me?"

"There is a 'but' coming here, right?"

"Yes, there is." Kaiser sighed. "Despite all your hard work, the ratings—and, as a result, the advertising revenue—isn't quite at the level we need at Kaiser Media to run a profitable news operation. I want to do better. I think we can do better."

The waiter brought our food. We both ate in silence for a few minutes. I waited to see what Brendan Kaiser would say next. I didn't really have anything to say. So I stuck my fork into the tortellini and bit into a piece. Pretty tasty. Good cream sauce too. Almost as good as the sauce on a Big Mac.

"I've decided to make some changes at Channel 10 News," Kaiser said finally, nibbling on a shoestring potato.

"What kind of changes?"

"Changes at the top."

"Wait a minute—are you firing me?"

"No, of course not."

"Demoting me? Is that the reason for this lunch?"

"You're still going to be the news editor."

"But you said you were making changes at the top so . . ."

That's when it hit me.

"Jack Faron?" I asked.

"Yes."

Jack Faron was the executive producer at Channel 10 News. My boss.

"I'm replacing Faron. Jack's done a good job, but he's more old school than we need right now. I'd like to put someone in the job with more drive, more energy, more new ideas. So I've hired a new executive producer. Jack will still be with us at Channel 10 News. But moving forward, he's going to be in a more . . . uh, advisory role."

"Does Jack know about this?"

"Not yet. I know you're close to him, so I wanted to make sure you were the first to hear about this."

I wasn't sure what to say. Jack Faron had been my mentor at Channel 10 News. The one who had hired me when the newspaper I worked for went out of business. The one that stood by me when my early on-air appearances as a TV reporter bombed. The one who promoted me to news editor and had backed me on every story and crisis since then.

And now he was not going to be there for me.

At least not in the same way.

I asked Kaiser the obvious question.

"Who's replacing him as executive producer?"

"Susan Endicott," he said. "Do you know her?"

"Not really."

"I think you two will get along really well. That's why I wanted to have this conversation with you. I want you to accept this. I want you to understand the reason for it. I want you to be happy. I want you to help make Susan Endicott feel welcome here. Are you good with all that, Clare?"

"Hey, you know me—I'm a team player."

"No, you're not."

I sighed. "Yeah, you're right, I'm not."

"Let's try to make this work, huh?"

I wasn't sure what to say next, but it turned out I didn't have to. I got a break. My phone rang, and—when I looked down at it—saw it was from Maggie Lang, my top editor at Channel 10 News.

"Where are you?" Maggie said.

"At lunch."

I hadn't told anyone who I was having lunch with.

"We've got a big story breaking. A murder. Female college student found murdered near Washington Square Park."

"Who is she?"

"Her name's Riley Hunt. She came here from Ohio to go to school at Easton College, not far from the park. Family has money, it sounds like. Her father's a doctor back in Ohio, her mother a lawyer."

"All hands on deck for this one," I said.

"Already done. We're gonna lead the newscast with it at 6."

After I hung up with Maggie, I told Kaiser what was happening. I said I needed to get back to the station right away to direct the news coverage. That wasn't totally true. Maggie could have handled it on her own. But I wanted to get out of here, and this seemed to be the perfect excuse. I didn't like what was happening to Jack Faron. I didn't like the fact I knew about it before him. And I was pretty sure I wasn't going to like Susan Endicott, even though I'd never met her.

And so I did what I do anytime I can't deal with problems in my life. I threw myself into a big story. And this murder sounded like a big story.

I said goodbye to Kaiser, walked through Tri-Bar and out the front door to catch a cab back to the Channel 10 newsroom.

The maître d' didn't bother to say goodbye.

CHAPTER 2

RILEY HUNT TURNED out to be a classic New York City crime story.

She was a beautiful girl. Blonde hair, blue eyes, people who knew her said she always had a sweet smile for everyone. A young woman who came to the city from the Midwest with stars in her eyes and determined to make it big. She'd finished at the top of her academic class during her freshman year at Easton College in Manhattan, where she was majoring in political science. She was elected to the Student Council as a sophomore, starred on the women's basketball team, and played music too—both with the school orchestra and in a band she belonged to off campus.

Her father was a plastic surgeon who specialized in Botox and other beauty treatments for wealthy people back in Dayton, where the family lived. Her mother was an attorney with a law firm there.

There was a color photo of her that appeared in one of the Easton publications after she joined the Student Council. Looking at it now, you could see much more than just her physical attractiveness there. Riley Hunt's eyes were bright and friendly; her smile infectious; and she had a determined look on her face that told the world this was a unique, interesting woman with a big future ahead of her.

No question about it, Riley Hunt sure seemed to have everything going for her in life.

That's why it was going to be such a big story for the media—including us at Channel 10 News—after someone took it all away from her with a violent, deadly, and tragic attack on a New York City street.

The facts we knew about the Riley Hunt murder went something like this:

She was last seen alive during the early morning hours of April 13, leaving a bar called the Cutting Edge in the West 30s near Herald Square. Someone thought they spotted her trying to hail a cab on the street outside after she left between 1 and 2 a.m. But no one was able to confirm that or whether or not she ever got into a cab.

The night had started for her much earlier at an awards dinner for the women's basketball team she played on. It was held at a restaurant on Broadway in Times Square, and she was one of those honored with trophies for her achievements on the court that season. After that, she had drinks at another bar nearby in Times Square with some of the people from the party. This lasted until the place closed a little after midnight. Then a handful of people made their way down to the Cutting Edge, about ten blocks south near Herald Square, which stayed open until 2 a.m.

While she was there, she received a phone call on her cell phone. She told people after the call that she was going to meet someone else later before she went back to her dorm. She didn't say who it was or where she was going. That was how everyone left her.

It gets murkier after that.

One account claimed she'd stayed at the Cutting Edge until 2 a.m., drinking alone until they told her they were shutting the doors and she had to leave. Another account—as I mentioned earlier—said she was seen trying to get a cab on Seventh Avenue during this time period.

There were other reports of her leaving the bar earlier.

What was known for sure was that the dead body of Riley Hunt—badly beaten—was discovered by a jogger not far from an entrance to Washington Square Park early the next morning, only a short distance away from the dormitory where she lived. An autopsy later showed that the most serious wound—and presumably the fatal one—had come when the killer struck her in the head with a hard object. But there were numerous bruises on her face and other parts of her body too from the attack.

One theory was that she had simply gotten drunk, left the bar alone, and made it downtown somehow to Washington Square Park, where she'd been accosted by an unknown assailant whose motive was robbery or rape. The problem with this was that her purse, with all the money and credit cards inside, was found with her. Her jewelry seemed untouched too. And there was no evidence of a sexual attack.

Another theory was that she had met up with her unknown caller, the person who called her at the last bar, and the encounter turned out badly. Her cell phone was not found with the body. Whether it was taken by the killer or just lost during the struggle was not clear. And no one was able to say who it was she had talked with and agreed to meet later that night after leaving the bar.

A third theory was that the report of her trying to hail a cab outside the Cutting Edge was correct, and she had managed to find one. That the cab driver was the one who accosted her on the deserted early morning streets, then dumped her body in the park. But there are hundreds of cab drivers on the streets of New York, even at that hour. If it was a cabbie who did it, finding the right one would not be easy.

And then there was the bar itself. The people who worked at the Cutting Edge. Here was this beautiful, sexy young woman drinking at the bar. Did she have too much to drink? Did she get drunk? What if someone there decided to take advantage of the situation and she fought back?

Everyone at the Cutting Edge seemed to have a different version of the night's events.

The bartender said he'd stopped serving Riley Hunt well before the legal closing time at 2 a.m. A waiter said she was still drinking there when the place closed. The manager at first refused to talk to police at all. Then he opened up and told a story about how he thought he remembered seeing the bouncer for the Cutting Edge helping to walk Riley out onto the street to look for a cab. The bouncer said it never happened that way. He said she left by herself and he never had any contact with her. A bus boy who had been cleaning up the place at closing time didn't remember seeing her at all.

Whether or not these things had anything at all to do with the murder of Riley Hunt remained unclear in those early hours of the murder investigation.

There have always been certain kinds of crime stories that really grab New Yorkers' interest in the media.

Crimes like the Preppie Murder Case, when a college coed was strangled to death during sex by an Upper East Side guy she'd just met at a Manhattan singles bar.

Or the Central Park Jogger case, where a young woman investment banker was brutally attacked while running one evening in Central Park.

Many of these fit into the category cynically known by some media critics as Blonde White Single Female crimes—when the victim was a pretty young girl, often from a wealthy background, who met a violent fate on the streets of New York City.

Riley Hunt was blonde and beautiful.

She came from money.

And she was dead.

She fit the category perfectly for a big, sensational crime story at Channel 10 News.

Yes, I know that sounds like a terrible thing to say.

But it's what I do for a living.

I cover death, and Riley Hunt was about as newsworthy a death as we'd had for a long time.

CHAPTER 3

"WE HAVE AN exclusive interview with the father of Riley Hunt, the murdered girl," Maggie Lang said at the news meeting.

"How did we manage that?" I asked.

"I hired a freelance film crew in Ohio. Sent them to the address outside Dayton that we had for the Hunt family. The father answered the door . . . and, well, we got lucky. It's pretty emotional stuff, Clare."

"Okay, good job. Let's see what we've got."

We had a big video monitor in the Channel 10 conference room, and Dr. Robert Hunt—the father of Riley Hunt—appeared on it now. He looked like I'd expect a doctor—especially a plastic surgeon—to look. Very distinguished, with some flecks of gray in his hair. Probably in his late 40s, although he appeared younger.

But it didn't take long for that facade of a professional doctor to fall apart in this situation. Soon after he started talking about his daughter, he began to cry. Quietly at first, but then with big sobs as he talked about her life—and about her tragic death.

"Riley was the shining light of our life," Dr. Hunt said during the interview. "She loved going to school, she loved reading books, she loved music, she loved animals—and she loved people most of all. Everyone who met her loved her back.

"I still remember so much about her growing up—she was the most beautiful little girl in the world. She was everything we ever wanted. And, for those next twenty years of life that she was given, she was all that we ever hoped for—and so much more. I still can't believe she's gone. Or how something like this could have ever happened to her. She loved New York, she loved being in college, she loved that campus. And now . . .

"I feel that this is all some horrible nightmare that I will wake up from. And that Riley will be here with us again. Except . . . except I know that will never happen. I will never see my little girl again. She's with the angels now. My little angel is an angel herself in heaven. But I want her back. I just can't handle this, I just . . ."

That's when he broke down in tears as the camera kept rolling.

"Pretty great stuff," I said. "What about the mother? Where is she?"

"Father said she was at her law office."

"She went to work after finding out her daughter was murdered?" someone asked.

"We all grieve in our own way," I said.

I had an idea. Something I hadn't done on the newscast in a long time.

"Let's do a cold open tonight," I said.

"With the father's interview?" Meg asked.

"Right. What do you think?"

"I love it!"

A "cold open" is a technique in TV where you go directly into a story at the beginning of the show without any opening credits or theme music or anything else. It's done to grab the audience's attention right from the start so they don't switch channels. You see it every week on *Saturday Night Live*. But sometimes a news show will do it, too to promote a really big story or exclusive.

"We open with the father on camera talking about his daughter, then breaking down in tears," Maggie said excitedly. I loved her enthusiasm. "Then, after that emotional scene, we come in with the Channel 10 News theme music and introduction of our anchor desk and news team.

"After that, there's also good video from the Easton campus. Students have erected a makeshift memorial for Riley Hunt— flowers laid there, pictures of her and placards with tributes and messages of love. There's also a ton of stuff on social media with more pictures of her, plus messages praising her life and lamenting her death, sad messages about her heartbreaking murder."

"What about the police investigation?" I asked.

"Still nothing solid there. They figure right now that it was a random murder. Riley Hunt was simply in the wrong place at the wrong time. That it was a murder which took place for no real reason that made any kind of sense. Those are the toughest kind of murders to solve, as you know, Clare."

I nodded.

"Okay then, that's the plan—we do the 'cold open' with the father's interview. After that, we'll go to the campus for the tributes and stuff there. Finally, talk about the police investigation—maybe they'll know more by then—and whatever else we can come up with about her murder for the rest of the day."

"So we're gonna milk this story for everything we can, huh?" one of the editors in the conference room said.

"You betcha!" I told him.

* * *

We went through some of the other stories for the broadcast.

A looming strike by sanitation workers. We generally didn't cover labor negotiations too much on TV news, because people didn't care that much. But a lot of New Yorkers would be upset if the streets suddenly were filled with garbage. There was a big fire in the Bronx that had destroyed a couple of warehouses, but no people had died. So it was mostly a video story showing all the flames. The election for mayor was heating up, and our political correspondent had an update from the major candidates' camps.

Oh, and we even had another murder—except this was a very strange one. A man and his wife in Bay Ridge had gotten into an argument about what numbers to play in the lottery. It was settled when he took out a gun and shot her to death.

"So did he have a winner?" I asked.

Everyone laughed.

"Damn, that is crazy though that a husband would kill his wife over something like that," I said.

"Not crazy to me," Brett Wolff, one member of our anchor team, said."

"Me either," said Dani Blaine, the other anchor. "Believe me, some of the things Brett does make me want to murder him too."

"Me? What about you?"

I sighed. Brett and Dani were married to each other, as well as being the Channel 10 co-anchors. They'd had an affair when Brett was married to another woman that was very tumultuous, to say the least. Once he divorced his wife, Brett married Dani and now they had a little baby daughter too. I had sort of hoped that the drama between them would quiet down after that.

But instead, they seemed to be fighting even more. So far they had managed to hide their differences from the audience when they were on camera doing the news. What happened if one of them suddenly snapped and killed the other one—as happened with the Bay Ridge couple—only they did it while they were on air?

Well, on the positive side, it would be a real ratings grabber.

I mean, we're talking about true reality TV!

An editor—an older guy named Bob Gleason—stuck his head into the conference room now and said to Maggie, "Clawson's script is ready. You said you wanted to read it before he went on air tonight."

Maggie called the script up on a computer and read through it quickly. She frowned. It was an investigative piece on political corruption—and we needed to make sure everything was accurate and buttoned up before we ran it.

"Bob, has anyone called the donor we mention in the story yet?" she asked.

He shook his head no.

"Did we google previous stories about this for background?"

Another shake of his head.

"This isn't ready to put on the air. Go back to Clawson and get some facts for me the next time before you turn in a story, okay?"

Gleason—clearly rattled—departed in a hurry. Maggie shook her head in frustration.

"Can you believe that guy is an adjunct professor of news editing at the Columbia J-School three nights a week?" she said.

"Well, you know what they say," I told her. "Those who can, do. Those who can't, teach. And those who can't do either, teach journalism."

"I like Gleason," Dani said. "His wife works as a chef at a fancy restaurant uptown and he brings in those great pastry spreads we have in the break room every Friday afternoon. Those chocolate truffles filled with cream cheese are simply to die for."

"Always good to work with a journalist who has her priorities in order," I said.

At the end of the meeting, we went through the story rotation again for the night's broadcast.

"Basically, it's Riley Hunt all the time for as long as we can—we'll fit in all the news after that. Let's go put out a newscast. And people," I said, doing my best impression of the classic line from the old *Hill Street Blues* TV show, "let's be careful out there."

Everyone laughed again.

Which was nice.

Because I wasn't sure how much laughing we'd be doing around here once Susan Endicott arrived.

CHAPTER 4

I WAS EATING pizza at home with my friend Janet Wood—talking about the Riley Hunt story, my lunch with Brendan Kaiser, the current state of my love life, and how good the pizza was. Not necessarily in that order of importance.

My place is a two-bedroom apartment in a high-rise just off of Union Square Park on the East Side of Manhattan. I've been here for a while now. There used to be a time when I moved every time a relationship ended with a guy I was living with in a place. Too many memories and all that sort of thing. But since I've been married and divorced three times—not to mention the other relationships I've had along the way—I abandoned that idea. The moving costs would have been prohibitive.

Janet was a very successful attorney in New York. She was happily married, had two daughters, and basically seemed to be in control of everything in her life. In other words, she was the exact opposite of me. Sort of like a Bizarro World version of Clare Carlson. Which probably was why we got along so well together.

Right now, we were doing a Top Ten list. It's a silly game we play sometimes—based on the old Top Ten lists of David Letterman. Top Ten reasons not to marry Brad Pitt. Top Ten things to say if you ever meet a Kardashian. Stuff like that. Yes, it was silly. But Janet and I had a lot of fun doing it.

Tonight the list was:

"Top Ten Fun Things About Being a TV Newswoman"

So far we had eight . . .

10. Breaking into regular programming with urgent news bulletins. We just love to scare the crap out of people.

9. Watching yourself on YouTube is too cool for words.

8. Mobile news van great for picking up hunky guys outside of singles bars.

7. Slow news days mean more time to watch Dr. Phil.

6. Flaunting tricky leg-crossing technique in wide camera shots.

5. Special discount when streaming *The Morning Show* with Jennifer Aniston.

4. Hoda Kotb initiation generally works as first date tension breaker.

3. Superficiality means big buck contracts. Just ask Megyn Kelly.

Janet came up with reason 2:

2. Sending subliminal messages through TV screen that make people do wacky stuff in their living room.

Then it was up to me:

"And the No. 1 fun thing about being a television reporter—drum roll, please."

1. Nobody parties like us TV chicks!

I picked up a piece of pizza and bit down into the cheese. Some of it wound up on my chin. Janet, on the other hand, ate her pizza like she did everything else. Neatly and completely in control. She even used a knife and fork to cut the pizza into tiny slices before eating them. Damn, that drove me crazy. Pizza was not meant to be eaten like that.

"What did you find out about this Susan Endicott woman who's going to be your new boss?" she asked.

"Endicott is all about ratings bait," I said.

"Huh?"

"Ratings bait. Like the term 'traffic bait' for digital when websites use some sort of over-the-top headline to get you to click on the item. Same with TV. She'll do anything for ratings, people say. She's all about big ratings."

"Aren't good ratings important?"

"Of course they are. But there's more to TV news than just ratings. It's supposed to be about journalism too."

"Where does she come from?"

"A station in San Francisco. Before that she worked at one of the cable news channels. She had a lot of success. I want to get more people to watch our newscasts too, but I also want to produce good journalism. I'm worried that Susan Endicott doesn't care about that part of the business very much. Not like Jack Faron did."

"Have you talked to Faron about this?"

"Not yet."

"Why not?"

"He hasn't said anything to me. I'm not sure if he knows yet. And, if he does, I'm not sure I want him to know I know too. And

I don't want him to know that I knew before he did. Does that make sense? Anyway, he'll tell me about it when he's ready."

"In the meantime, you'll throw yourself into that college woman murder story instead of having to deal with the rest of it, right?"

"You know me well, Janet."

"Any idea yet who killed her?"

"Nope. It's a mystery. Which is the best kind of story. The longer the questions remain in the story, the better the story is for us as news. Riley Hunt's murder is a pretty sensational crime, Janet. It will draw some good ratings."

"That sounds like what you were just accusing the Endicott woman of doing."

"There's a fine line of distinction between sensational journalism and irresponsible journalism."

"Where exactly is that line?"

"I'm never sure." I sighed.

She cut off another slice of pizza, picked it up with her fork, and popped it into her mouth. Dainty-like. She chewed it carefully. I wondered if she ever spilled anything on herself like I did all the time.

"What else is going on with you, Clare?"

"Meaning?"

"Well, your love life."

"My love life is kind of like the moon right now," I said.

"Huh?"

"Lifeless and barren."

"Don't complain to me. I tried to help. I set you up with that lawyer I knew a few weeks ago. Ted Glazer. But Glazer said you never even returned his calls after the first date. Why not?"

"Ted Glazer was boring, Janet."

"That guy makes $300,000 a year, owns a duplex in Battery Park, and is in line to become a full partner in his law firm very soon."

"B-o-o-o-ring."

"Okay, maybe he was a little dull."

"Thank you."

"No one else—no other men—on the dating horizon for you?"

"Nah. All of my ex-husbands seem to be happily married to their new wives at the moment, so they're out. Not that I'd be particularly interested in a do-over with any of them anyway. The one guy I would be interested in—the FBI guy/ex-cop Scott Manning I had the affair with—is married too. Not happily, but he's sticking with his wife to try and make it work. I still have some hopes there though. I'm kinda waiting that marriage out to see what happens."

Janet shook her head.

"You're amazing, Clare."

"Thank you."

"I didn't mean it as a compliment."

There was one piece of pizza left. I thought about being polite and offering it to Janet. Or at least splitting it with her. But instead, I grabbed it before she could get to it with that damn knife and fork. I ate it all in a few bites, then licked the excess cheese off of my fingers. Good to the last bite.

"When do you meet Susan Endicott?" Janet asked.

"Not sure."

"You really need to be careful here, Clare."

"What do you mean?"

"It's important to make a good first impression in a work situation like this with a new boss."

"Hey, I'll just be myself."

"That's what I'm afraid of," Janet said.

CHAPTER 5

AT A LITTLE after 9 the next morning I walked into the Channel 10 newsroom wearing a lavender gauze sundress with a jacket, a pair of oversized sunglasses, and a big smile.

It was a beautiful spring day, with the sun shining and birds chirping and flowers blooming all over. I'd bought my outfit at Saks one bitterly cold day during the depths of winter to cheer myself up.

"Nice outfit, Clare," Wendy Jeffers, the Channel 10 weather reporter, whistled in admiration as I walked past her desk.

"Thanks, Wendy. It's new."

She looked at me more closely now.

"A little tight though, isn't it?"

"What do you mean?"

"The jacket."

"I just bought this before Christmas."

"Well, maybe you put on a few pounds over the winter."

Actually, the jacket did feel a little tight. But then it was supposed to be European tailored.

"That's the way a tailored outfit is," I explained to Wendy. "Sometimes you've got to sacrifice comfort for fashion."

"Sure, I guess that's it then," she said.

I went into my office, hung the jacket on the back of my chair, and checked my messages.

The inbox on my computer was filled with email, news releases, and the other usual stuff. I skimmed through it quickly. There was a memo from the Fire Department with 10 tips for keeping your home safe; an invitation to a dog spring fashion show; an email from a man in Bogota, NJ, who was willing to reveal to Channel 10 News exclusively how the Russians had implanted a spy device in his wisdom tooth. Eight million people, eight million stories. I deleted them all with a single key stroke. A cluttered inbox is a cluttered mind.

The door to my office opened and someone came in. It was Jack Faron. I was surprised to see him.

"What's happening, Jack?" I asked, since I couldn't think of anything else to say at the moment.

"You tell me."

"What do you mean?"

"The murder. The woman from Easton College. It's the biggest crime story we've had in a while. We did a great job covering it last night, but now we have to keep it going. Tell me about the coverage you're planning for today."

I told him what I knew.

"We're all over the Easton campus today. Talking to friends, other students there, people in the neighborhood. She supposedly had a boyfriend too. We're trying to track him down. Don't worry, we'll have a lot of good coverage tonight."

"What about her family? What's going on there?"

"The family—her father, the one we had the interview with last night, and the mother—are on the way to New York to claim the body. They'll take her back to Dayton for a formal funeral. But there's going to be a big memorial service here too. The details are still being worked out, but it should be in the next day or two. Right now, they're talking about it being in the evening with a candlelight process up Sixth Avenue. Now that should be really good video for us."

Faron nodded.

"Yep," he said. "This has everything you can ask for in a crime story. Beautiful girl victim. Money. Nice neighborhood. Senseless crime. Anything more from the police on who did it or why?"

"Publicly, they say it's an ongoing investigation and they're pursuing a number of possible leads. Which is no surprise they'd say that. But our police sources with the NYPD say they're saying the same thing privately too. Which is surprising. They don't seem to have any idea on this one yet, Jack. It could well be just a random, crazy attack. Which is tough for two reasons: 1) there's no substantial trail of evidence to find the killer and 2) this crazy person is still out there and might do it again. I'm going to check to see if there were any similar cases like this that had happened around the city. You never know. Someone does something like this one time, they're not likely to stop doing it."

"But that does make it a better story," Faron said. "Let's keep pushing on it all as hard as we can. Of course, I don't have to tell you that, Clare, do I? Who's working on it for us?"

"Anyone in the newsroom who's available, Jack. But Janelle Wright will be the main reporter on the newscast tonight. Brett and Dani will introduce the story from the anchor desk, then go to Janelle and the other reporters around the city working on this."

"God, I wish it was you instead of Janelle on air with this story."

"So do I. Do you want me . . . ?"

"No, you're the news director. We've been through all this before. You're a terrific reporter, Clare, and you've broken some big stories for us. But I need you in this job. So let Janelle handle it. Just keep an eye on her."

Janelle was very popular with our viewers, a beautiful blonde newscaster—like so many other people on TV—who was easy on the eyes. Problem was she wasn't a very good reporter. And she sometimes had a lot of trouble avoiding on-air gaffes when she was talking in front of the live camera.

"Maggie and I are writing all her scripts," I said. "All she has to do is read our words off a teleprompter."

"What could go wrong?" Faron said.

"I don't even want to think about that . . ."

We talked a bit more about the story until I asked him the question I wanted to ask him: the white elephant in the room.

"Is everything okay with you?" I asked.

"What do you mean?"

"Is there anything you want to tell me?"

"What is it you want me to tell you?"

That's when I realized Jack Faron didn't know. He didn't know that he was about to be replaced by this Susan Endicott woman. Kaiser hadn't told him yet. But Kaiser had told me. That made for a really awkward situation.

So when was Kaiser going to tell Jack Faron the news?

I found out a few minutes later when Faron's phone rang. He answered it, talked for a few minutes, and then said he had to leave.

"That was Brendan Kaiser's office," he said. "He wants to see me right away. He's been on me about our ratings not being everything he hoped they would be. I guess it's going to be more of that. No big deal. I've dealt with station owners my entire career. I know how to handle Kaiser."

"Let me know what happens, Jack," I said as he walked out of my office.

"I'll get back to you as soon as I'm finished with Kaiser."

*   *   *

After Faron left, I walked back out into the newsroom and stopped at Wendy Jeffers' desk again.

"Dammit, that really bummed me out," I said to her.

"What?"

"Your comment about me putting on weight."

"I was probably just imagining it."

"What if you weren't?"

"Then it's only a pound or two."

Maybe Wendy was right. Maybe I was making a big deal over nothing. Maybe I was stressed out over this Faron business. Maybe I'd feel better about everything once it was resolved. Maybe I could even stop at a Baskin-Robbins store for some ice cream later. That ought to cheer me up.

"I saw Faron in your office," Wendy said to me now. "Anything going on?"

"Might be. Not sure yet."

"When will you know more?"

As it turned out, it didn't take very long. A short time later, I heard the sound of a ping on my phone. It was a text to me. A text from Susan Endicott.

"You and I need to talk," the text said.

"When?" I texted back.

"Right now."

"Where are you?"

"Sitting in Jack Faron's old office."

Well, that didn't take long.

CHAPTER 6

SUSAN ENDICOTT WAS on the phone when I walked into what until now had been Jack Faron's office. She kept talking and waved me to sit down. I sat down.

Endicott was not what I expected. She was hard to describe. Not pretty, not unattractive. Not dressed fashionably, not like a slob either. She had on some kind of drab gray gabardine pants suit that was not very flattering; she seemed to have used almost no makeup; and she wasn't wearing any jewelry that I could see. Clearly, this was a woman who did not spend a lot of time on her appearance.

She also had a pair of eyeglasses pushed back onto the top of her head. I've always disliked people that wore their glasses pushed back onto the top of their head like that. I know it doesn't make a lot of sense, but that was a pet peeve of mine. Not a good sign about Susan Endicott.

She was talking with someone on the phone about the apartment she was going to rent here in New York City.

"I want three bedrooms, not two," she said now. "And a terrace, if you can. Need a parking space for my car. And there has to be a doorman. I'm not schlepping my own packages and dry cleaning in there. Oh, it should be somewhere on the Upper East Side—70s or 80s—but no higher. Maybe with a view of the East River."

Well, one thing I knew—Brendan Kaiser was paying her a lot of money to do this job.

As she talked, I noticed the furniture in the office was different. Jack Faron's old desk was gone, and she had replaced it with one of her own. All his pictures and other decorations on the walls and desk had disappeared too. Even the rug had been changed. Everything about the place was different.

This woman was sure making herself at home in a hurry.

She held up her hand again now as she talked to indicate I should keep waiting for her to finish.

I waited.

After a while, I started to get bored. I passed the time by trying to rank—in order of desirability—the ten men I'd most like to sleep with. I was at a tie for third place, trying to decide between Ben Affleck and Bradley Cooper, when Susan Endicott finally hung up and looked over at me.

"Hi, I'm Clare Carlson, and I—" I started to say.

"I know who you are."

"Uh, okay."

A no-nonsense woman.

"I wanted to see you right away because I think it's very important that you and I get off on the right foot together," she said.

I thought about suggesting that keeping me waiting while she took care of her personal business on the phone wasn't a great way to do that. But I didn't say anything.

"I know you were close to Jack Faron, Carlson," she said. "And I know Faron let you get away with a lot of crap because of that. Well, those days are over. There's a new sheriff in town, and that's me. You're going to do what I want—or else. My way or the highway, Carlson. Let me make that perfectly clear right now. Any questions?"

"Just one."

"Go ahead."

"When do we get to the part about starting off on the right foot?"

Endicott shook her head.

"I've heard that you think you're a funny lady. Charming people with a lot of snappy comebacks and a smart mouth and your jokes. Some people probably think that's cute. I'm sure Jack Faron did. But not me. I don't like jokes. And I don't want you doing any laughing or joking in my presence. If I want jokes, I'll watch goddamn Ellen DeGeneres. Is that clear?"

I nodded and smiled.

I hoped the smile was okay with her.

"Any other questions?"

"Yes, what happened to Jack Faron's stuff that was here?"

"I've replaced that with my own things. I'm the executive producer now. This is my office. You don't think I have a right to redesign it so quickly?"

I shrugged.

"You have a right."

"Then what's your problem?"

"Oh, I just think it shows a certain lack of class."

"Let me explain something, Carlson. There's going to be a lot of changes around here. And they're going to happen very fast. We need to boost the ratings of our news shows. That's why I'm here."

"Our ratings aren't that bad," I pointed out. "They're decent."

"Well, Brendan Kaiser wants more than 'decent.' He wants to be at the top of the market. And so do I. That's why I'm here. To make whatever changes are necessary to put us there. I'm going to start these changes with you."

Whoa! Was she going to fire me?

"I know all about you, Carlson. You're a pain in the ass, but you're a star. You've broken big stories in the past. Become a national celebrity with them. That's what I need you to do now. Break a big story for me. This Riley Hunt murder is a big story. Who's the lead on-air person doing it for us right now?"

"Janelle Wright. She's—"

"Replace her."

"Replace her with who?"

"You."

I stared at her.

"You want me to go on the air to report this story myself?"

"Of course. It's a big story, you're a big star. I need you on it to boost the ratings. So you're back on the air with this story."

"Jack Faron never liked me to go on the air. He wanted me to concentrate on being the news director."

"Jack Faron isn't the executive producer here anymore."

"Right."

I thought about what she was saying. I wasn't terribly unhappy about the idea. I always liked being a reporter better than being just the news director. In the past, I always had to fight Faron to do that. But now this woman was pushing me in that direction herself. For her own reasons, of course.

"What about my job as news director?"

"You'll keep doing that. But delegate a lot of that to someone under you. I can always get a news director. On-air TV news stars are harder to find. And, whatever I think of you, you are a star, Carlson. Now tell me where we are on the Riley Hunt story."

I told her everything I knew.

"So from now on, you're the lead on-air personality for Channel 10 with this story," she said when I was done going through it all. "Understood?"

I tried to think of a snappy comeback, but I couldn't.

"Understood," I said.

"Meanwhile, as news director, I want you to give me a list of all the Channel 10 personnel—particularly the prominent on-air people like the anchor team, weather, and sports. Understood?"

"Uh, understood."

"Along with that, I want an evaluation from you of everyone's performance. Understood?"

That I didn't understand.

"An evaluation?"

"Yes, I want to know what you think of all of them."

"Is this for some kind of pay raise?"

"No, it's for deciding who we need to replace."

"But . . ."

"Like I told you before, I'm here to jack up the ratings. To do that, I need to make changes. Some of these changes might be painful, but they have to be done."

"These are all good people. None of them deserves to be fired."

Endicott shrugged.

"You can't make an omelet without breaking a few eggs," she said.

CHAPTER 7

THERE WAS A news meeting coming up later after I left Endicott, and I wasn't looking forward to that meeting.

Normally, I love the news meetings—they're the highlight of my day. I get to talk about my favorite part of my job, covering the news—instead of worrying about ad rates or budget numbers or marketing shares.

But this was going to be different.

People in the newsroom were going to figure out very soon that Jack Faron was gone—and another person was sitting in his office. There'd been no official announcement from Kaiser or anyone else yet. But this was a newsroom filled with reporters. Reporters picked up on that kind of thing in a hurry.

I knew I'd be peppered with questions about what was going on at Channel 10 News—and what was coming next.

I didn't really have any answers for those questions.

There was also the harsh truth that not all of these people would be a part of Channel 10 News going forward. Endicott had made it very clear to me that big changes were coming. I couldn't be sure who was staying and who was going. And it seemed like I wasn't going to have much final say about that either.

As Susan Endicott said, she was the new boss—the new sheriff in town. She wasn't going to care much about my opinion on this. But I knew it was all going to fall into my lap at some point. Then—like it or not—I would have to get involved in the blood-bath of people here that I feared was coming. Cleaning up the mess that was left after people here got fired or forced out in some other way.

I couldn't do anything about that.

So I concentrated instead on what I could do something about.

The big story.

Riley Hunt.

That was my priority right now.

*   *   *

I went downstairs and brought back a big cup of coffee, shut the door to my office to make sure I wouldn't be interrupted, and began going through everything I could find on the Riley Hunt murder.

There was stuff from our reporters at Channel 10, from other media, and from websites I found online too.

I went through everything, making notes as I went.

Everything I read and saw confirmed the idea we'd heard from the beginning that Riley Hunt was some kind of golden girl, on an upward trajectory toward a successful career and a happy life and an overall bright future—until someone inexplicably murdered her that night on a Greenwich Village street.

Valedictorian of her high school back in Dayton, president of her class there, senior prom queen—she had her pick of colleges to attend. She chose Easton, which was not as well known as some of the other New York schools like Columbia, NYU, and Fordham— but still very highly regarded in the world of higher education.

It turned out her mother had attended Easton too, years earlier, so that probably played a role in her decision to attend the college. The same mother, I thought to myself, who went to work at her law office on the day that she found out her daughter was dead. I wondered what that was all about.

There was going to be a memorial service with the parents present on campus before they took the body back home to Ohio. I definitely planned to be there. Riley's teachers and friends and classmates would be attending, so I'd get lots of good on-air interviews remembering her. We'd already interviewed the father on air, but I wanted to talk to the mother too.

Riley's major at Easton had been political science, and she'd told people she hoped to work in the diplomatic world—at the State Department or maybe the UN—once she graduated. She even had some dreams about maybe running for political office herself sometime. She'd campaigned for Hillary Clinton in 2016 when she was barely in high school and again for Elizabeth Warren during the 2020 primary race.

"I want to be one of those women who help break through the glass ceiling of the political world," Riley had been quoted as saying about her future in her high school yearbook.

She also had a big interest in music, and she was taking enough courses for a minor in that as well as her political science major. There were several professors and musicians I found who had worked with her in the classes at Easton. But she had also been the lead singer in a band that played at events on and off campus.

The band was called Fallen Sky—and they featured a lot of '80s music from Pat Benatar and Blondie and ZZ Top. They had a website that listed the names of everyone in the band. I wrote those down too. I had a feeling they might be more informative than even the people she played music with in the school curriculum.

There were the names of friends she had at Easton—along with her roommate in the dorm there—that I added to my list. In terms of men, it appeared she was in a relationship with a guy named Bruce Townsend. He didn't go to Easton; he was a student at Baruch College. I definitely put him on my list.

The bottom line, of course, was that most of these people weren't going to tell me anything that would help the investigation.

They'd just tell me all over again what a wonderful person Riley was and how tragic it was for her to die this way. In some random attack by what presumably was a madman roaming the streets.

But that was okay.

A senseless death like this on the streets of New York always turned into a big news story.

I remembered a case a number of years ago where a teenaged tourist from out West somewhere was stabbed to death as he walked with his family through a subway station. No reason. No motive. Simply another random crime in the big city for an innocent victim visiting for the first time.

These kinds of crimes had happened before, but this one had really captured the public's attention, and the media all played it up in a huge way. There'd been a tremendous amount of reaction and outrage over the young tourist's senseless death. And that eventually led to lot of police changes in terms of bolstering law enforcement protection on trains and in stations around the city.

Maybe the same thing would happen—more police on the street protecting people—after Riley Hunt's murder.

Especially if I—and the rest of the media—turned it into a big story.

And a big story was exactly what I needed in my life right now.

A big story cheered me up no matter how many other things were going wrong around me.

Yep, a big story always made everything better.

CHAPTER 8

THE FIRST THING I needed to do was find out exactly where the police were in the investigation of Riley Hunt's murder. That meant talking to my sources in the department. Or, to be more specific, my source—as in a single source. But there was a slight problem with this. Because my police source was also my ex-husband, Homicide Sgt. Sam Markham.

There was another problem for me too.

I wasn't sure if Sam was still mad at me or not.

Our divorce had gone pretty amicably, as divorces go, and it had been mostly my fault. Sam, like my previous two ex-husbands, was a decent guy. The problem wasn't that he hadn't been a good husband; I hadn't been a very good wife. Not that I cheated on him or anything, it was the job—my job—that caused all the problems. I always put my life and career as a journalist ahead of everything else. Chasing after news stories was the biggest excitement of my life, and no man could ever compete with that feeling. At least none of the men I'd been married to.

I always tell this story about Sam and me—because it sums up our relationship so well—of him serving me with divorce papers. He had them delivered by the process server to the Channel 10 newsroom, not where I was living. That was the one place he knew

I'd be sure to get them. I was directing coverage of a plane crash when that happened, and I didn't open up the envelope with his divorce papers until it was over. That should give you an idea of how tough I was to live with as man and wife.

Sam and I have experienced ups and downs in our relationship since then. He is remarried now, with a young child, and I think he's happy. Most of the time anyway. But every once in a while, especially when he's had a bit too much to drink, Sam has made a pass at me again. Nothing serious, but I think he just missed all the fun we had in bed and elsewhere. I always tried letting him down gently. But, sometimes after I rejected one of his amorous advances, he would get mad at me and lash out angrily in frustration and, I suppose, a bit of embarrassment too.

The last time was at a bar where I was with a group of media people and Sam came in. I think he was looking for me that night. When I said "no" to him, things escalated quickly and it got very ugly between us.

We hadn't talked since then.

So I wasn't sure what his reaction was going to be when I went to the detective squad room at his station house.

It didn't take long to find out.

"Look what just crawled out from under a rock," he said, glaring at me now. "My snooping reporter of an ex-wife. Man, did I dodge a bullet when I got myself out of that marriage to you. What in the hell do you want?"

I was pretty sure Sam was still mad at me.

"I'm working on a story," I said.

"What story?"

"Riley Hunt," I told him, even though I knew he'd figured that out already.

"The Public Relations Department is at 1 Police Plaza. They'll tell you anything there is to announce about the Hunt murder case. They deal with the media, not me. So go bother them for a while, Carlson . . ."

I sighed.

"Look, Sam, could we just skip past this part and get down to business. I like you, and I know you like me. Even though it doesn't seem that way a lot of the time. I have a couple of questions about the Riley Hunt case, that's all. What do you say we have a professional discussion about it without all of this drama?"

Sam hesitated for a few seconds, then nodded. I was always able to get through to him.

Always able to convince him in an argument that I was right. Maybe that was one of the problems with our marriage. I always thought I was right, and he compromised a lot of times with me. But that was all water under the bridge now.

"Okay, tell me what you want to know from me, Clare."

I went through everything I'd found out so far about the Hunt girl and her murder. I asked him what else the police had found out. He said—and I believed him—that there wasn't much. They were still operating on the theory of a random killing by someone—possibly an out-of-control drug addict or deranged person—who attacked the girl for no real reason when he spotted her walking along on the street at that hour of the night. The fact that there was no indication of robbery or sexual assault seemed to back up that idea.

I asked about her cell phone, and he said that it hadn't been found yet.

"Doesn't that seem strange?" I asked Sam. "What happened to it? Whoever killed her left her handbag, her wallet with credit cards and money in it, her jewelry. But there's no cell phone. Why not?"

"Maybe she dropped it during the struggle and someone picked it up afterward. Or she left it behind somewhere at one of the bars or other spots she'd been in that night. It will probably turn up sooner or later."

"What about devices in her room—computer? IPad?"

"There were none."

"What twenty-year-old doesn't have a computer or an iPad today?"

"Her roommate said she had a laptop but she lost it—or it was stolen—before the murder."

"Doesn't that seem suspicious?"

"Look, Clare, I don't know where you're going here or what you're looking for with this. But whatever it is, there's nothing there. Someone attacked this woman on the street—without any logical reason in all likelihood—and we'll eventually catch that person. I doubt we'll find any of the answers on her computer or her iPad or anything else like that."

I wasn't so sure.

"Any possibilities of a personal motive? That she might have been killed by someone she knew?"

"Who?"

I shrugged. "Friends, family, boyfriend. The usual suspects. Have you talked to the parents, Sam?"

"Yes."

"Father and mother?"

"Both of them."

"The mother went to work on the day she found out her daughter was dead."

"So?"

"It seems odd to me."

"Listen, there's no law against plunging yourself into your work to avoid dealing with all the trauma in your personal life. Hell, you're a perfect example of that, Clare."

I didn't respond to that one.

"Friends? Other students? Anyone who might have had some kind of a grudge against Riley?"

"She was popular with everyone."

"Maybe too popular. Maybe someone got jealous."

"C'mon, you're really reaching here now."

There was one other question I wanted to ask.

"She had a boyfriend, right?"

"Yes."

"Have you interviewed him?"

"Of course we have.'

"What did he say?"

"He's shocked and heartbroken."

"Does he have an alibi for the time of her murder?"

"Actually, he does. A pretty damn good one too. He was with his father all night at the family house on Long Island."

"The father confirms that?"

"Totally."

"Maybe the father is only covering up for the kid. The most obvious suspect in a murder case like this is always someone the victim has been romantically involved with. You know that as well as I do, Sam."

"Do you know the kid's name?"

I checked my notes.

"Says here his name is Bruce Townsend," I said.

"Right. His father is Hugh Townsend. Sound familiar?"

"The deputy police commissioner?"

"Uh-huh. And Deputy NYPD Commissioner Hugh Townsend has taken over the investigation of this case himself personally. He wants to make sure that no evidence—no lead of any kind—gets overlooked. He wants to find out who murdered his son's fiancée more than anyone else does. Believe me, Clare, we're going to pull out all the stops on this one—it's definitely top priority—until we catch the person who killed her."

"*Fiancée?*"

"They were supposed to be married."

"I hadn't heard about that anywhere."

"The son, Bruce Townsend, proposed right before she was killed."

"Interesting timing."

"Meaning?"

"It just seems like it might be significant . . ."

"We're done here now, Clare," Sam said.

CHAPTER 9

"How did your first meeting go with the new boss?" Maggie Lang asked me.

"Badly."

"How badly?"

"Remember those old news clips about the crash and burning of the *Hindenburg*? Where all those people died. And how the announcer kept saying: 'Oh, the humanity...'"

"That bad, huh?"

"Even worse."

I'd told Maggie about Susan Endicott before anyone else. She was my number one deputy and also a voice of sanity and reason in our often-chaotic newsroom. I wanted to have her on my side, no matter what. I went through a lot of stuff about Endicott's obnoxious behavior and her obvious ego. I did not tell Maggie about Endicott's threat to start making changes and firing people though. I didn't want to set off a full-scale panic in the newsroom. No sense in yelling "fire" until the blaze breaks out.

"Where's Jack Faron?" she asked.

"No idea."

"He's not fired?"

"Technically, no. He's a consultant now. Whatever that means."

"I hope he's okay."

"Me too. I like Jack."

"And you don't like this Endicott woman who's taking his place?"

"That about sums up the situation pretty well, Maggie."

*   *   *

I went through it again with everyone at the news meeting afterward. About Susan Endicott's arrival and Jack Faron's departure. At least his departure from an active role in the Channel 10 news operation. I also said how I was taking over the on-air coverage myself of the Riley Hunt story.

"Why?" they asked, especially Janelle Wright—who had been the on-air person reporting the story for us so far.

"Susan Endicott asked me to."

"But you're the news director."

"I've covered stories on air before. You all know that."

But there were a lot more questions and comments from the room about my announcement that I was going back on the air to lead the coverage of this story.

"Yes, only that was because you wanted to do them, right?"

"This time you're being assigned to do it. That's different."

"How do you feel about this?"

"I'm always happy to work on a big story," I said, and left it at that.

Obviously, there were plenty of questions too about Susan Endicott. People here had already looked up information online about her, and knew about her obsession with ratings and her ambition in the TV news business. I didn't go into any specifics about my meeting with her, telling them even less than I did Maggie. I didn't want to upset anyone more than necessary. But it didn't hold back the mounting anxiety in the room.

"One thing that bothers me is that she still hasn't met anyone or introduced herself to us," someone said. "She's just sitting in that office. Jack Faron's office. When is she going to reach out to us and tell us more about what she's going to do here as executive producer?"

There were nods of agreement around the room.

"Yes, why hasn't she talked to any of us?" said Brett Wolff, the co-anchor of Channel 10 News.

"She's talked to me," said Dani Blaine, the other co-anchor.

"What do you mean?"

"Susan Endicott talked with me. She called me into her office before this meeting. Told me I was doing a great job as news anchor here. Told me how much she liked my work and my on-air performance."

"She hasn't talked to me yet," Brett said.

"What do you want me to say?" Dani smiled.

This was trouble on a lot of fronts. Brett and Dani were very competitive, not just as co-anchors but also as husband and wife. If Susan Endicott liked one of them, but not the other—well, that was bad. Not only because it would break up our anchor team. It could also break up Brett and Dani's marriage. Jeez.

"What about the rest of us?" said Steve Stratton, the sports reporter. "Does that mean she doesn't have any use for us? That we're not worth talking to? I don't know about the rest of you, but I think I'm going to start updating my job resume right away."

It went on like that for a while. I let everyone talk and rant about the changes happening at Channel 10 before getting down to business. That business was putting on a newscast that evening.

"Let's talk about the Riley Hunt story," I said. "What have we got for tonight?"

*　　*　　*

A few hours later, there was the pulsating theme music and introduction to the 6:00 p.m. newscast:

> ANNOUNCER: "It's the News at 6, with the Channel 10 news team: Brett Wolff and Dani Blaine at the anchor desk; Steve Stratton with sports; and Wendy Jeffers with your up-to-date weather forecast. If you want to know what's happening—you want it fast and you want it accurate—Channel 10 News has got you covered.
>
> "And now here's Brett and Dani . . ."

> BRETT: There's a spring heat wave headed our way. The Yankees and Mets are off to great starts to the season. The mayor and the governor are feuding again about who's to blame for transit system problems. But the big story continues to be the murder of Easton College student Riley Hunt on a New York City street.

> DANI: Riley Hunt's murder has shocked a city that has seen many other horrifying crimes committed—but this one is particularly tragic and heartbreaking. Our own news director at Channel 10, Pulitzer Prize–winning journalist Clare Carlson, is leading the team coverage of this story. Clare?

> ME: Riley Hunt was in a band that was supposed to play at a campus event this week. She was planning on being married.

And she was about to finish up her sophomore year at Easton College on the honor role. But, instead, there will be a memorial service for Riley Hunt this week on the Easton campus. Here's what we know so far about her murder and the investigation into finding out who killed her . . .

CHAPTER 10

"I NEED TO find you a man," Janet said.

"Words of doom."

"What do you mean?"

"I've met some of your blind dates before, remember?"

We were sitting outside eating breakfast at a café on Park Avenue South, not far from my apartment near Union Square. It was a beautiful sunny day with the temperature in the 60s and no humidity whatsoever. The kind of day that made you love living in New York City in the spring.

"Well, you're not the easiest woman to match up with a guy, Clare."

"What's wrong with me?"

"You're judgmental about people, overly critical, and set unrealistically high expectations," she said. "Plus, you're very immature about the whole thing."

"Am not."

"Am too."

I thought about coming back with another retort, but I was afraid that might bolster her "immature" argument.

"So do you want me to try and fix you up or not?"

"No, I do not."

The waiter brought our food. I'd ordered the big breakfast special—an omelet with plenty of cheese, a big order of bacon and buttered toast on the side. I was still a bit concerned about my new jacket fitting too snuggly, so I put Equal into my coffee instead of sugar. That ought to take care of it for me. Janet had ordered some kind of vegetable dish that looked really unappetizing. I dug my fork into the eggs along with a big hunk of cheese, and I gobbled it down. Hmmm, good. I was glad I had made this my breakfast choice instead of whatever the hell it was Janet was eating.

I wanted to steer the conversation away from my love life. Or, more specifically, my lack of a love life. I told Janet a bit about the story I was working on and about my meeting with Susan Endicott. I specifically mentioned the fact that Endicott pushed her glasses onto the top of her head when she wasn't using them.

"What does that have to do with anything?"

"It irritates me."

"She's not the only person in the world who pushes their glasses onto the top of their head. Other people do it too."

"And I don't like any of them."

Janet shook her head.

"Like I said, you're judgmental, over-critical, and you set unrealistic expectations for people."

"Have I ever been wrong about anyone?"

"Plenty of times."

"Well, no one's perfect."

Janet ate some more of her breakfast. She sure seemed to like it. I was working my way through the cheesy omelet and the bacon, leaving the buttered toast to the end. You have to pace yourself when eating a good breakfast. I thought about the best way to do this. I thought about how eating a balanced meal for breakfast was important for the rest of the day. I also thought about asking the waiter for a second order of bacon.

"I'm not sure I understand your anger at this Endicott woman," Janet said. "Yes, she seems crude and egotistic and not exactly a people person. But she's going to give you the chance to do what you always want to do. Go back to reporting. And on a big story like this Riley Hunt murder."

"I know, it's a conundrum. But when I get involved in a story, it's my idea. This is hers. I also worry about the woman's judgement because of her obvious zeal for ratings. Jack Faron was always the voice of reason if I went too far. Now I feel like I'll have to be the voice of reason with her. That's not a good role for me, Janet."

"Have you talked to Faron?"

"Not yet. I think he's avoiding me. Avoiding everyone. He hasn't been seen at the station since Endicott arrived. He's supposed to be in some kind of consultant role, but I think that's a made-up job. Susan Endicott doesn't look like the kind of person who's going to want any kind of 'consulting' done on her work. I imagine Jack is really embarrassed right now. That's why I haven't heard from him. I hope to be able to talk to him soon.

"My biggest concern is about the other people on the staff. Endicott wants to fire some people, change things up. They don't know that yet, but I do. Which puts me in a tricky situation. I want to protect everybody there as much as I can. I really like them all. Even some of the ones I bad-mouth at times like Janelle Wright. But I'm not sure what kind of say I'm going to have over the staff situation."

"You still have Brendan Kaiser, the owner, on your side, right?"

"I hope so. I think he still likes me because of the stories I've broken for the station."

"And if you break this big story—the one about the Riley Hunt murder—he'll like you even more."

"I guess."

"So put all your effort into that, and everything will be fine."

"Easier said than done."

"Not for you—you're a hotshot reporter. You've told me that many times."

"That I am," I agreed.

In the end, I resisted the temptation to go for the second order of bacon. I was very proud of myself for doing that. Very proud of my willpower and my self-control. I would have been even prouder if I hadn't ordered something from the pastry tray to take with me before I left.

On the way out, I said to Janet: "Do you really think I'm judgmental?"

"Yes."

"Over-critical?"

"Definitely."

"Set my expectations unrealistically high for people?"

"Without a doubt."

I nodded.

"Okay, just confirming," I said.

CHAPTER 11

THERE HAD ALREADY been several memorials, vigils, and events for Riley Hunt. But none like this one that was being held tonight near the Easton campus in Washington Square Park.

This was the official ceremony by the college as New York City's farewell to the slain coed before her body was taken back to her hometown in Ohio.

Everyone was there. The mayor. Lots of other politicians. Hundreds of Easton students and faculty. And, of course, the media. We were out in full force from Channel 10, like every other news outlet in town.

I recognized some of the specific other people there too. Riley's mother and father. Well, at least I assumed it was her mother. I knew the father's face from our interview with him that first day, and she was holding onto him now for support. She was somewhere in her 40s, very attractive and immaculately dressed, but she kept a tight hold on her husband the whole time I watched them. She appeared to be in a state of shock. Yet this was the same woman who apparently went to work as usual on the day she found out her daughter had been murdered. I couldn't quite figure that out.

Riley's boyfriend—and I guess fiancé—was there too. Bruce Townsend. I'd seen a picture of him, and he was easy to spot. A big guy, maybe 6 foot 5 at least, with high, thick curly black hair. He stood out even with a crowd so big around him.

Someone also pointed out a girl to me that they said had been Riley's roommate at the Easton dormitory. She had bright red hair, but otherwise was kind of ordinary looking. I couldn't help but think how she must have been overshadowed next to her more glamorous roommate.

I wanted to talk to all of them. Riley's parents, especially the mother. The boyfriend. The roommate. But I knew I wouldn't get much of a chance to do that in the media frenzy around here now. The best I was going to do was a quote or two for on-air tonight. I'd have to figure out how to approach them all on my own later.

There were lots of pictures of Riley posted on trees and fences and walls around the park. Photos of her playing basketball; photos performing with the rock band where she was the lead vocalist; photos of her walking on campus with books on her arm; pictures too from that last night where she was celebrating with friends—unaware that it would be the last night of her all-too-short life. Even pictures of her growing up in Ohio—one particularly poignant one of her as a little girl hugging a dog under the Christmas tree.

I was struck again by how pretty she was. A kind of fragile beauty. Not overtly gorgeous or sexy—but more of a wholesome, All-American girl type quality that is rare these days. It reminded me in a way of my own daughter, who was nearly 30 now—but still had those youthful-like qualities.

And made me think of my granddaughter, who in a few years would be a teenager and thinking about going to college. She looked like that too.

This girl's death—Riley Hunt—had affected me deeply. I wasn't exactly sure why.

Maybe it had something to do with how she reminded me of my own daughter and granddaughter.

But, for whatever reason, I found myself really relating to the dead Riley Hunt, even though I never knew her. This was more than just a big news story now. I wanted to find out the truth about what happened to her. I couldn't bring Riley Hunt back to life, but I could do this—discover the answers about her death—in her memory.

The most amazing part of the memorial event was the lights. Lights that lit up the park in honor of Riley. Not real lights. Some were candles, but much of it came from cell phones people held high in the air that lit up the sky. It was like there were lit cell phones as far as I could see. One thing for sure—that was going to provide some spectacular video for our Channel 10 newscast.

The speeches were emotional, of course. Many of them focused on the future that seemed so bright for Riley Hunt that she would never see now.

"That is the saddest part of it," one of her political science professors from the college said. "She had so much to look forward to. And we had so much to look forward to seeing from her. She wanted to devote her life to public service. Maybe she would have had a wonderful career in the State Department. Or maybe she would have been ambassador to a foreign country. Or maybe even Senator Hunt or President Hunt. That's how much potential this remarkable young woman possessed. But now we are left to just wonder 'why?' Why something like this could happen . . ."

Bruce Townsend, the boyfriend, talked about how they met at a performance of her band. How he'd fallen head over heels in love with her that night. About how he nervously asked her out on a date after the band performance was over. About how much time they'd spent together. About their plans to get married. And about all their dreams for the future and raising a family and so much else.

"It's not only Riley that died," he said. "A part of me died along with her."

It was a very poignant moment in a very moving, emotional ceremony.

Riley's parents spoke too. The father repeated some of the same things he'd said during that initial interview we aired from Ohio. He talked about how Riley always wanted to make the world a better place. How she volunteered at a soup kitchen on McDougal Street to help the poor. How she regularly visited the animals at abandoned pet shelters. And how she spent several hours every week working with an organization to aid homeless military veterans on the streets of New York City.

At the same time, Robert Hunt also said Riley would not want everyone there at the service to cry for her.

"I think if Riley is looking down on this now, she won't be sad . . . she will be happy. Happy to see this outpouring of love for her. And, because I knew Riley so well, I am telling you that she absolutely wouldn't want any of us to feel sad. She'd want us to celebrate her life, not mourn her death. I know that's difficult for us to do, but that's what Riley would have wanted."

Riley's mother stood up to speak next. Elizabeth Hunt looked wobbly and her eyes didn't seem to focus on anyone or anything. Had she been drinking or taking too many drugs to relax or something? That might make sense given the situation, I suppose. Her husband stood next to her, almost holding her up.

She started to get a few words out. "My daughter . . . my Riley . . ." and then she stopped. Her body began to sway even with her husband holding on to her. Then she started to cry. Uncontrollable crying. It was a shocking moment. Her husband and a few others finally led her away from the podium.

It was an understandable reaction, of course—she'd suffered the devastating loss of her daughter from a tragic and violent death.

And one thing was for certain—it was a great media moment for us and Channel 10 News and everyone else. That poignant scene of the devastated mother—breaking down in tears at her daughter's memorial service—would lead every newscast in town later that evening and be on the front page of every newspaper.

But I still didn't really understand about Elizabeth Hunt, Riley's mother.

I mean, this woman had gone to work as usual on the day she first heard about her daughter's murder.

Now she was so grief-stricken she couldn't even stand up on her own or get any words out before collapsing.

There was something going on here that didn't make sense to me.

CHAPTER 12

"TAKE BACK NEW YORK," Susan Endicott said.

"Excuse me?"

"That's going to be our new editorial slogan here at Channel 10 News."

"Take Back New York," I repeated.

"Yes. And the Riley Hunt story is going to be the focus of it and what we put on our newscasts going forward."

To say I didn't understand what she was saying would be an understatement. But I didn't bother to ask. I knew Susan Endicott would tell me more on her own. This woman loved to hear the sound of her own voice.

"New York is supposed to be the greatest city in the world, right?" she said. "Broadway theaters, museums, restaurants, stores, sporting events like the U.S. Open and everything else. Not only Manhattan, but places like Brooklyn and the Bronx are rich in wonderful character and history."

"Don't forget Queens."

"Okay, Queens. I've never been to Queens, but I'm sure it's wonderful too."

"Have you ever been to Brooklyn or the Bronx?"

"Uh, not yet."

"And there's Staten Island."

"Okay."

"That's a borough of New York City too."

"The point is . . ."

"Here's a way to remember it. Just sing the line: 'The Bronx is up, the Battery is down. New York, New York, a helluva town.' You see the Battery is in Brooklyn so . . ."

I should have kept my mouth shut and let her talk. But I simply couldn't help myself. The woman really annoyed me, and I've never been able to hide my distaste for someone like that. It didn't seem to bother Susan Endicott though. Maybe she was used to it. Or maybe she didn't even care what people thought of her. It was all about Susan Endicott.

"The point is," she said again, "the Riley Hunt murder has exposed to everyone the seamy underbelly of New York. All the ugliness that has taken over here. The crime. The lawlessness. The fear that anyone can become a victim. It brings back memories of Son of Sam and the Summer of '77. No one is safe. This crazed killer is still out there, maybe looking for a new victim to kill at random. Just like he did with Riley Hunt. That's a terrifying situation for this city. But it's also good ratings for us."

"We don't know for sure she was killed by some crazy person at random," I pointed out.

"What is the police theory at the moment?"

"That it's a random killing by some crazy person on the street."

"That's good enough for me."

I didn't say anything.

"We'll keep hammering away on the newscast about how we need to get these type of people—the crazy people, the killers, the homeless—off the streets of New York so hardworking, decent New Yorkers can enjoy this city again. We want to take our city back and make it the greatest city in the world again. That will be our slogan each and every night when we present the news to our viewers."

"Take Back New York," I said.

"That's right. What do you think?"

I shrugged. "It sounds kinda naive and simplistic."

"What do you mean?"

"What about all these people that you seem to want to rid the streets of? These undesirables who ruin it for the rest of us or whatever it is you're saying. Aren't they a part of our city too? For better or worse. That's a lot of the beauty and wonder of New York, this mix of all different sorts of people living here. What happens to all these people that you don't want to be a part of New York anymore?"

"I don't care."

"You should."

"Listen, this campaign will make us very controversial and very prominent in TV news. Everyone will be talking about us. And that's all that matters. It will put Channel 10 News at the top of the media world. That translates into big ratings."

"So that's what this is all about? Ratings?"

"What else is there?"

I wasn't sure if she was kidding or not.

"We had a case like this in San Francisco when I worked there," she said. "Young college girl gets attacked, raped, and murdered on a jogging path near the campus. Everyone was terrified. We played on that terror element night after night on our newscasts. How there was some crazy person out there stalking women on the streets. People were afraid to leave their homes for weeks.

"But let me tell you something they did do . . . they watched TV. And a lot of them watched our newscasts because we were reporting it bigger and better than anyone else in town. I personally took charge of that news campaign at the station. We even had a theme—we called it 'City of Fear.' That ran at the bottom of the screen for all of our reporting.

"The result? Our ratings went through the roof. That's what happens when people become afraid. They want to see more of what they're afraid of on the TV news. We milked that sucker for everything we could for as long as we could."

"How did it turn out?"

"What do you mean?"

"Did the police ever catch this crazy stalker before he attacked any more women?"

"Funny thing about that. It turned out it wasn't a crazy stalker at all. It was a boyfriend of the girl. They had sex—consensual sex—then got into a big argument. He killed her in a rage, then dumped the body on the jogging path so everyone would think that was where she'd been killed."

"So your TV news campaign there—the whole City of Fear thing—was wrong?"

"Didn't matter." Endicott shrugged. "We still got all the great ratings while the stalker scare was happening. And a lot of those viewers stayed around for us afterward. It was a win-win, all the way around. And, like I said, that City of Fear campaign—and all those huge ratings it drew—was all my idea."

"You must have been very proud," I said, trying to keep the sarcasm in my voice as subtle as possible.

"Yeah, it was great."

I guess subtle sarcasm didn't register with this woman.

CHAPTER 13

I MADE A list of people I'd seen attending Riley Hunt's funeral that I most wanted to talk to individually about her.

There were three names at the top of the list:

1. Bruce Townsend, Riley's fiancé.

2. The woman who was her roommate at the Easton dorm.

3. One—or any—of the band members of the group she played with at campus and off-campus events.

I started out with the Townsend kid, and he turned out to be the easiest to contact. I simply called the NYPD Public Information office and asked to speak to his father, Deputy Commissioner Hugh Townsend. He told me that he would make his son available to me for an interview in his office later that day. He said that he wanted to be there too. That was fine. In fact, it was even better than I hoped. I got two for one with the interview—the son who was engaged to Riley, and the father who was in charge of investigating the murder case.

"I understand you need to do your job, just like I need to do mine," Deputy Commissioner Townsend said to me when I got there to see him and his son at 1 Police Plaza. "I've always had a great—and a very respectful—relationship with the media. Obviously, this has been a very traumatic experience for my son, but I encouraged him to talk to you. Isn't that right, Bruce?"

"Yes," his son said. "I want to do anything I can to honor Riley and keep her memory alive."

He looked even bigger than I remembered him being from the funeral. Maybe 6 foot 6 or 6 foot 7. Hefty, but not fat—like he probably worked out regularly. But it was his hair that was his most conspicuous feature. Big, dark brown, bushy hair that made him seem even taller than he was.

His father was tall too, although not quite as big as his son. But he didn't have big, bushy hair, he had no hair at all. His head was shaved bald. Maybe that's why the son wore his hair so long, he figured the family genes might not let him keep it too long.

The father was wearing his uniform, complete with medals and insignias, and he looked very much like the top figure in law enforcement that he was. The son was dressed more casually, like a college student might look, wearing a plaid sports shirt and jeans. He said he was taking criminal justice courses at Baruch College. I guess he hoped to follow in his father's footsteps with a career in law enforcement.

I'd brought my film crew with me. Before we started though, I asked Deputy Commissioner Townsend a few questions about the status of the investigation. Hoping he might give me something off the record that he hadn't said to anyone else. But he pretty much stuck to the standard line that was coming out of the NYPD.

"It really all points to her just being in the wrong place at the wrong time," Townsend said. "Normally the streets near the campus are safe, even at that time of night. Students walk there all the time without incident.

"We're still working on the theory that it was a random attack—presumably by some deranged person since nothing was taken from her. There's no other motive or possible suspect we've been able to find who might have wanted to kill her.

"As you probably know, these are the most difficult types of cases to solve because there's no clear or logical trail of evidence in a random attack like this. But I assure you we will find the person who did this. And I hope—and I believe—that will be very soon."

"What about the girl's cell phone?" I asked when he was finished.

"What about it?"

"You said nothing had been stolen or taken from her. But she had a cell phone. And it wasn't there with her body. Do you have any idea yet what happened to it?"

"Maybe the killer did take that, for some reason."

"Or someone else picked it up later and never told anyone."

"That's possible too."

I had another question for Townsend before I interviewed his son.

"Do you think there's any conflict of interest in you heading up this murder investigation since the victim had such a close personal relationship with your own son?"

"This is my job," he said. "I bring people to justice who do bad things to other people. Sadly, this time it has happened close to home for me. But I will do my job as a professional law enforcement officer just like I do every day and in every case for this department."

The interview we taped with his son after that didn't reveal any big surprises. Still, it was good TV. He said a lot of the same things he'd said at the funeral. But he was very emotional and clearly grief-stricken over Riley's shocking murder. He seemed like a nice kid. Riley seemed like a nice kid too. Maybe they would have had a happy marriage. Except now, we'd never know.

I asked him how they met. He elaborated on the story he'd told during the funeral.

"I went to one of the concerts for her band on campus. I was blown away. They were good, but I didn't care much about the music. I couldn't take my eyes off the lead singer. She caught my eye in the audience too, I guess I was watching her so intently. We had a drink afterward. Then it just went from there for us.

"She was so full of energy and drive and ambition. For the music. For her school work. For the sports she played like basketball. And most of all for the future. That's why she was majoring in political science. She said she wanted to make a difference in the future for the world. To make the world a better place."

She wanted to make the world a better place. A lot of people said that about her. I remembered at the memorial service where they talked about her working at soup kitchens, pet shelters, and a group to help homeless military veterans.

Riley Hunt sure sounded like a helluva young woman.

"Tell me about the last time you saw her."

"Not much to tell. It was all very casual. We had no way of knowing that it would be our last time together. We grabbed some sandwiches at a deli, then ate them in Washington Square Park. She loved to hang out in the park. She talked about how she had that big basketball awards dinner, and she asked me again if I could be there. But I'd already made plans to go home to my parents' house on Long Island, and my mother had been looking forward to seeing me. So I went there instead of being with Riley. If I'd just been with her instead that night, maybe . . ."

He shook his head sadly.

"The next morning, my father got a call from his office about it and told me what happened to Riley. I'm not quite sure what I said or did—it all seemed so unbelievable that Riley could be gone like that. I still wake up sometimes in the morning, and I think that this must all be a bad dream that I'm going to wake up from. But then I realize it is no dream. Riley is really dead."

I nodded sympathetically. There didn't seem to be much else to do.

"When was the wedding going to be?" I asked.

"We hadn't made any specific wedding plans yet."

"I understood you were engaged."

"We were, but . . ."

"They were sort of engaged to be engaged," his father interrupted then. "They'd only known each other for a short time. I convinced them to hold off for a while on anything specific, marriage-wise. After all, people need to know each other well before getting married. I told them that was important for a healthy marriage. Don't you agree?"

"I'm not the best person to ask about healthy marriages," I said.

"The bottom line is Riley and I planned to spend our entire lives together," Bruce Townsend said. "I keep thinking about those last moments we spent eating lunch in the park. I never could have imagined everything that happened afterward. I wish I could go back in time and tell her I was going to be with her that night. Tell her how much I loved her . . ."

He shook his head sadly.

"I thought we had sixty years together ahead of us, Riley and me. But we only got a few months. It's just not fair . . ."

That's the sound bite which led our newscast that night.

CHAPTER 14

I MET RILEY Hunt's roommate on a park bench outside her dormitory on the campus of Easton College.

She told me her name was Brianna Bentley. She said she was a junior—a year ahead of Riley—and was majoring in theater arts.

"Brianna Bentley?" I said. "That's a pretty name."

"You think so?" Her face brightened. "It's actually my stage name. I changed it when I got into theater arts to something that I thought would be good for my career."

"What's your actual name?"

"Nancy Guntzler. I think Brianna Bentley is much better for me. So that's what I go by now."

I had a video crew with me, but I told her I wanted to interview her a bit one-on-one before we did something for on-air.

Not that it took much prodding to get Brianna Bentley/Nancy Guntzler to do it. She seemed eager to be on TV.

Which I quickly found a bit weird and off-putting.

"I want to look my best for this," she said. "Is there anyone who can put makeup on me or do something with my hair for the camera? A lot of people are going to be watching. Maybe some important people who can help me break into show business. It could be a real opportunity for me."

I said we didn't do that kind of thing for these kinds of interviews.

"Do I look all right though?"

"You look fine."

"Are you sure?"

I didn't know how to respond delicately. The truth was she didn't look that good. She was a bit overweight—not exactly fat, but definitely pudgy—and her face had a pasty white pallor, which made her red hair seem out of place. I wondered if she'd dyed the hair red as part of her "actress look." But I ignored her question and told her: "This isn't about you. It's about your roommate, Riley Hunt. Who was brutally murdered here a few nights ago. That's what we want to talk to you about."

"Okay, but I'm studying to be an actress. I'm a good actress. I just need someone to notice me. And this could be my big chance for that to happen."

If she was grief-stricken at all about the murder of her roommate, she sure didn't show it.

I asked her about their relationship.

"We were roommates," she said.

"Were you friends?"

"You don't have to be friends with someone to be their roommate. The school sometimes assigns roommates. That's what happened with us."

"So you wouldn't say you and Riley were friends?"

"No, not friends."

She smiled, like she thought there was something funny about that.

"Definitely not friends."

"Were you enemies?"

"We used to be friends. Then we were enemies. But mostly we stayed out of each other's way as much as possible. Let's just say I wasn't Riley's biggest fan. But then a lot of people felt like that about her."

"I thought she was very popular on campus."

"That's what she wanted people to believe."

"Is that what you plan to say on the air?"

"What do you want me to say?"

"I want you to tell the truth."

She laughed now. "The truth? The truth about Riley? What's that line from Jack Nicholson in the movie? 'You can't handle the truth!' Well, I don't think you could handle the truth about Riley. Your viewers wouldn't believe me anyway. They want to buy into this myth about Riley Hunt being this lovely, popular golden girl of a college coed, just like you do."

None of this was what I was expecting. But then the whole experience of talking with a college student and being on a college campus was weird for me too. I hadn't spent much time at colleges since I went myself years ago. And that had been a kinda strange experience too. Me, I had a traumatic experience when I went away to college a long time ago. I got pregnant my first year there, my father cut off my money—and I worked for a year before going back to school to get my journalism degree.

That was a lot different from this woman or Riley Hunt.

And it was a different time back then in the '80s too.

But none of this explained the roommate's seeming lack of grief or emotion—and frankly her hostility—about the dead girl.

"Were you with Riley at all that last night when she went to several bars before she was attacked and killed?" I asked.

"Me? Never? I wasn't part of her crowd."

"When was the last time you talked with her?"

"The day before, I guess."

"Not that day?"

"I'm involved in rehearsals for a major campus theatrical production. I've got a big actress role," she said proudly. "I was busy in class or working at the theater all day. So no, I didn't see Riley. At least not that I remember. We didn't spend too much time together—even as roommates. More just like two ships passing in the night, as they say. I did my thing, and she did her thing. Whatever the hell her thing was."

I asked her about Riley's cell phone and her computer. The fact that both were missing bothered me. But she told me the same thing I'd heard from Sam—Riley had lost her laptop computer a short time earlier, or more likely it had been stolen, and Riley had never replaced it. She said she had told the police this when they asked about Riley's computer or other devices. As for the cell phone, she had no answer for that. Other than to say Riley always carried it with her. Which made me wonder even more who had it now.

"Anything else you want to tell me about Riley?" I asked her.

"Oh, I could tell you a lot of things, believe me."

"Like what?"

"You wouldn't believe me."

"Try me."

"C'mon, I know what you want. Like I told you before, I know what your viewers want. An interview with me about what a wonderful person Riley was and how her death is a tragic loss and how much we're all going to miss her—and all that kind of crap. So put me in front of the camera, and I'll tell you what you want to hear."

Sure enough, once the camera was rolling, the young woman who called herself Brianna Bentley was like a different person talking about Riley Hunt.

"Riley and I had lived together all year," she said then. "When you live with someone, you get to know them really well. She was a beautiful person, inside and out. And she had such a bright future ahead of her. Riley was a true light of hope in this world. I simply can't believe she's gone.

"Who would want to do something like that? I wish Riley and I could be together again in our room. Talking and laughing and gossiping about people we know like we had such fun doing. Except I know that will never be happening again. Riley is with the angels now. And that's what she was—an angel. I miss her so much!"

I thought she was going to cry at that point. She never did, not quite. That might have been too obviously theatrical for her. Instead, she managed to have a single tear come out of her eye, roll down her cheek—and she wiped it away with her hand for the camera. It was a nice touch, I had to admit.

This woman was right about one thing.

She was a damn good actress.

But, before she went into her act, she'd told me stuff about Riley Hunt that raised more questions I hadn't heard before.

And I was pretty sure she had other secrets about Riley that she was hiding.

About what Riley was really like.

About her life.

And maybe about her death too.

CHAPTER 15

THERE WERE FOUR other members besides Riley in Fallen Sky, the band she had played with at on-campus and off-campus events. Three men and a woman who played drums. The woman's name was Ellie Feldman.

She was working part-time at a music store in Greenwich Village off Bleecker Street, and I convinced her to join me at a coffee shop on MacDougal to talk about Riley.

"I'm really serious about making music my career," she explained to me. "That's why I'm in the band, I work at the store, and why I major in music at Easton."

"What about Riley? Did she take music seriously too?"

"Nah, it was just something she did to have fun between those political science classes she took. That's where her ambition was. She really thought she was going to be a congresswoman or a senator or even the first woman president someday. But instead . . . well, this happened."

"What about the other people in the band?"

"Hey, they had their own interests too. Like Riley did. I'm the only one in the band who is really committed to music. Have you talked to anyone else from Fallen Sky yet?"

"You're the first."

I asked her some more questions about the group. She explained how Fallen Sky played a lot of '80s and '90s pop music in their performances because that's what people seemed to like—even more than the current songs and groups on the charts now.

"Was Riley a good lead singer?"

"She was sexy."

"That's not the question."

"With a group like ours, being cool and sexy is important. Riley could pull that off. She had that Debbie Harry, Chrissie Hynde, Belinda Carlisle look that fit in well with a lot of those old songs we did from women like that. Her voice didn't matter that much. Men loved her at our shows. All sorts of guys in the audience had crushes on her. They all wanted to be with her."

"Enough to stalk her one night and maybe kill her?"

Ellie didn't say anything back. But I felt like I'd struck a nerve.

"There was someone?"

"Like I said, men were always interested in Riley."

"But was there anyone in particular?"

"I think there might have been."

"Someone who could have become obsessed with Riley?"

"Maybe."

"Enough to track her down on the street and kill her?"

She shrugged.

"All I know is that Riley told me not long ago she felt like someone was following her. Stalking her, was the way she put it. She wasn't 100 percent certain, but she said she had this feeling she was being watched. She assumed it was some fan of hers from the band who had a crush on her or something."

"Did you tell this to the police?"

"Yes, but I don't think they took it too seriously. They said she was most likely killed by a random crazy person on the street—not someone who knew her."

"That's the prevalent theory."

"But you don't agree?"

"I'm checking out all the possibilities. Did she tell you anything at all more about this stalker of hers she thought might be out there?"

"No. And, in fact, even after she brought it up, she kind of laughed and said it was probably only her imagination."

*   *   *

I tracked down the rest of the members of Fallen Sky too. The most interesting was the lead guitar player. His name was Jamie. He said he was the closest person to Riley in the group. "Not romantic or anything," he explained. "I have a girlfriend. But just because Riley and I did a lot of stuff together onstage—me on lead guitar and her as the lead singer."

"When is the last time you saw Riley?"

"We had a band rehearsal a couple of nights before she died. We were supposed to play some gigs later in the week. Of course, those were all called off after Riley's murder. God knows if Fallen Sky will ever perform again. Without Riley . . ."

His voice trailed off.

"Did you notice anything unusual about her at that last band rehearsal?"

"What do you mean?"

"Did she seem upset about anything? Nervous?"

I told him the story from Ellie about how she had a feeling that she was possibly being followed or watched by someone.

"Nah, nothing like that," Jamie said. "She just seemed . . . well, preoccupied."

"Preoccupied?"

"Yes. Like she had something else on her mind. She wasn't very focused on our rehearsal. I eventually cut it short because she didn't seem in the right frame of mind to sing that day."

"Any idea what was bothering her?"

"Not really. I figured that whatever it was would go away and she'd be fine for our next appearance. Maybe I'd ask her about it then at a later time. Of course, there was no later time for Riley, was there?"

"And you never saw Riley again after that?"

He hesitated before answering me, like he was trying to decide how to answer my question. Which is always a pretty good indication to an interviewer that the answer will be an interesting one.

"Jamie?"

"I did see her."

"Where?"

"I saw her in Washington Square Park. The day after our band rehearsal. She was talking to a guy. A guy who . . . well, I'm pretty sure he's a drug dealer."

Wow! A drug dealer? This sure didn't fit the image of the wholesome girl that Riley Hunt was supposed to be.

"Was Riley into drugs?"

"Not that I ever knew about. Oh, she smoked a bit of pot once in a while. We all did. But no heavy-duty drug use. Or so I always thought."

"Do you know the name of the man she was talking to?"

"No. But I'd seen him dealing drugs in the park before."

"Do you think Riley was buying drugs from him that day?"

"I don't know. It didn't look like that was what was happening at all. They weren't passing any money back and forth or exchanging any packages or doing anything like that at all."

"What were they doing?"

"They were just talking."

"Talking?'

"Yes, like they were friends or something."

CHAPTER 16

I FINALLY FOUND Jack Faron. Or rather he found me.

"I'm at Max's Pub," he texted me. "Remember that place? Near the old newspaper office where you and I won a Pulitzer a long time ago? Well, okay, you won the Pulitzer. Can you meet me here?"

Jack Faron had been my editor at the newspaper when I won that Pulitzer as a young reporter. He moved on to television news and—after the paper went out of business—gave me a chance to break into TV as an on-air reporter at Channel 10. That didn't go too well at first, but he kept me there as part of the production team and eventually named me news director. We'd broken some big stories since then, me and Jack. I owed him a lot. And it felt strange not to be working for him anymore.

Faron was at the bar working on a big plate of chicken wings when I walked in—dipping them in blue cheese dressing and washing it all down with a beer.

"Want some wings?" he asked when I sat down next to him. "This blue cheese on them is incredible."

"No thanks."

"Why not? You like chicken wings."

"I'm trying to watch my weight these days," I said, remembering the tight jacket on my new spring outfit.

"Me too."

"Interesting approach to dieting," I said as he dipped another wing into the blue cheese dressing and then chewed on it hungrily.

Faron had been trying to lose some weight for the past year or so. Nibbling on fruit and cottage cheese at lunch, drinking Slim Fast—stuff like that. He wasn't terribly obese, but he'd developed a middle-aged paunch that he'd been concerned about. Apparently, he wasn't too worried about it now though.

But what the hell, the guy just lost his job.

Some people drown their sorrows in drink.

He seemed to be doing it with food.

"Can I at least buy you a drink, Clare?"

"I'd love a beer."

"You still drink Corona, right?"

"Yep, with a lime. That would be great."

A few minutes later, I was sipping on my beer and talking to Jack Faron about everything that had happened to him since that day he left my office for his meeting with Brendan Kaiser.

"I didn't see it coming. Can you believe that? After all these years in the business, I had no clue. Anyway, that's why I didn't come back and talk to anyone about it. I was embarrassed and I guess I was in a state of shock. Oh, they gave me a nice severance package so I'm okay financially. And I even have the fancy title of 'consultant.' But I don't think I'll be doing much consulting with the Endicott woman around. What do you think of her?"

I told him everything I knew about Susan Endicott. He didn't seem surprised. Endicott had built up quite a reputation in the TV news business at her previous jobs. Great for boosting ratings, not so great as a human being. The transition from Jack Faron to Susan Endicott was going to be tough for all of us at Channel 10.

"Oh, and she wears her glasses up on top of her head," I said.

"Huh?"

"I hate it when someone wears their glasses on top of their head like that. I find it really, really annoying."

"From what you've told me about Susan Endicott, it sounds like you've got a lot more to worry about than that."

I asked Faron about his future.

He laughed. "Future? What future? People forget about you very quickly in this business, you know that. It's like that story you always tell about Kathleen Sullivan. The 'didn't she used to be Kathleen Sullivan' line. I figure that people will be saying the same thing about me: 'Didn't he used to be Jack Faron?'"

"You could get another job, Jack."

"C'mon, let's be realistic. I'm an aging white male. Not a lot of demand in this business for old men like me. Look at me . . ."

"You still look good for a man in his 60s."

"I'm 57, Clare."

"You look good for that age too," I said quickly.

The chicken wings were gone now. So was my beer. Faron looked like he wanted to order another round of chicken wings. Maybe keep on eating chicken wings all night—or until he exploded. But he didn't. He ordered another beer for himself and for me. I drank some more beer and said to him: "You're a consultant now, Jack. So how about doing some consulting?"

"I told you—Endicott doesn't want to hear my ideas."

"I know, but I do. I could really use some input—I could use someone like you to consult with—on this Riley Hunt story."

Faron thought about it briefly and then shrugged. "I'm on the Channel 10 payroll as a consultant anyway. Why not? Tell me about it all."

I told him everything I'd found out and the people I'd talked to so far. And why some of it bothered me. The mother's reaction to her daughter's murder. The hostility of the roommate. The people in her band who told me about a possible stalker and saw her talking with a drug dealer in Washington Square Park. Plus, the fact that her fiancé's father was a high police official who was overseeing the murder investigation.

"What do you think all of this means?" he asked after I was done.

"I have no idea."

"Maybe nothing at all."

"You think?"

"Sure. If it was just a random attack on the street like everyone else seems to think, then all these things—all your questions—are irrelevant."

"I guess."

"You're not buying the random murder theory?"

"I don't know, Jack. I have a funny feeling about all this. My news instinct just . . . well, my news instinct tells me there might be a lot more to the Riley Hunt story than any of us know about so far."

"Your news instinct? That's it?"

"Yes. I've talked about my news instincts with you on other stories before this. Have my news instincts ever been wrong?"

"Yes, plenty of times."

"Okay, but sometimes I'm right."

"What does Susan Endicott think about your news instincts on this?"

"She likes the idea that Riley was killed by a crazed person on the streets of New York. It terrifies everyone and builds ratings. It backs up her 'Take Back New York' idea. She wants me to push that angle, and not get off track with other possible scenarios."

"So what are you going to do?"

"I'm going to keep digging on the Riley Hunt story," I said. "Every part of it. Not just what Endicott told me to do."

"Even if Endicott doesn't want you to do that?"

"Hey, Jack, I've ignored executive producers before. You know that better than anyone, right?"

He smiled.

"Let me know what you find out."

CHAPTER 17

I DECIDED TO go back and retrace Riley Hunt's steps on the night that she died.

Starting at the restaurant in Times Square where she'd attended the awards dinner for her basketball team.

There were still pictures posted up there from the event that night. All the women on the basketball team, including Riley. There was a photo of her on the basketball court in her uniform playing in a game. Another from that night at the banquet, proudly holding up a trophy she had won. She looked so pretty and full of life in both pictures. It was still hard to believe her life had been snuffed out so soon afterward.

I didn't find out much there that I didn't already know. One person said she seemed very quiet that night, like she had something on her mind that was bothering her. There was no indication of what that might be. But it was similar to what Jamie, the guy in Fallen Sky, had said about her at their most recent band rehearsal.

There wasn't much more I learned at the restaurant. The same at the next place I went to. A bar down the street from the restaurant where Riley and some of the other people at the awards dinner had gone for more drinks afterward. It was an Irish pub called Patsy's. Not much help, but I had to try.

My last stop turned out to be more interesting. The Cutting Edge, a bar on Herald Square several blocks south. The final place where we knew that Riley Hunt had stopped that night before she was murdered.

The woman behind the bar at the Cutting Edge was very friendly and helpful. Especially after I told her I was a TV newswoman from Channel 10. She said she wanted to get into TV news one day too. Ah, the dream of being a TV newswoman. Everyone thought it was so glamorous. But I needed her cooperation so I encouraged her in the TV newswoman dream, offered to give her any help I could— and then finally got around to the real reason I was there.

She said she was working there that night and remembered Riley Hunt.

"I couldn't believe it when I saw on the news that she was dead. Murdered too. I'd just been serving her drinks only a few hours earlier."

"What was she drinking?" I asked, just out of curiosity.

"Gin and tonic. I remember she wanted a specific kind of gin too. Lincoln Blue. She said that was the way she liked her gin and tonic."

I asked her how many drinks Riley had ordered.

"One. Maybe two." She shrugged. "She wasn't drunk or anything."

"Did she talk to you about anything else?"

"Not really. She was with a group of people. They came in here together after some party at a restaurant. That's what she was doing at first. Then, later, well, she seemed preoccupied with a guy that came in at some point after that."

"What guy?"

"I don't know. Just a guy."

"Do you think she knew him before?"

"I assume so. He and Riley were really talking with each other. They spent some time together, the two of them alone. She didn't . . . she didn't seem happy with him."

I thought about her fiancé, Bruce Townsend.

"Was he a big guy?" I asked.

I described Townsend to her.

"No, that doesn't sound like him."

"Did they leave together?"

"No, he left alone."

"And Riley?"

"Uh, she left afterward."

So who was this mysterious guy?

And there was something else bothering me.

This woman behind the bar had suddenly gone from giving me expansive answers to short, terse replies. I had a feeling that she might know more than she was telling me. Maybe she even knew the identity of the man Riley was talking with at the bar not long before she was found dead downtown.

I confronted her with that now.

"Look, I don't want to talk to you anymore about Johnny . . ." she started to say.

"Johnny?"

"Oh, I shouldn't have said that."

"His name is Johnny?"

She didn't answer me but gave a slight nod with her head.

"Do you know Johnny's last name?"

"No."

But she said it in a way that made it obvious to me that she was lying.

"You said you wanted to get into the TV news business. You said you wanted to work with me on this story. So work with me here now. I could really use your help."

"I'd like to help you. I really would. But I'm afraid of getting involved if I talk any more about Johnny. I've got my own life here ahead of me to think about. I don't want to get messed up with certain kinds of people. They come after you. They might come after me if they knew I was talking about Johnny."

"We could do it off the record."

"You mean I'd be an unidentified source?"

"No one would know it was you."

"Like Deep Throat."

Damn. A half century after Watergate, people still knew about Deep Throat as the ultimate media source.

"Absolutely," I said.

She thought about it briefly and then said: "His name is Johnny Steffano."

That name sounded familiar to me, but I couldn't quite place it at first.

"His father is Anthony Steffano. You know who he is, don't you?"

I sure did. Anthony Steffano was reputed to be one of the top crime bosses in the city. On the surface, he was a legitimate businessman—owning restaurants, real estate property, and lots of other companies, plus working with and donating money to a lot of philanthropic organizations. But the reality was he made his money and gained his power through crime activities like drugs, extortion, robbery, and even murder.

"Riley Hunt was hanging out with Anthony Steffano's son?" I asked.

"That's right."

"And it didn't look like they had just met?"

"Oh no, they knew each other."

"How well do you think they knew each other?"

"He tried to put his arm around her at one point and tried to kiss her. She let him, even though she didn't seem all that enthusiastic about the kiss. But it seemed clear to me that they had—or at least they had had in the past—some kind of a romantic relationship between them."

Wow!

Now there was the son of a mobster in the picture.

Plus, a drug dealer from Washington Square Park.

And, of course, the fiancé whose father was a top police official.

Riley Hunt sure had made a lot of interesting friends during her time here in New York City.

CHAPTER 18

I ASKED MAGGIE to find out as much as she could for me about Johnny Steffano. She pulled some stuff together and brought it to my office.

"What do you want to know about Johnny Steffano?" she asked.

"For starters, how do I find him?"

"You don't want to find him."

"Why not?"

"He's a tough guy."

"How tough?"

She opened up her laptop and began to read from the information she'd gathered about him.

"Johnny Steffano is 24 years old, and he's already put together quite a record of achievements. Criminal achievements, that is. He was arrested for shoplifting when he was 16, stealing a car when he was 17, weapons possession—a handgun, along with a pair of brass knuckles—at 21, then busted for assaulting a guy in a bar who accidentally spilled a drink on him last year. He served time in juvenile detention, then did a couple of stints in state prison on the assault and gun possession convictions."

"How would he and someone like Riley Hunt ever know each other?"

"He's also a student at Easton College at the moment."

"You're kidding?"

"Majoring in sports administration. Anyway, I guess that's how they met."

I thought about that. It still didn't make sense. Riley Hunt and Johnny Steffano. The engagement to the police commissioner's son made sense. But not this.

"Does somebody with a record—convicted of felonies like Steffano—even get admitted to a college like Easton? Wouldn't that be a red flag enough to disqualify him?"

"Apparently not in Steffano's case."

"Because of his father?"

Maggie nodded.

"Anthony Steffano is on the Board of Trustees and is a major contributor to Easton."

"A quid pro quo," I said.

"I would imagine."

"Isn't higher education wonderful?"

"Wait, I've got more. I found a source who said about six months ago the kid got suspended after a complaint filed by one of his teachers. The teacher reported that Steffano threatened him with bodily harm—the exact words were 'he told me he was going to smash my face in'—if the teacher didn't reverse a failing grade he'd gotten for one of his courses."

"What happened then?"

"Nothing. Like I said, the Steffano kid was suspended at first. But then the dean of students reversed that and reinstated him. All the charges were dismissed. They said Steffano was joking when he said that, he wasn't really serious. Then later it was discovered that Steffano's father had made another contribution to the school, a big money grant to help build a new wing of the Easton library."

"I'm beginning to see a pattern here."

"Do you think Johnny Steffano could have been responsible for the Hunt girl's murder?"

"Well, we know Johnny Steffano is a violent person who has beaten up people in the past. Riley Hunt died after being beaten up. So yes, the possibility of that does cross my mind."

"What are you going to do now?"

"Go ask Johnny Steffano about it."

* * *

First, I had to find Steffano. I could go looking for him on the Easton campus, but it was a big place. I didn't figure I'd find him studying at the library or anything, even if his father did help build it. No, the easiest place to look for Johnny Steffano was at a restaurant called Steffano's that his father owned in Little Italy. The kid worked there for his father, I found out. So all I had to do was go to Steffano's, order a bowl of spaghetti, and shoot the breeze with Johnny Steffano. Easy. Except it didn't turn out to be so easy.

When I got to the restaurant, I met a big guy—maybe 6 foot 5 and nearly 300 pounds—who looked like he could have doubled as an actor on *The Sopranos* before taking this job. He had long hair, pulled together in the back with a ponytail. He didn't look like the kind of guy who would be sporting a ponytail hairdo—but, given his size, I figured not a lot of people would question him about it.

He was very nice to me at first. He sat me at a good table near the door. He even held my chair for me. And he ran through all the specials on the menu, recommending that I try the Fettuccine Alfredo. "It is simply exquisite," he said to me. "Rich, but so good you'll think you died and went to heaven."

But that all changed when I told him who I was and why I was there.

"Johnny is not here," he said stiffly.

"When will he be here?"

"Johnny is a very busy young man."

"Probably cramming for finals, huh?"

He glared at me.

"Look, all I want to do is talk with the kid. Find out more about how he knew Riley Hunt and what he knew. I'll put him on TV talking about her. It'll be great. I'll make him famous. Everyone's following this story about Riley Hunt's murder."

"Johnny doesn't know anything about it."

"But he did know her, right?"

"I think you should leave now."

"Before I get my fettuccine?"

"I'll walk you to the door."

I took out my business card with my name and contact information at Channel 10 on it—then handed it to him. "Call me when Johnny gets here. Let me know."

The guy looked at the card carefully, like he was memorizing my information, then ripped the card up into little pieces and threw them down on the table in front of me.

"We're not getting along too well, are we?" I said.

"On the contrary, we're getting along fine, Ms. Carlson. As long as you leave quietly, and you never come back here again."

He walked me to the door and out onto the street.

"By the way," I said, "I'll bet your fettuccine alfredo special wasn't that good anyway. Probably tasted like something that came out of a can."

"If I see you here again, your departure will much more unpleasant," he said. "Do you understand what I'm saying. I'm not a person you want to mess with."

I made an imaginary gun with my hand, pointing the index finger at him and using my thumb to pretend to pull the trigger.

"Right back at you, big guy," I said.

CHAPTER 19

THERE WAS A fancy Mercedes-Benz sitting in front of the Channel 10 building when I came out the door after work. It was dark blue. Really big. And very expensive-looking. An impressive vehicle, no question about it.

There were four men inside. One of them opened the passenger door as I walked by, as if to let me in to join them. Wow! A luxury car waiting to whisk me away. How great is that? Of course, it would have been even greater if I had any idea who was in this car or why they might be waiting for me.

"May we have a word with you, Ms. Carlson," the man in the passenger seat said. He was about 60, distinguished-looking with gray hair and wearing a fashionable tailored suit and tie. Just the kind of guy I'd expect to be in a car like this.

"What about?" I asked, keeping my distance from him and the car as best I could.

"We have a question for you."

"I'll bet I know what the question is: Can you have my autograph? Sorry, not now. I'm in a hurry. Big-time TV star and all."

He didn't laugh or even smile.

"That's not the question."

"Oh, I've got it now—" looking over the expensive car. "You want to know how to get to the auto show. I think it's at the Javits Center this year. Good luck. You ought to do great there with this big, beautiful sucker of a car."

Still no smile. Instead, he said to me: "I've been told that you fancy yourself as a bit of a wit."

"I amuse myself sometimes."

"May I ask you a question?"

"Sure."

"Why are you so interested in Johnny Steffano?"

I looked closer into the car now. Besides this guy and the driver in the front seat, there were two more men in the back. I recognized one of them as the big guy with the ponytail from Steffano's restaurant. I didn't know his name, but I decided to call him Fettuccine Guy. I was pretty sure at this point that being a restaurant employee was not his only responsibility for Anthony Steffano.

Next to him was an older man. I could tell—based on pictures I'd seen—that this was Anthony Steffano himself. There was no sign of Johnny Steffano though.

I wasn't quite sure what to do next.

I mean, I could run.

But I was interested in seeing where this all led.

Besides, I was standing out here on a public street right in front of my office building so I didn't figure anyone was going to shoot me down or kidnap me in front of all these potential eyewitnesses. At least I was counting on that.

I waved now to Fettuccine Guy in the back seat. I guess he'd remembered who I was and where to find me before he tore up my business card.

"Hey, good to see you again," I shouted at him. "Did you come to deliver me some of that fettuccine alfredo in person. I bet it really is to die for. Oops, bad choice of words I guess with you guys . . ."

He didn't laugh or smile either.

Damn, this was a tough audience.

I decided to suspend the comedy routine and get down to business.

"Let me talk to Johnny Steffano about Riley Hunt," I said.

"Who is Riley Hunt?" the guy in the passenger seat said with a smirk.

"She was a woman at Easton College, the same school Johnny Steffano attends. She was murdered a few nights ago, as I'm sure you're well aware. I'm told Johnny Steffano had some kind of a relationship with her. Ergo, I want to interview him to see if he can shed any light on the story I'm working on about Riley's murder. Can you arrange an interview for me with him?"

The back passenger door of the car opened now. The man I knew to be Anthony Steffano got out. He walked over to me on the sidewalk.

"My son doesn't know anything about it," he said.

"But he did know her, didn't he?" I pointed out. "Maybe even known her in the biblical sense?"

"I am warning you: do not involve my son or my family in this manner."

Anthony Steffano didn't exactly look like an underworld boss. He wasn't particularly big or tough-looking or scary like you see in movies and on TV. Based on his physical appearance, he could have been anyone—a lawyer, real estate broker, accountant, or whatever. But I knew from what I read about him what a powerful, ruthless man he was—and what he could be capable of doing.

Still, I wasn't going to let him—or anyone else in the car—intimidate me.

"And if I don't?"

"Let's not consider that possibility."

"Or what? Are you going to sic Fettuccine Guy in the car there on me?"

Steffano sighed.

"Ms. Carlson, I'm friendly with the owner of your station. Brendan Kaiser. Brendan and I belong to the same country club. We've played golf together. We are on the boards of major charities together. I can reach out to Brendan Kaiser and—"

"I wondered when you'd get around to that. I figured it had to come sooner or later. I guess when a man like you can buy so many things with money—like keeping his son as a student at a prestigious university like Easton College—well, that man just assumes everyone can be bought. Threats don't work on me, Mr. Steffano. They just make me mad."

Steffano did smile now.

The first time I'd gotten a smile from anyone here.

I hoped that was good for me.

"Look, my son has made some mistakes," he said. "But he's young, he's still growing up. Didn't you do things you regretted when you were young? That's really all these things with my son have involved."

Car theft? Assault? Threatening your teacher with bodily harm? Oh, well...

"Just some high-spirited, youthful hijinks, huh?" I said to Anthony Steffano.

"I want him to get back on track with his life. That's why I helped him get back into the college. I don't want him involved in any more trouble or scandal. Not now. But that's what would happen if I let you talk to him or you talk about him and this case on the air. Even if it became clear that he knew nothing about it or the murder, which he doesn't. So why do we have to do this?"

"Because he did know her, Mr. Steffano. That's all I want to talk with your son about. All he has to do is tell the truth."

Steffano thought about that for a few seconds.

"If I make Johnny available to you, will you promise to try not to drag him into this if you are convinced that he has no involvement or knowledge whatsoever about the girl's murder?"

"I can't make that promise to you, Mr. Steffano."

"I'm trying to work with you here."

"I'll do the best I can to protect your son," I said.

"That's really not enough."

"It's all I can do."

CHAPTER 20

"DO I HAVE a guy for you to meet!" Janet said.

"Not interested."

"Let me tell you a bit about him."

"No."

I said it as emphatically as I could, hoping that would convince Janet to end this topic—even though I knew it wouldn't.

"His name is Pete Bevilacqua," she said.

"Janet!"

"I figured you'd want to know sooner or later."

"What does Pete what's-his-name do for a living?"

"He's a professor of Spanish. At Princeton."

"Oh God, an academic. Does he smoke a pipe and have patches on the elbows of his sports jackets?"

"Well, I've never actually met him."

"And yet you're trying to fix me up with this guy?"

"He's a friend of a friend."

"My God, I'm not that desperate, Janet."

"C'mon, he's seen you on TV and he says he really wants to meet you. So he reached out to the friend. Because he knew the friend knew me."

"Sounds like a stalker."

"So is that a definite 'no' on meeting him, Clare?"

"Maybe." I shrugged.

"I'll give him your number."

*   *   *

"I hardly ever do this sort of thing," I said to Pete Bevilacqua.

"Me either."

"It seems pretty desperate."

"Almost pathetic."

"And yet here we are doing it."

I was on a blind date with Bevilacqua, the professor from Princeton Janet had eventually set me up with. Well, it wasn't really a blind date. More like a blind meetup. We were at a Starbucks on Sixth Avenue around the corner from the Channel 10 office.

Pete Bevilacqua turned out to be a decent enough looking guy. Not a gorgeous hunk, but no slouch in the looks department either. He had curly brown hair, a neatly trimmed beard, and was wearing a denim sports jacket and a pair of beige slacks that made him look . . . well, professorial. I'd rate him maybe an 8 out of a possible 10 on my sexual attraction meter for desirable men.

No question about it, Pete Bevilacqua would be fine for any woman looking to start up a relationship. Which I wasn't. At least not at the moment. I did my best to make this clear to him now.

"Let's not waste any more time on this than we have to," I told him.

"What do you mean?"

"Janet just won't quit trying to be a matchmaker for me."

"You mean I'm not the first?"

"Oh no. I've gone out with her neighbor, her eye doctor—once even with a guy who came to her house to sell her insurance. A long list of losers."

"Do I seem like a loser to you?"

"Given Janet's track record, I figure you'll turn out to be A) married, B) gay, or C) a psychopathic stalker."

"Is there an option D?"

"Boring as hell. Janet's fixed me up with them too."

He had ordered some kind of a latte, along with a cinnamon bun and a bottle of spring water. I just had coffee. Black coffee. I wanted to keep this as simple as possible.

"If we don't go for any kind of refills on our drinks or order any more food, we can probably get through this in five or ten minutes. That should satisfy my obligation to Janet. Then you and I can go our separate ways and we'll never have to see each other again."

He smiled.

"Well, before you force-feed me this cinnamon bun on your way out of here, is it okay if I ask you one question?"

"Go ahead."

"Are you always in attack mode like this?"

I sighed.

He was right.

"Look," he said, "I took an hour train ride in from Princeton to do this. You walked a half a block from your office. Give me a little break here, huh?"

"I'm sorry. You didn't deserve any of that. It's just that . . . well, I'm working on this big story and I've got a new boss and so I'm really under a lot of pressure right now. I'm not looking for a new man in my life at this moment."

"I understand."

"You must think I'm a really horrible person."

"Actually, I think you're kinda cute."

"Really?"

"Really."

"Okay," I said, "you got yourself another fifteen minutes with that remark."

He asked me some questions about my job. I told him a bit about the Riley Hunt story and how we were focusing on it big-time. I also talked about how much I loved being a reporter, no matter how long I'd been doing it.

I asked him about teaching at Princeton. He talked about the thrill of dealing with young students and about teaching and about his job there in the Spanish languages department. I didn't really care that much. I was only trying to be polite since he asked me about my job. But he seemed truly interested in what I did for a living.

"I wanted to be a journalist once a long time ago."

"No kidding?"

"Yeah, I thought it sounded really romantic to be a reporter."

"What happened?"

"I wasn't very good at it."

"How long did you try?"

"About six months. I got a job one summer while I was at school for this small daily in upstate New York. Mostly writing about weddings and obits and small stuff like that. But then one day there was this big fire downtown, and four people died. I didn't put that in the lead of my story. It was like in the eighth or ninth paragraph. That's when I—and I guess my editors—decided that I didn't have what it takes to be a newspaper reporter."

"You couldn't pyramid," I said.

"Huh?"

"That's what we call it in the news business. Putting the main facts in the opening of any story. Then filling in the lesser facts below. Pyramiding. It's a crucial skill for any reporter."

"And I'll bet you can pyramid . . ."

"Oh, I pyramid with the best of them."

We were on our second coffee refills when we started to get to the personal stuff.

"How do you pronounce your name?" I asked him. "It's a tough one."

"Nah, its easy."

"Tell me."

"P-e-t-e."

I rolled my eyes.

"Your damn last name!"

"Oh, that is a bit tricky." He pronounced it for me. "It's Scottish. My wife always had a lot of trouble pronouncing it whenever she introduced herself as Mrs. Bevilacqua."

"Wife?"

"Ex-wife. We're divorced."

"Because she couldn't pronounce Bevilacqua?"

"Well, let's just say there were other issues between us. I guess I'm not always the easiest person to live with. We got divorced last year." He looked at me across the table. "Does it bother you at all that I'm divorced?"

"Hardly. I'm the queen of divorce."

"You too?"

"Three times."

"Wow!"

"Yeah, I'm not that easy to get along with either."

We'd been here for more than an hour now. Pete Bevilacqua finished off the rest of his drink, looked across the table at me, and said,

"So basically, both of us are impossible to live with, we don't really have much in common at all with our work—and you wouldn't even be here except for that goddamned Janet Wood woman. Would you say that's a good appraisal of the situation here between you and me?"

"That sums it up pretty well, I think."

"Do you want to do it again?"

"Meet here again for coffee?"

"Listen, I understand there's a real pecking order when it comes to dating. There's the real date, like dinner or a movie. There's the lunch date, which is less formal because it's in the middle of the workday. There's drinks, which sometimes leads to dinner—but can also only occupy a shorter amount of time. And then last—the least risky of all—there's the coffee date. Like we're having today. Like you said, we could have ended this after five or ten minutes. But we didn't. How about upping the ante a bit next time? Lunch? Drinks? Maybe even dinner?"

"I'm not sure of my schedule at the moment . . ."

"This requires a 'yes' or 'no' answer."

"Yes or no?"

"I'd prefer yes so if you're undecided . . ."

"Maybe."

He laughed.

"You're a really interesting person, Clare Carlson."

CHAPTER 21

Susan Endicott wanted to know about the evaluation ratings of our on-air personnel and others that she'd asked me to compile for her.

"I'm working on it," I said.

Which wasn't true. I hadn't done anything.

"When can I see it?"

"Oh, soon."

"You've got until the end of the week."

"Why?"

"Why what?'

"Why are we doing this?"

"I want your evaluation on everyone so we can decide how to move forward with making changes to the newscast."

"I'll give you my evaluations right now. We have a great team here at Channel 10 News. Every one of them. I give them all my highest rating. How's that for an evaluation?"

"Oh, c'mon. You don't really think what's his name, the sports guy, is any good."

"His name is Steve Stratton," I said.

"Whatever, Steve Stratton," she said, waving her hand contemptuously to make it clear to me she didn't care what his name was. "Jeez, what a Neanderthal."

Steve Stratton had been reporting sports news in New York for the past 30 years. Sure, time had passed him by in some ways—he didn't like covering soccer or women's sports or political activism among athletes, all the stuff that had become part of TV sportscasting in recent years. But he was still a highly regarded sportscaster, a sort of legend in the business. He gave our sportscasts an air of professional authority based on his years of experience. Not everyone on a TV newscast has to be a wisecracking young kid.

I told that to Endicott now.

But she wasn't impressed in the least.

"He's a boring old guy who looks like he should have been on TV news in the 1950s or '60s. Let's get someone new, someone fresh, someone different to do sports for us."

"Anything else?"

"Yeah, what's the deal with the two Barbie Twins?"

The Barbie Twins was the term people dismissively used—behind their backs, of course—for Cassie O'Neal and Janelle Wright. Sure, it was totally inappropriate language in the modern workplace. But it pretty well summed up Cassie and Janelle who were strong in the looks department on TV but not so much when it came to journalistic skills. And they weren't exactly the brightest bulbs in the room.

For Cassie, it was always a challenge for her to pronounce any words longer than two or three syllables accurately. Some of her on-air malaprops were funny, but definitely cringeworthy. As for Janelle, she once did a live remote from the Brooklyn Bridge in which she said: "Behind me you can see the beauty of the Queens skyline."

"Believe it or not, Janelle and Cassie get the highest popularity ratings of anyone on our news shows," I said. "Which probably says something about the quality of TV news and the people who watch it. I've thought more than once about getting rid of them, but their popularity—"

"Why would you do that?"

"Do what?"

"Think about getting rid of them."

"I told you . . . they mess up on air a lot."

"But they look good on the air. That's what is important. So we want them both. Just write everything out for them before they go on air. Make them read it from a teleprompter. Put cheat notes on the teleprompter screen so they get it all right if you have to. Now let's talk about the weather girl."

"Weather woman," I said.

"Right. What's her name?"

"Wendy Jeffers."

"Tell me more about her."

"Well, she's an experienced meteorologist who—"

"Oh, c'mon, Carlson. She looks good too. That's what I really like. A good-looking female weather reporter. Do you realize how much of a rating spike we can get in our male viewership if we play her up prominently on the show? Let's give her more time on the newscast. And let her talk about more than the weather. Have her do some exchanges on other topics too—traffic, news, entertainment, or whatever—with the anchor desk or various reporters. Let's make her a real on-air personality."

That shouldn't be a problem, I thought. Wendy Jeffers always wanted to do more than just the weather. She envisioned herself as a kind of female Al Roker. Well, now it looked like she was going to get her chance.

"How about Brett and Dani?" I asked.

I remembered the scene in the news meeting when Dani said Endicott had praised her, but she ignored Brett.

"What about them?"

"They've been our anchor team since I got here and—"

"Fire one of them."

"What? Now wait a minute . . ."

"One of them has to go."

"Why?"

"To shake things up."

"Which one do you want me to fire?"

I figured she'd say Brett, but she didn't.

"Doesn't matter. I want one of them to stay and one of them to go—you can flip a coin if you want to. I want to shake it up, get some controversy going. No better way to do that than fire one of the anchors. Only one of them gets to stay."

"Brett and Dani are married," I pointed out.

"Even better."

"This could affect their marriage."

"Wow, that would be terrific publicity if they got divorced . . ."

I shook my head sadly.

"And you figure that would get us even bigger ratings with the one who's still here because of all the marital controversy?"

"Exactly."

"Is there anything you won't do for ratings?" I asked her.

Susan Endicott laughed now. It was the first time I'd heard her laugh since I met her. But it wasn't a "ha ha" funny kind of laugh.

"Let me get back to you on that." Susan Endicott smiled.

I got up and started to leave her office.

"Let's start with Stratton," she said. "Fire him first. Let me know as soon as it's done."

"I don't want to fire Steve."

"I don't care what you want, Carlson. Just do it."

"What if I refuse?"

"Then I'll fire you," Endicott said.

I thought maybe she was kidding.

But she wasn't laughing anymore when she said it.

CHAPTER 22

"ENDICOTT JUST DROPPED the big one," I said to Maggie in my office afterward.

"What do you mean?"

"She used the F-word on me."

"She said . . . ?"

"Fired."

"Oh, that F-word."

"She said it's either me or Steve. If don't fire him—and I'm sure there'll be others after Steve—then she'll fire me."

Maggie asked the obvious question next. "What about me?"

"Your name didn't come up, Maggie. I don't think she even knows who you are."

"Is that good?"

"When it comes to Susan Endicott, the answer is yes."

Maggie shook her head.

"She can't fire you, Clare. You've broken all those big stories for the station. You're a star. And Brendan Kaiser, the owner, loves you. You're bulletproof. Even someone like Susan Endicott can't hurt you."

"I suppose."

"You don't agree?"

"I hope you're right about that, but I really don't want to test it out."

"What are you gonna do?"

"Keep working on the story."

"I mean about Steve."

"That's what I mean too. I'll keep holding Endicott off as long as I can. While I dig into the Riley Hunt story until I break something—something really big—that makes such a media splash she can't get rid of me. Then I can use that to try to save Steve's job."

"That means there's a lot riding for you on this story, Clare."

"Always is," I said.

*   *   *

There was a stack of that morning's newspapers on my desk. I'm one of those people who still like to get the print version of the paper, even though I do read them online a lot too. I feel it's easier to find stuff—and also not miss anything—when I'm holding the actual paper in my hand.

After Maggie left, I picked up the *New York Times* and began paging through it. Just for the hell of it, I turned to the employment section of the Want Ads. In case I really did get fired, I wanted to be ready. Maybe there was someone out there looking for an out-of-work TV news director with a Pulitzer Prize.

The first thing that caught my eye was a big ad for computer data entry operators. Computer data entry operator. I said that to myself a few times, getting used to the sound of it. It had a nice ring. Maybe this could be a career opportunity for me. Something a woman like me could really sink her teeth into. Make something of herself.

I read the ad: "Data entry operators needed for temporary or permanent work in the computer industry. Top pay rates, benefits, good working atmosphere. Call Marilyn." There was a telephone number for Marilyn at the bottom.

Good working atmosphere, the ad said. I could use a good working atmosphere. This computer data entry job might be just what I needed. There was a problem though. Before I called Marilyn, I needed to find out what a computer data entry operator actually did. If I asked Marilyn that question, I figured it might hurt my chances for getting the job. Marilyn might even get mad at me.

There were lots of other jobs listed too. Legal secretary. Quality control inspector. Waitress. Waitress, now that didn't sound like a bad idea. Tips, food around whenever you wanted it, customers to talk to. I could tell them all about my Pulitzer and TV news career while I served them grilled cheese, and maybe they'd give me a big tip.

Thinking about being a waitress started to make me hungry. I went downstairs to a place in the lobby of our building, bought a chocolate Chipwich sandwich, and brought it back to my desk.

While I was eating it, I decided to take stock of what I knew about the Riley Hunt story. That should be easy because I didn't know very much for sure. Especially about her relationships with men. Riley Hunt was:

A. engaged to the son of the deputy police commissioner

B. maybe going out with a guy whose father was a mob bigwig

C. hanging out with a drug dealer from Washington Square Park

D. being stalked by some unknown admirer—or potential
     killer

Pick any of those answers.

Or maybe all of them.

I checked my watch. A little after noon. I still had a few hours
before I had to run the afternoon news meeting. What should I do
until then? Maybe call Marilyn about the computer data entry
operator job. Probably a bad time though, Marilyn might be out to
lunch. I couldn't think of anything else to do. Except maybe go
downstairs and get another Chipwich.

I looked at the empty ice cream wrapper in my hand, crumpled
it up, and aimed it at a nearby waste can. It hit the rim and bounced
out. A near miss, but still a miss. Just like everything I'd done on
the Riley Hunt story. I still had a feeling there was something out
there that I was missing. Something big. I really did.

That's when I suddenly thought again about computers.

Not Marilyn's computers.

The computer that had never been found for Riley Hunt.

The one that had been lost or stolen a few days before her
murder.

I made a few phone calls. After that I stood up, put my handbag
on my shoulder, and walked out of my office.

"Where are you going?" Maggie asked as I walked past her desk.

"To go see someone about a computer."

CHAPTER 23

THE PERSON I was meeting in Bryant Park was a man named Todd Schacter. Schacter knew a lot about computers. Let me be more specific: he knew a lot about other people's computers. Todd Schacter was a computer hacker.

Of course, not everything he did was illegal.

But not all of it was legal either.

He operated, legally speaking, in a kind of . . . well, a gray area of the law.

Which was fine with me right now.

I met Schacter a few years ago through my friend Janet, the lawyer. She'd represented him after he'd been arrested for breaking into a Fortune 500 company's computer files. He posted a lot of the confidential details online about the company's top officers—including salaries, perks, expense accounts, and more for all the stockholders to see.

Schacter didn't do stuff like that for the money.

I wasn't exactly sure why he did it.

And I guess I didn't really want to know.

But, after Janet got him off the computer violation charge, he helped me get information from a powerful senator's secret computer emails that resulted in me tracking down my long-lost daughter, Lucy.

I convinced him to help me then by selling him on the challenge of whether or not he could really do it.

Now I had to sell him on the challenge of helping me by using his cyber skills for more information about the dead Riley Hunt.

I'd called Janet to get the latest contact information—it always kept changing—and I got a message to meet him here in the middle of Bryant Park.

"Why Bryant Park?" I asked Schacter when we were sitting on a park bench on the north side of the park, behind the New York Public Library.

"This is my office these days."

"Didn't you used to work out of Starbucks locations?"

That's where I'd met up with him the first time.

"Not secure enough. Outside is better."

Schacter was a tall, skinny guy with uncombed and wild-looking hair. I never was sure exactly how old he was—he could have been anywhere from his late 20s to his 40s. His eyes had kind of a near-deranged look to them. The most noticeable feature of him though was the constant twitching he did. This guy was really wired.

"What are you trying to get information about this time?" he asked.

"Riley Hunt."

"The girl who was murdered near Washington Square Park."

"Ah, you watch TV news."

"Actually, I read it in the *New York Post*."

"Will you help me?"

"There's an active police investigation going on with that case. It's dangerous for me to get into anything like that with the law."

"Yeah, you're right. Definitely too dangerous and risky for a guy like you. I mean, you'd never do anything that wasn't strictly legal, right, Todd?"

He smiled. Sort of smiled. I was hoping I could get him interested in the challenge of this, the same way as I did last time when he helped me find my daughter.

I gave him as many details about Riley as I could—where she went to college, where she was from, the music and sports she played, and so forth.

"What about her cell phone?" he asked.

"Missing."

"Computer?"

"No one has found a computer for her yet."

"Tablet?"

"Not that I'm aware of."

"That seems crazy for a college student today."

"You know, I said the same thing."

I said I wanted him to find out whatever he could—anything at all—from Riley's emails or social media postings online.

"Maybe one of them will be a clue about what happened to her."

"Except her death was supposedly a random murder on the street—which would not have anything to do with this or anything else about her life."

"Everybody keeps telling me that."

"So why bother?"

"I like to cover all the bases before I make up my mind. Will you help me?"

He didn't answer my question.

Not then.

"How's your daughter?" he asked instead.

That surprised me. I didn't think that this guy had any emotional feelings or attachments about anything like that. But he remembered about Lucy.

"She's good," I said. "She has a daughter too, Emily. My granddaughter. I couldn't have found them without you, Todd." I tried to sound as sincere as I could. Which wasn't hard to do because it was true. "Will you help me again this time?"

The twitch suddenly started again.

He looked more nervous and tense and worried than ever.

I waited and waited for a long time until I got an answer from him.

"I'll get back to you," he said finally.

I was just about to ask if he wanted to be paid this time—I figured I could get him something from the Channel 10 News budget for helping us on the story—when a bicyclist sped past us and nearly knocked a cup of coffee out of my hand.

I managed to hold onto the cup, then yelled some New York–style insults at the back of the departing biker. When I turned back to Todd Schacter, he wasn't there anymore. The bench was empty.

"Working with someone like Todd Schacter for secret information is like going down a slippery slope," Janet had told me when I asked her that first time to set me up with him to find Lucy. She'd repeated the warning with me again this time when I called her about Schacter too. "You never know where this is going to go, Clare. Are you willing to take that kind of a risk?"

The answer was yes.

I'd take the risk of working with Todd Schacter.

I needed to do whatever it took to put together the missing pieces of the Riley Hunt puzzle.

CHAPTER 24

I DECIDED TO go back to the scene of the crime. The place where Riley Hunt's body had been found was on Sullivan Street just south of Washington Square Park, a few blocks from Easton College.

I wasn't sure what I was going to find there, but I've learned in the past that it's always useful to go to the scene of a crime—to see and experience that spot on my own.

Sometimes you get lucky and stumble onto something you weren't expecting.

It was midafternoon, and there were a number of stores and other businesses that were open in the area. Obviously, none of them had been open in the middle of the night when Riley was murdered. But I talked to the store owners anyway, hoping they'd give me something that might help. The police would have done all this too. But maybe they missed something I could pick up on. Maybe I was smarter than the police. I always like to think that I'm smarter than most of the other people I deal with.

I got a break when one of the store owners mentioned to me how they'd seen a lot more crime in the neighborhood recently.

"I blame this permissive society," he said. "No one says 'no' to anything anymore. People feel like they're entitled to take whatever they want. No one goes to jail—they're back on the street the next day after a robbery or whatever. That's why I had a security camera put in. So I can see everything that's happening in my store—and outside on the street too if I see anyone suspicious."

Security camera.

Of course.

There were security cameras everywhere now. In stores like this. On street corners. There were probably plenty more of them around here. Possibly the one at this store—or in other places—had picked up something that night that might give me new information about Riley Hunt.

It turned out to be true. The police had watched the video, the store owner said. But he shared it with me too. The good part was that Riley was definitely in it. The bad part was it didn't really show me anything more about what happened to her.

There was a timeline running at the bottom of the video. He fast-forwarded it to earlier in the night and we watched the empty street together for a while. Then, at 2:23 a.m., a woman came into the picture. Riley Hunt. The quality of the video was not great and it was dark, but I recognized her. Besides, how many other women would have been out walking alone at that time of night?

There was no indication of anything wrong. She walked steadily north on Sullivan Street past the store, headed presumably to Washington Square Park and then her dormitory. She moved at a steady pace—not too fast and not too slow—without any indication she was drunk or under the influence of anything else. Finally, she disappeared from the screen when she moved out of the camera's range.

There was nothing after that.

But I did now know the exact time—or close to the time—when she was murdered: 2:23 a.m.

And I knew for certain she had been walking in the direction of Washington Square Park and the Easton campus in the final moments of her life.

When I left, I kept walking in that same direction. But there were no more stores or apparent security cameras I could see between that spot and the location where her body was found.

Another dead end.

Just for the hell of it, I began tracing her steps—or her presumed steps—in the other direction. Before she got to the place where she was seen on the store security camera. Maybe at least I could figure out where she might have been coming from.

Several blocks away from the Sullivan Street location where her body was found, I found a bodega with a security camera outside. At first, the guy behind the counter was reluctant to show me any video from it. But then I told him I'd interview him on-air about it for Channel 10. He agreed. Ah, the power of the press. Or at least the power of the TV media.

We went into a cubicle in the back of the store where he had the video monitoring equipment. I asked him to find some spot in the video before the 2:23 a.m. time when she'd passed by the other store several blocks away.

While he was doing that, I asked him if the police had watched this security video too—as they did with other store owners.

He said no one had asked him about it until I did.

Which made sense, I suppose.

This wasn't the crime scene—or even that close to it—so I wasn't sure why the police would think it was important.

I wasn't even sure why I was doing this.

But that's the way I cover a story. I try to find out every fact, every piece of evidence, every possible lead—no matter how far-fetched or obscure—in the hopes it will lead me somewhere that I wouldn't have gone otherwise.

There was nothing on the video at first.

Just a dark street.

No Riley Hunt

No murderer.

No nothing.

The bodega guy had rewound it all the way back to 2 a.m. I asked him to go back even further, just to see what was there.

He was back to 1:54—I made a note of it from the timeline, only a half hour or so before Riley Hunt was killed—when I saw something.

A man walking past the bodega in the same direction as Riley Hunt had been that night.

A big man.

With big hair too.

Like with the other security camera, it was dark and the quality of the video wasn't perfect—but it was good enough for me.

I recognized him from the hair.

It was Bruce Townsend.

Riley's boyfriend.

And he'd been walking on the same streets as Riley Hunt not long before she was murdered.

So much for his alibi about being home with his big shot police brass father on Long Island.

CHAPTER 25

"Did you check the security cameras?" I asked Sam Markham, my ex-husband and one of the homicide detectives on the Riley Hunt case.

"What security cameras?"

"Uh, the ones around the area where Riley Hunt's body was found on the street."

"Jeez!" Sam said, slapping his hand to his forehead. "Why didn't we think of that? The security cameras, of course. Hey, I'm sure they can show us exactly who did this killing. All we have to do is watch the security camera video and we'll be able to figure the whole damn case out right now."

"You checked the security cameras," I said.

"We did. It's one of the first rules in the crime fighter instruction manual they make us all read."

"You don't have to be so sarcastic about it."

"That's funny coming from you."

"Okay, so what did you find out?"

"What do you think we found out?"

"Nothing."

"Bingo! Are we done here?"

"I'm just trying to help."

"And believe me, we appreciate it. Otherwise, Larry and me here would be aimlessly muddling around in the dark trying to solve crimes in our own amateurish ways without your perceptive guidance. Right, Larry?"

Larry Parks, Sam's partner, snorted. We were sitting in the squad room where they worked. I got special access that a lot of the media didn't because I used to be married to Sam. But it didn't get me much respect or goodwill. Larry Parks was definitely not a fan of mine. And Sam—who could be friendly or unfriendly, depending on his mood—seemed to be in a particularly bad mood today.

Maybe this case was getting to him.

Like it was getting to me.

But I kept going anyway.

I had to be careful about how I said what was coming next.

"How far away from the crime scene did you check the security cameras?"

"Why?"

"Well, something might have happened—there might be something interesting to see on a video—before she got to the spot where she was murdered."

"We checked all the cameras in the immediate area."

The security camera I saw with Riley's fiancé on it was outside the immediate area.

I didn't want to tell Sam I'd seen what I saw on it—namely, Bruce Townsend, the son of the deputy police chief who was in charge of the entire investigation.

No cop ever wants to hear anything like that. No cop wants anyone to raise questions about another cop. Or a member of another cop's family that might reflect badly on that cop. Especially if the other cop is a top brass in the NYPD. No, Sam and Larry would not be happy if I told them that. They'd probably want to "blame the messenger" for even bringing up such a thing. And that messenger would be me.

They needed to find out about the kid on the video the same way I did, by watching it on their own.

"We got a report at the station—albeit an unconfirmed one—that a woman was seen walking in an area a few blocks away not long before the murder."

I gave him a few specific blocks, including the one where I had watched the security camera at the store.

"I'd check those security cameras out too, if I were you."

Sam gave me a funny look.

Like he knew something was up.

That's the problem when you're dealing with an ex-husband. They know you too well.

"Is there something you're not telling me?" he asked.

"No, only trying to be a good citizen and help you out."

"We don't need your help," he said with a grunt.

"You never know. Maybe you missed something. Hey, it's happened before where you should have listened to me . . ."

Yes, I'd broken a couple of big murder cases in the past that the police hadn't been able to crack. Probably not a good idea to bring that up now though. It certainly didn't make me any more popular in the room.

"You got lucky with those," Parks snapped at me. "That's all it was. Just blind, stupid luck. You walk around like you're some sort of hotshot investigator, Carlson. Some big-time crime fighter. But you're not. You're not a cop at all. You're a goddamn TV reporter. I'm not sure why my partner here even talks to you like this. You have any thoughts or questions—take them to the NYPD public relations department. Or ask them at a press conference like everyone else. Let us do our job."

"Good advice, Clare," Sam said. "Anything else before you leave. If not . . ."

"Is her cell phone still missing?"

"Yes, it is."

"And her missing computer never turned up either?"

"Nope. But, like I keep telling you, I doubt there's going to be anything on a computer that would explain why she got beaten to death on the street in the middle of the night. Presumably by someone she didn't know or ever had any contact with until that moment."

"Then you still believe her murder was totally random?"

"Yes."

"I'm not so sure."

Parks sighed loudly.

"You know what your problem is, Carlson?" he said now.

"No, tell me my problem."

"You're sexually frustrated."

"What?"

"Sam here is happily married to a good wife now. That's gotta drive you nuts. All of your other marriages have gone down the drain too. So you take out all your anger and hostility on Sam and the rest of us to make up for the fact that you're nothing but a damned sexually frustrated bitch."

"I don't think you're supposed to say that to a woman—especially a professional media woman doing her job—in this day and age, Larry," I said.

"Why not?"

"It's sexual harassment."

"So?"

"Sexual harassment is against the law."

"Then go call a cop," he said.

CHAPTER 26

"Ms. Carlson, we have a situation down here at the front entrance," the security guard for Channel 10 News said to me on the phone.

"What's going on?"

"There's a man demanding to see you immediately. But, when we said we needed to check with you before letting him pass, he became belligerent and angry and a bit violent. He's already pushed one of the security guards here and threatened to hit me if I didn't let him up to see you right away. I'm afraid we might have to call the police."

"Who is this person? Did he give you a name?"

"Yes, it's Johnny Steffano."

"I'll be right down."

* * *

Steffano was still agitated when I got to the lobby. He was engaged in some kind of an animated conversation with the security guard I'd been talking to on the phone. He was a good-looking enough guy, dark, swarthy, very Italian. But he had this expression on his face like he was mad at the world. Based on what I knew about his background and criminal record, it seemed like he had that bad attitude a lot. He was a big guy, not tall like Bruce Townsend, but more hefty and muscular. He was screaming at the security guard now, but stopped when he saw me—and turned his wrath in my direction.

"Mr. Steffano, my name is—" I started to say.

"I already know who you are. You're the one who's been making all this damn trouble for me!"

"My name is Clare Carlson, and I'm a journalist for Channel 10 News working on the Riley Hunt murder story. I understand you knew Ms. Hunt."

"Who told you that?"

"You were seen with her on the night that she died."

"I've been seen with a lot of people."

"Witnesses say the two of you seemed to know each other quite well."

"What does that mean?"

"You were seen trying to be affectionate to her so . . ."

"Affectionate, how?"

"Uh, you kissed her."

He didn't say anything.

"So you can see why I'm interested in talking with you about anything you remember from that night?"

"I don't know anything about what happened to her afterward."

"Well, she was murdered—shortly after being with you in that bar."

That comment seemed to shake him up a bit. For a second, the look of anger on his face disappeared—and I saw uncertainty and maybe even a bit of fear there.

But then the angry scowl was back.

"I'm not talking to you anymore about Riley Hunt," he said. "I'm not telling you anything else."

"You haven't told me anything yet."

"And I don't plan to."

"Then why are you here?

"Huh?"

"You came to see me."

"My father made me come. Said you were harassing him and people at the restaurant about me. Said I should come meet and talk with you to clear the air. What is it you want to know from me?"

"How about what you did—and where you went—after leaving that bar where Riley Hunt was. And where you were when she was murdered downtown later."

It was the worst question to ask.

At least it was for him.

"Goddamn you!" he shouted.

He started moving toward me menacingly with his fists out in front of him. The security guard—who was about half the size as Steffano and twice as old—valiantly attempted to step between us.

"Get out of my way," Steffano yelled.

When the security guard didn't move, Steffano grabbed him, shoved him against the wall, and then threw him to the ground.

"Stay away from me, stay away from my father, stay away from our restaurant—just stay the hell away," he said, snarling at me.

The security man had gotten up and was on his phone now.

Calling the police for help.

But, as it turned out, we didn't need the police.

Steffano stood there in front of me briefly, his fists doubled up in anger, and glared at me while the security guard was on the phone with the cops.

Then Steffano turned around and stalked out the door.

He slammed it so hard that he cracked one of the panes in the glass on the door.

Damn.

This was a guy with a real temper.

I'm not the greatest judge in the world when it comes to evaluating men for personal relationships.

But, based on what I'd seen so far . . .

Well, let's just say I was pretty sure Bruce Townsend would have been a better choice for Riley than Johnny Steffano.

CHAPTER 27

"THIS IS NICE," Pete Bevilacqua said.

"The place?"

"Oh, that too. No, I meant it was nice that you and I are getting together again. Drinks this time. Not just coffee. So I guess I passed the first test in your dating rating meter, huh?"

"You did all right." I smiled.

"I must have. The next step after coffee was supposed to be lunch, then drinks if that went okay. According to what we talked about anyway. But I flew right past the lunch requirement to drinks. Does that happen very often?"

"Nope, it's almost unheard of."

"If I don't screw this up, maybe its dinner next with you. And then who knows what might happen after that? Now that's real uncharted territory."

"It's a murky mystery."

We were sitting outside at a bar next to Rockefeller Center. 30 Rock, as they call it. Just like the TV show. This has always been a very special New York City place for me. I was a little girl when I won a national writing contest that got me a trip to visit NBC News here as the prize. I knew right then that I wanted to live and work in the media here in New York City, and nowhere else. I still feel the same way.

I told that to him now.

"All I know about newswomen is what I see at the movies or on TV," he said. "So who did you identify with on-screen? Murphy Brown? Jane Craig in *Broadcast News*?"

"Actually, my first women journalist heroes on TV and at the movies were from newspapers. Lois Lane. Hildy Johnson in *His Girl Friday*. Now there was a woman who was way ahead of her time!"

"Is that your favorite newspaper movie?"

"My favorite is one you maybe never heard of. Called *Deadline USA*. From the early '50s, with Humphrey Bogart. Bogart plays the city editor of a newspaper that's about to go out of business—but he still wants to break the big story the paper is working right to the very end. On the last day the newspaper is in business, a young guy comes in to ask him for a job. Want to know what Bogart's response was? 'Son, being a newspaper reporter isn't the oldest job in the world, but it's the best.' God, I love that sort of stuff."

"Did you ever think of going back into the newspaper business?"

"Newspapers are disappearing pretty quickly now."

"And you like TV news?"

"Not everything about it. There's a lot of BS and crap in TV news. But I try and bring some of the journalism things I learned at newspapers to my job at Channel 10. It's not exactly like working at a newspaper, but it gets damn close on good days."

"You've had a lot of good days."

"I've done all right."

"C'mon, you've solved a bunch of murders, put some corrupt politicians in jail—and you even tracked down your own daughter twenty years after she was supposedly kidnapped. That was a big story!"

"You've been checking up on me?"

"Not hard to do. You're pretty famous, Clare."

I shrugged. "Fame is fleeting in my business. You're only as good as your last story. That's why I'm so focused right now on the story about the murdered Easton girl, Riley Hunt."

I told him about a lot of the things I'd been doing to chase the story. He asked me some questions about it. He genuinely seemed interested in my job. Okay, maybe he was pretending to be interested to get on my good side, but that didn't matter. It was good for me to talk about all this stuff. Maybe saying the facts out loud would help me sort it all out in my own mind.

"Do you get this passionately interested in every story you cover?" he asked.

"No, I don't usually . . ."

I paused.

"Well, sometimes."

Another pause.

"Yes, I guess I do."

He smiled.

"I need to find out everything I can about Riley Hunt. I need to get into her head. I need to understand what her life was all about before someone took it away like this. I think that's a real story if I can manage to do that. And I believe that maybe these answers about her life will also lead me to figure out who murdered her and why."

"But it seems like it was simply a random murder on the street by some crazy lunatic or something—so none of that stuff really matters, does it?"

"That's what my boss told me."

"Is that good for me that I think the way your boss does?"

"Not if you hope to have dinner with me."

I asked him some stuff about Princeton and his life there. He said he lived in a condo right near the campus that he bought after he and his wife got divorced. She was on the Princeton faculty, too. He talked about how much he loved working with young students and teaching them. Not only Spanish, he said. He loved all the romantic languages.

"Do you speak any languages?" he asked.

"English."

"Never took any Spanish at all?"

"Oh, I did a year or so. My freshman year in college. We had to take a foreign language as a mandatory requirement. I picked Spanish because people said it was the easiest language to learn. I picked up some of it and could speak a few sentences here and there. But I probably wouldn't remember any of it now."

"Let's test you on that."

"You're going to give me a Spanish test?"

"Bear with me."

"Okay, give it a shot."

"*¿cenarás conmigo la próxima vez?*"

I shook my head. "What does that mean?"

"Will you have dinner with me next time?"

"Si," I said.

He laughed.

"We're making progress, Clare."

"On my Spanish lesson?"

"On everything."

CHAPTER 28

"MEET ME IN Madison Square Park in an hour," Todd Schacter said to me on the phone.

"You mean Bryant Park, right?"

"Madison Square Park. South end. Next to the Shake Shack on East 23rd Street."

"I thought you said Bryant Park was your office."

"I change it up sometimes."

"Why?"

"One hour. Be there. I won't wait."

Then he hung up.

* * *

An hour later, I was sitting on a bench there eating a cheeseburger and French fries from the Shake Shack. I knew the place, it had terrific cheeseburgers. No sense letting a good lunch opportunity go to waste. And it was a working lunch. So I kept working on my cheeseburger until Todd Schacter showed up.

"Todd, how are you?" I said.

"How I am is not really relevant."

"I was only trying to make polite conversation."

"I'm here. That's all you need to know."

Social exchanges were clearly not a strong point for Todd Schacter.

"The cheeseburgers here are great," I said. "You want one? I'll buy."

"No."

"They're the best burgers in town."

"I don't eat meat."

"There sure are a lot of things you don't do, Todd."

"Do you want to find out what I know about Riley Hunt from online?"

"Absolutely."

"Did you ever hear of something called Orion in connection with Riley Hunt?"

"Orion?"

"Right."

"What's Orion?"

"Take a guess."

"There's the constellation Orion."

"Nope."

I thought about it some more.

"There's also been a NASA mission named Orion."

He shook his head.

"Are you gonna tell me or what?"

"There's a number of companies with the name Orion," he said. "One of them turned out to be very interesting."

He took out his laptop computer, opened it up, pressed a few keys, and then a website appeared on the screen. The website had the name Orion in big letters at the top. Then he began to scroll through the site.

There was an array of people in pictures there. All of them women. Very good-looking women. There were names underneath the pictures along with personal information—height, weight, measurements, likes and dislikes. There were also dollar amounts listed for each woman: hourly, nightly, even weekend rates.

Schacter scanned through the pictures until he came to one and stopped.

The name underneath the picture said Casey O'Keefe.

Except I knew her by another name.

That was Riley Hunt.

It wasn't only the name that was different though. She looked different too. The clean, wholesome Midwestern look was gone. She looked glamorous here, she looked sexy, she looked damn hot.

"Is Orion what I think it is?" I asked.

"What do you think it is?"

"As escort service."

"It calls itself a dating service. Sort of like Tinder or one of those other websites where people go to meet up with other people. The difference here is the women charge the men for their time. They agree on a price up front online before they ever meet. Orion delivers a date—a glamorous date—to a man's door. But for a price. According to the information on the site, the prices these girls charge range anywhere from $250 to $1,000, depending on the length of the date that's agreed upon."

"And that's not prostitution?"

"Not according to the site. They insist they're not an escort service. That it's up to the woman if she wants to have sex or not. All they do is facilitate the process for a man to meet an attractive woman. But, of course, most men believe they're going to have sex when they sign up with one of the women. It's kinda brilliant actually, when you think about it. A really good business model. Someone described it as 'Uber for escorts.'"

I wrote down a bunch of information, including the URL for the website—along with the sign-on name and password he'd used to access it.

I asked him about email or posts on social media from Riley Hunt. He said he hadn't found anything recent that was relevant yet. Not on Facebook or Twitter or Instagram or anywhere else where she might have posted in the days before her death.

"Don't you find that unusual?" I asked.

"Very unusual."

"You think she never posted in any of those places?"

"Or else someone deleted all her posts."

"But not the stuff on Orion?"

"Probably couldn't be deleted. Because it was already on the Orion website."

"And there's no trail or evidence of anything else from her online?"

"Not yet, but I'll keep looking."

I asked him again if he wanted to be paid for his work, but he seemed almost insulted by the idea. I guess he just enjoyed doing this sort of thing for the challenge; nothing else mattered to him.

Even the time he'd gotten arrested—and eventually acquitted thanks to Janet—was like that. He'd broken into the confidential computer files of the executives for a Fortune 500 company and then posted salaries, perks, and other personal information online, which caused an uproar among stockholders in the company. He didn't do this for any personal profit or gain. He simply wanted to show he could do it. Which he did.

I really didn't know very much about the guy.

I didn't know how he really made a living.

I didn't know anything about his personal life.

No, I didn't really want to know any more details about Todd Schacter.

"Orion," I said, looking at the picture of Riley Hunt displaying herself to men for money on the website.

"Orion," he repeated.

"But what does it all mean? Does this have anything to do with her murder? Could the killer have been someone she met up with on this site?"

"Hey, I just tell you what's online," Todd Schacter said. "It's up to you to figure out the rest."

CHAPTER 29

I HAD A decision to make.

I had uncovered several significant things about Riley Hunt that I had not yet revealed to the police or to the Channel 10 News audience or—maybe most importantly—to my own boss, Susan Endicott.

They were:

The presence in the neighborhood right before the murder of Bruce Townsend, Riley's fiancé and the son of the top police officer who just happened to be overseeing the NYPD investigation.

Her encounter at the midtown bar earlier with Johnny Steffano, the volatile and troubled son of reputed mob boss Anthony Steffano.

The discovery that Riley was working as an escort for Orion, presumably taking money to go out on dates with men she met online.

Oh, and you can also throw in the stuff from her bandmate about her maybe hanging out with a Washington Square Park drug dealer.

And the potential stalker.

All interesting stuff, but none of it confirmed yet to have had anything to do with Riley Hunt's murder.

So what did I do with this information?

In the past, I would have gone to Jack Faron, my executive producer, and asked his advice. Except Jack Faron wasn't my executive producer anymore.

But he was still supposedly working for Channel 10 News as a consultant, right?

So I called up Faron to "consult" with him on the story.

When I was finished running through it all, there was a long silence on the other end of the phone.

"Jack?" I asked.

"Have you told Susan Endicott about all this?"

"No, I haven't."

"Why not?"

"Because I don't trust her, Jack."

"Maybe not, but you have to do what she says since she's the executive producer."

"I didn't always do what you said when you were the executive producer."

"No, you didn't." He laughed.

"Look, Jack, here's my dilemma. A lot of this stuff is pretty explosive. But it might not be relevant to the murder, especially if she was killed by some random person in the street. If I go public with this on the air, a lot of people could get hurt. Bruce Townsend, for one, along with his father, the deputy NYPD commissioner. Do I really want to suggest that he might have had something to do with his fiancée's death? Same with Johnny Steffano. Okay, he had the scene with her in the bar a few hours earlier, but that doesn't mean he had anything to do with her death later in another part of town. I know it seems weird for me to worry about damaging the reputation of someone like the Steffano kid, but I promised his father I'd do my best to keep him out of it. I gave Anthony Steffano my word. I take my word seriously, even to someone like Anthony Steffano. And then there's the escort business and other stuff with Riley: that's ruining the reputation of a dead girl that everyone loves right now. Not to mention causing more pain for her parents. On the other hand, this is a big story. A potential ratings blockbuster. Susan Endicott is going to tell me to put it all on the air. Hey, I like big ratings too. But I want to do the right thing here, Jack."

There was another long silence on the line.

I knew Jack Faron was thinking it over.

The way he used to do when I brought a problem like this to him in his office.

"Do the police know about any of these things?" he asked.

"Not that I'm aware of."

"But they're going to find out sooner or later, right?"

"Right. The police aren't stupid, Jack. They'll be talking to the same people, following the same trail of evidence that I am. Maybe they already have."

"So you can't hold onto this big scoop forever?"

"No."

"But, if you tell Endicott everything you've told me, she'll order you to put it all on the air right now—with no concern about how it could affect the people involved. Even if it turns out none of them had anything to do with Riley Hunt's murder."

"That's my problem, Jack. What's the solution?"

Faron sighed. I understood this was difficult for him. He had no reason to talk to me about any of this, given his current situation. In fact, he could get himself in trouble he didn't want in terms of violating some terms of whatever settlement agreement he'd made with Brendan Kaiser and other top executives at Channel 10.

But I was hoping I could count on Jack Faron, like I had in the past. He always told me to do the right thing whenever I brought him a problem like this. And I wanted to do the right thing now.

"Okay," Faron said, "here's what I think you should do . . ."

*   *   *

At 6 p.m., the red light went on and the intro for the evening newscast began to roll:

> ANNOUNCER: This is Channel 10 News.
>
> With Brett Wolff and Dani Blaine on the anchor desk, Steve Stratton with sports, and Wendy Jeffers from the Accu 10 Weather Center.
>
> We tell you about New York, we love New York, we are New York—just like you.
>
> And our goal each day is: Take Back New York.
>
> Let's make it the wonderful city again that it once was.
>
> And now here's Brett and Dani . . .
>
> BRETT: Good evening. Here's what's happening. A fire at a Queens apartment building leaves one person dead and six injured. The mayor is talking about raising some taxes again to help keep cash-strapped small business owners afloat. The Mets won again, and are on their best opening season hot streak in more than 20 years; and Wendy Jeffers will give you some tips for dealing with the hot summer months ahead.
>
> DANI: But first, we start with an update on the tragic murder of Easton College student Riley Hunt. Clare Carlson, the Pulitzer Prize–winning news director of this station, has an exclusive report.

ME: Although police have maintained they believe the murder of Easton College student Riley Hunt was a random attack late at night near Washington Square Park, Channel 10 News has uncovered puzzling new details about the dead woman and her actions in the last days and hours of her life.

Here's what we now know . . .

I reported on how a man known to Riley had been spotted on a security camera in the area just before her death; how another man, an Easton College student with a history of violent behavior, had been seen with her in a bar several hours earlier that night; and finally how Riley had been active on a social media dating site that may have led to her encounter with someone that killed her.

I did not identify Townsend or Steffano. I also did not say anything about her possible relationship with a drug dealer. Nor did I mention that the "dating site" was really an escort service where Riley might well have been taking money to go out on dates with strange men she met on the site.

That was the plan I worked out with Faron.

Give out enough details to grab people's attention—and let them know there could be a lot more to this story than we already knew.

But hold back other information like identifying Townsend or Steffano by name—or suggesting Riley Hunt was some kind of a prostitute.

That might come out later.

But right now I only wanted to light a fuse and see what kind of fireworks my report set off.

I figured that would happen pretty quickly.

And I was sure right.

The fireworks started as soon as the newscast was over.

CHAPTER 30

"WHAT THE HELL were you doing out there?" Susan Endicott screamed at me.

"My job."

"Your job is to work for me."

"My job is to be the news director for this station. To find and break news. That's what I did out there on the newscast."

"Without telling me?"

"That would seem to be the case."

We were in my office, not hers this time. She had stormed in to confront me as soon as I got off the air. Her face was red, she was flailing her arms in the air, and she didn't sit down—just paced back and forth in front of my desk. I had a feeling—call it a crazy hunch—that she might be upset with me.

"You really screwed up this time, Carlson," she said.

"How did I do that?"

"First off, if you're going to get off our message—about Take Back New York from the crazy killers out there on the streets—you should have done it right. At least taken advantage of the opportunity better than you did. Instead, you throw out a bunch of random facts without any specifics. I wouldn't have let you do that."

"I know. That's why I didn't tell you first."

She sat down in a chair in front of my desk now. Then she quickly stood up again. I guess she realized that the dynamics of sitting in a chair while I was behind the desk—not her—put me in the power position. I wasn't sure, but I figured Susan Endicott thought about stuff like that a lot. Anyway, she was back up and pacing back and forth in front of me again, gesturing wildly as she talked.

"Do you know the name of the man on the security camera who knew Riley Hunt and was in the neighborhood that night?"

"I do."

"And the name of the man in the bar before that?"

"Yes."

"And more details about this dating service she was involved in?" I nodded.

"Actually, it was more like an escort service. Women going out on dates with men for money. Not exactly prostitution, but not exactly *not* prostitution either. Sort of a gray area in the middle, legally speaking."

"You're going on the air with all of this. The 11 p.m. newscast tonight. We'll tease it during the evening programming and that should get us some gigantic ratings with all this exclusive information."

"Not going to happen."

"What?"

"I'm not doing it. Not yet. I may well air all of this at some point in the future. But not right now. Not until we know more about the case."

I explained to her, the same as I had explained to Jack Faron, about my concern for destroying the lives of both men and also about tarnishing the reputation of the dead Riley Hunt if it turned out later that there was no connection between any of these things and Riley's murder.

But her reaction was a lot different than Jack Faron's.

"I don't give a crap about any of that," she said. "I'm telling you to put all this out on the 11 p.m. newscast. That's not a request. That's an order. A direct order from your superior."

"I won't do it."

"Okay, then I'll have someone else do it. Janelle or Cassie can go on the air and do the same thing if you refuse."

"No, they can't."

"Why not?"

"Because they don't have the information. I'm the only one who knows all the specifics about the men and the dating/escort agency. You can't put Janelle or Cassie or anyone else out there to do what you want in place of me." I smiled as I saw the look of shock and discomfort on her face. "Kind of frustrating for you, huh?"

She started to sit down in front of my desk again, then she suddenly stood up—and finally she sat back down again, glaring at me. Jeez, this woman was up and down more than a jack-in-the-box.

"That's insubordination," she said." Rank insubordination. You realize that, don't you?"

"Oh, yes. I'm very well versed on insubordination. And I'm very good at insubordination too. It's one of my specialties."

"Insubordination is a fireable offense," she said.

"You're threatening to fire me? That's the second time you've made that threat. First, when I refused to get rid of Steve Stratton—and now you're doing it again. That's a lot of tough talk, but—"

"I can fire you, Carlson!"

"Then do it."

"What?"

"If you really think you can fire me, go ahead and try."

She shook her head.

"You think you're invulnerable, don't you? Because you once won a damn Pulitzer Prize and broke some big exclusives that made you a star and buddied up with Brendan Kaiser at various points. You figure you can do anything you want. Well, no one is irreplaceable, not even you. And whatever you think your relationship is with Brendan Kaiser, know this: Kaiser hired me to do whatever I needed to do at this station to push up the ratings and the revenue. That's what I'm doing. I think that's more important to him than you or your reputation or all your big scoops in the past."

"Let's find out," I said.

She looked confused. "What do you mean?"

"Call up Brendan Kaiser right now—tell him you want to fire me, and see if he lets you do it. If he doesn't, then you go back to your office and let me do my job."

I started to reach for the phone.

It was a game of chicken, of course.

I had no idea what Kaiser might have done if we did call him with this.

But I wanted to see who blinked first—me or Susan Endicott.

Only I never got the chance.

Because something happened then that changed everything.

Maggie stuck her head in the door and announced big breaking news.

"They just arrested someone for the murder of Riley Hunt," she said.

CHAPTER 31

THE PERSON THE police arrested for killing Riley Hunt was not her fiancé, Bruce Townsend. It was not Johnny Steffano. And it was not anyone she met online from the Orion website dating service.

His name was Donnie Ray Bakely, and he was 25 years old. A veteran of both Iran and Afghanistan, he'd been discharged from the Army a year earlier for unspecified medical reasons. Now he was homeless and living on the streets of New York City.

He'd been arrested earlier that day at Tompkins Square Park in another neighborhood of Lower Manhattan—a number of blocks away from Washington Square Park—where he had attacked a woman sitting on a park bench.

According to witnesses and the police account, he'd begun screaming at her—calling her a "murderer" and a "traitor" and saying he was going to stab her to death with a bayonet. He did not have a bayonet, but simulated making a series of stab wounds with his hands on the terrified woman.

Fortunately, several men in the park pulled him off her before he could do any real damage, and someone called 911 for the police.

At first, Bakely was going to be simply taken into custody and then transported to the psychiatric unit at Bellevue Hospital.

But then police examined the belongings he was carrying—inside a battered Army knapsack—and found a cell phone. The cell phone turned out to be the missing phone that belonged to Riley Hunt.

There was blood on the phone and on the knapsack. The blood was Type O, the same blood type as Riley. It would take longer to do a complete check, but seemed obvious that the blood was Riley Hunt's—that it came from her as she struggled for her life that night on the street.

It was pretty strong evidence.

But, as it turned out, even that evidence wasn't needed.

Because Donnie Ray Bakely readily admitted to killing a woman—who clearly was Riley Hunt—on a Greenwich Village street that night near Washington Square and the Easton College campus.

He said she had to die because of what she did to him.

That's why he beat and murdered her when he encountered her on that lonely dark street, he explained.

But he couldn't quite remember exactly what she had done to him that set off his rage and murderous fury.

We immediately broke into the evening Channel 10 programming with breaking news headlines and live updates about the arrest.

I did the live spots myself, as I'd been doing everything on the Riley Hunt murder from the beginning.

And I came back on the 11 p.m. newscast with a full report on all the dramatic events that had occured.

*   *   *

The next day I was there in court—along with the rest of the media—to cover the arraignment of Donnie Ray Bakely.

His attorney was a legal aid attorney appointed because Bakely seemingly had no money or ability to find representation for himself. The attorney told the court of Bakely's impressive military record while serving in Iraq and Afghanistan, winning numerous medals for heroism and bravery in combat, before being seriously wounded in a land mine explosion near Kabul a few years earlier.

He said most of Bakely's physical wounds from the blast had healed, but he suffered severe brain damage that prevented him from living a normal life.

After his discharge from the Army, he'd been in and out of a series of VA hospitals until finally winding up homeless and confused and struggling to survive on the streets of New York City.

It was a tragic story.

For him.

And for Riley Hunt.

Donnie Ray Bakely was in the courtroom, but he didn't seem very interested in the proceedings. He was a slightly built young man, with long, unruly-looking hair, and he had a vacant look on his face. Almost as if he wasn't really here, at least in his own mind. He was somewhere else, a long way away. Maybe back in Afghanistan or Iraq.

The attorney for Bakely asked the judge to take all of his background and service for his country and sacrifices while in the military into consideration before making a final ruling on whether Donnie Ray Bakely should stand trial on a murder charge. The judge agreed to have him examined thoroughly in a prison psychiatric ward to determine if he was sane enough to enter a guilty plea.

I reported all this on that evening's Channel 10 newscast.

Endicott told me she wanted me to end my segment with the
"Take Back New York" slogan—especially since that's what this
story now turned out to be, a crazy person on the streets that took
a life for no good reason.

I did what she asked me to this time.

What the hell, it turned out she was right—and I was wrong—
about the Riley Hunt murder.

* * *

"So the story is over?" Janet asked me on the phone when I called
her that night to tell her everything that had happened.

"Right. All the exclusive evidence I turned up—the fiancé on the
security video, the mobster's son in the bar, the escort service money
connection with men online—all turned out to mean nothing in
the end. It was just a crazy guy who killed her. That's all. And now
he's in custody."

"You sound disappointed," Janet said.

"I guess I do."

"Well, at least cops got their man—the person who did it—
pretty quickly."

"Maybe that's what I'm so disappointed about."

I'd been thinking about this ever since the Donnie Ray Bakely
arrest happened. This story—the baffling murder of Riley Hunt—
had been just what I needed. A big story for me to go after exclusives
with. That took my mind off all the other stuff I was dealing with
in my life. The horrible woman boss I now had in Susan Endicott.
The departure of my friend and mentor Jack Faron. My struggles
to find some kind of romantic life again. And even learning how to
deal with being a mother—not to mention a grandmother—at this
time in my life.

"So what are you going to do now?" Janet asked.

"All I can think of is to do the one thing I always do that will make me feel better."

"What's that?"

"Find another big story to chase."

PART II

CLARE, WE'RE ON LIVE!

CHAPTER 32

THE NEXT BIG news story turned out to be about me.

It wasn't actually a real news story. But it sure caused a helluva sensation when it went viral on social media.

What happened was a case of the dreaded term in television broadcasting known as the "hot mic"—a microphone putting someone live on the air even though they don't realize they're on live TV until it's too late.

In this case, I was the victim.

Or, to put it more accurately, I was the culprit.

I was still appearing on air—doing other news stories—because Susan Endicott wanted to cash in on my reputation from all my previous scoops. At least that's the way she put it. So I was on the newscasts reporting a handful of big stories as well as working behind the scenes as the news director. It was a heavy load. I wasn't unhappy about it because I like to keep busy and I like to do real journalism. But it was exhausting juggling both roles, which is maybe why I screwed up that day on air.

We had gone to a commercial break, and I was waiting to be introduced by Brett and Dani after we came back on air. The two of them had been feuding off camera more than ever—I guess the marriage and parental responsibilities were really getting to them—and now they suddenly started bickering about which one was going to introduce me.

I was tired of all their arguments and I was tired in general from the demands of the two jobs.

And so, I sighed and said: "Would you two just stop it? If you've got problems in your goddamn marriage, go home and work it out in the bedroom with some mind-blowing sex—not here."

What I didn't notice was that Brett and Dani had stopped fighting at that point, and were staring at the TV monitor.

There was a red light on too, as I soon found out.

"Clare, we're on live," Dani said.

It was the moment every broadcaster dreaded—when an open mic sends out to the entire world what you thought was private.

I quickly issued an on-air apology, mumbling something about there being a technical mishap that allowed something to get on the air that shouldn't have. I followed up later with an official statement saying that I regretted the unfortunate incident and hoped anyone watching wasn't offended by it. Brett and Dani said they weren't upset and supported me.

But it didn't matter.

The excruciating exchange was captured on video by a viewer who put it out on Twitter.

The video of me quickly went viral and was trending at the top of social media on all sorts of platforms with the hashtag #Clarewereonlive.

Even worse, the #Clarewereonlive hashtag became a catchphrase people were laughing about for days on websites, Instagram, Twitter, and pretty much everywhere else on the internet.

"You're famous again," Maggie said to me as she sorted through it all on her computer screen.

"Or infamous."

"You know what they say, Clare. Bad publicity is better than no publicity."

"Yeah, well, I'm more like the guy in the old joke who got tarred and feathered and ridden out of town on a rail. When they asked him how he felt about it, he said: 'If it weren't for the honor of the thing, I would rather have walked.'"

*   *   *

I thought Susan Endicott might use this whole thing to try to get me fired—or at least suspended—by Brendan Kaiser, the Channel 10 owner.

But my on-air mistake—and all the furor it caused—didn't seem to bother her.

She actually seemed happy about it.

I'd come up with two possible reasons for that:

1. She enjoyed watching me squirm in embarrassment and took delight in my discomfort.

2. Like Maggie, she believed that any publicity was good publicity and all this attention helped the Channel 10 News ratings.

I figured it had to be one or the other of the two.

Or maybe both.

Otherwise, there'd been a sort of truce—or at least a temporary cease-fire—in our warfare since that last time in her office.

I'd been busy for the next few days covering the Donnie Ray Bakely arrest and the conclusion of the Riley Hunt murder story. I knew there would be more battles with Susan Endicott ahead. But I didn't want to fight with her right now. I was tired of fighting.

* * *

"You seem a bit down," Janet said to me one night when she called me at home.

"I'm not down."

"Well, you're not exactly 'up' in the temperament department these days."

"No, I'm not."

"What are you then?"

"Somewhere in the middle."

"Is this still about that Endicott woman?"

"Partly. But it's more than that, Janet. This whole story, the Riley Hunt murder, really got. to me. I thought there was a real story there—one of the biggest ever—and that was what I needed more than anything. I wanted to find out the real truth about Riley Hunt. I wanted to find the killer of Riley Hunt. I wanted to get justice for Riley Hunt. But then the story suddenly ended. There were no twists, no great deductions on my part—no nothing. Just a sad, crazy guy who took a beautiful beloved young woman's life for no reason. I'm having trouble getting past that."

"There will be other stories."

"I guess."

"You don't think so?"

"I have a lot of trouble imagining what my life will be like going forward under Susan Endicott. The Riley Hunt story was my lifeline. The one thing I could cling to and what I do best—report the hell out of a story—to make sure Endicott couldn't mess with me."

"And now the Riley Hunt story is over."

"Yes." I sighed.

She asked me about Pete Bevilacqua. I told her about our coffee meeting, our drinks together, and that he had been calling me since then to ask for a dinner date. Except I also told her how I'd been putting him off, telling him I was too busy at work right now to meet him for dinner.

"Sounds like you two got along pretty well at the coffee and drinks."

"It was fun."

"Then what's the problem?"

"The problem is I've been down this road too many times before. If we go out to dinner, the next step is he wants to sleep with me. That could be fun at first, at least I hope the sex would be fun, but it always leads to more problems. Sex complicates everything. And I don't need any more damn complications in my life right now. Maybe I'm better off being by myself."

"You don't have to sleep with him on the first date or even the second or the third, if you don't want to. Maybe he would understand that."

"Most men don't."

"I think you should see him. Only make sure that you decide whether or not to have sex, not him. That's the important thing."

"It's the same advice my mother gave me when I went to college. Look how that turned out."

"You got pregnant your freshman year."

"I'm still the same person as that nineteen-year-old girl was, Janet."

"No, you're not. That was a long time ago. You're older and wiser now."

"I'm damn sure older," I said.

*   *   *

"Have you ever thought about leaving all this news stuff in New York City behind and doing something else with your life?" my daughter asked me when I called her afterward in Virginia where she lived with her family.

"Like what?"

"I don't know. Maybe move down here. You could retire."

"I'm too young to retire."

"Well, you are a grandmother." She laughed.

"What would I do there?"

"Lots of things. Hike. Ride bikes. Write. Paint. Do whatever you want to do. Be a grandmother. Hey, be a mother too. You and I have never really had much quality mother/daughter time together. It would be fun. And you keep going on about how much you hate your new boss. Is there a man in your life up there, right now?"

I told her about Pete Bevilacqua. How he seemed to want to take our relationship to the next level. And I repeated what I said to Janet about how sleeping with him would just complicate my life right now in ways that I didn't need.

"You don't have to sleep with every man you meet, Mom."

Ah, words of wisdom from my own daughter.

Who would have ever figured that?

"And yet I seem to . . ."

"It's your decision."

"I guess."

"And who knows? Maybe this guy will be different. Maybe this is the one for you. Maybe this one really is a good man."

"I've found a lot of good men in the past," I said. "It never seems to last with good men though. At least for me."

*   *   *

After I hung up, I picked up a newspaper and began paging through it. Looking for some story that might excite me. But it all seemed to be the same old stuff I saw every day. I read the editorial page, the entertainment sections, checked my horoscope—it said *predictable* or *uninspiring routines in your world could be shaken with little or no warning*—hmmm—and finally turned to the Dear Abby column.

For a long time, I didn't even realize the Dear Abby column was still around. I figured Abby and her advice to the lovelorn had disappeared years ago. But the column was still there, in hundreds of papers around the country. The original Dear Abby was gone, but her daughter wrote the column now. Dishing out the same kind of advice every day to the people who wrote in with their problems.

Abby was in fine form today. A teenaged girl, signed "Confused in Kenosha," wanted to know if she should let her boyfriend have sex with her. The guy kept saying it was the only way she could prove her love for him. All the other kids in school were doing it too. The girl felt under pressure to have sex with him.

Abby told her to wait until marriage. That she didn't have to have sex to prove her love. If this guy really loved her, he'd wait until she was ready for sex.

Atta girl, Abby! You've got all the answers.

Just like Janet and my daughter have all the answers too.

Me, I've got no answers. No answers for moving on past the Riley Hunt story. No answers for dealing with Susan Endicott. No answers for my sex life. Yep, I was pretty much out of answers on everything.

CHAPTER 33

IT WAS A few weeks after the Donnie Ray Bakely arrest that Maggie stuck her head into my office and said there was someone outside who wanted to see me.

"She's the mother of the guy they arrested in the Riley Hunt murder. Her name is Ruth Bakely. She wants to talk to you about it. She said she'll only talk to you, none of the other reporters."

"Why me?"

"She saw an on-air editorial you did on the newscast after her son's murder arrest about the plight of military veterans living homeless on the street. And how we had to do better to take care of these people. I guess it had a big effect on her."

I looked out the open door of my office, saw a middle-aged woman sitting out there, and then turned back to Maggie. "Sure, what the hell. Send her in," I said.

A few seconds later, Ruth Bakely was standing in front of my desk. When I saw her up close, I realized she probably wasn't any older than me. But she looked and talked and acted like an older woman. Maybe she'd had a tough life. And now her son was charged with a horrible crime. I felt sorry for her.

"Hi, my name is Clare Carlson, and I'm news director here at Channel 10. Sit down and tell me what I can do for you."

The woman sat in a chair facing me, then looked at the computer on my desk.

"You're the one who did the editorial about veterans after my son was arrested?"

"That's right."

"Can you call that up for me on the screen of your computer?"

It took a few minutes, but I found the video file and called it up. I pushed *play* and it was there on the screen. It wasn't very long. Less than a minute. Just another element to the Riley Hunt case coverage we had done back then.

At the bottom of the screen, there was a crawl that said AN AMERICAN TRAGEDY. Then it showed me talking on air that day:

> The story about the arrest of a troubled Army veteran from the Afghanistan and Iraqi wars focuses our attention once again on one of our national tragedies.
>
> Whatever one's sentiments about the American military involvement abroad, there is little question of the debt we owe to the brave men and women who we send to fight in faraway lands like this.
>
> And there is also little question about the problems—psychological as well as physical—that these soldiers suffer when they attempt to return to civilian life.
>
> Maybe this tragedy will finally jolt us into trying to come to grips with such a very real national problem . . .

The editorial went on for a short time longer. When it was done, I clicked off the screen and looked back at Ruth Bakely, wondering what this was all about.

"I saw that the day you did it on TV and never forgot it. I wasn't sure if the person who said those words really meant them, but I could only hope they did. Did you mean what you said about helping people like my son?"

"Look, I'm sorry about your son," I said quietly. "What happened was a terrible tragedy. But your son was sick. There was something wrong with him that made him do this."

The woman stood up now. She was trembling as she spoke. "Let me tell you about my son. All the years he was growing up, he was the best son a mother could ever want. He was an A student, he played quarterback on the football team, he had lots of friends. He was going to go to college and become a teacher, but we didn't have enough money right away. So he went into the Army. We thought he could go to college later on the GI Bill.

"Then he got sent to Iraq. After that, it was two tours in Afghanistan. And when he came back, he was never the same. Never. It was like something was constantly tearing away at his insides, something that wouldn't let him alone. He couldn't forget. There were the flashbacks, the nightmares. I'd say, 'Donnie, honey, it's time to just forget about it.' And he'd look at me and say: 'I can't, Mom, I can't.' And then we'd both cry."

She looked down at her hands.

"A few weeks ago it got worse than ever. He went into the hospital for a few days—a VA facility here in New York City. I thought maybe they could help. But when he got out, he was worse. Then this thing happened."

I wasn't sure what it was she wanted from me yet.

But I soon found out.

"Talk to him, Ms. Carlson."

"Your son?"

"Yes. Go to the prison and interview him."

We'd made an obligatory effort for a prison interview after the arrest, but never got anywhere. Besides, Sam told me the kid was just spouting gibberish—nothing intelligible at all. I told that to her now.

"I can get you in," she said. "I'm his mother."

"But if he can't really speak . . ."

"He's better now. Something happened to him right before the arrest. But they've been treating him with different medication in prison, and he's much more under control now. He has things to say. I want you to hear them and put them on the air so others can see and hear him too."

The problem was the story was a bit off everyone's radar now. Maybe a jailhouse interview with the killer would have been great after the arrest, but now it seemed more like an afterthought. Besides, he'd already confessed to killing Riley Hunt. What was he going to tell me that was more explosive than that?

I guess Mrs. Bakely sensed my reluctance.

"Please talk to him. It's important that something good comes out of this. Maybe people can learn something from it, so that someday other mothers don't have to go through the heartache I have. I've lost my son, Ms. Carlson. First I lost him to that war—now he's in prison, and he probably will be in prison for the rest of his life. Do you have any idea what it's like to be a mother and lose someone you love like that?"

I looked out the window next to my desk. It was almost June now, and the first real feel of summer was in the air. The Manhattan streets outside would soon be clogged every weekend with people trying to escape to the Hamptons or Fire Island. I thought about another spring day when another mother lost her child—me and my daughter, Lucy. It had taken me twenty years to get my daughter back. But it was worth the struggle. For me. Or for any other mother.

"Yes, I do," I told her.

"So you'll go talk to Donnie?"

I thought for a moment, then sighed. "Okay, I guess so."

CHAPTER 34

IT TURNED OUT I couldn't get an on-air interview with Donnie Ray Bakely. Not yet. Even with his mother's permission. I needed official approval first. But she was able to get me in to see him as a friend of the family. Even though they weren't going to let me bring in a TV crew to film the interview.

I decided to go see him in jail anyway. Just to see what he had to say, in hopes I was able to do something on air later.

He was being held at Rikers Island, which is still the main correctional facility in New York City. It's about as bad a prison as you could imagine. Located on an island in the East River between Queens and the Bronx, and no way for a prisoner to escape until he tried to swim. Some had made the attempt, but few succeeded. Sort of like Alcatraz, New York style. Periodically, there was political debate about tearing down Rikers and replacing it with smaller, more modern jails around the city. But they'd been talking about that for a long time, and Rikers was still there.

Donnie Ray Bakely looked different from the person I'd seen in the courtroom that first day he was arraigned. Acted differently too. At least at first. In the courtroom, he had seemed strangely detached from the proceeding and almost unaware of his situation. Now he looked nervous and scared.

He was wearing a gray prison outfit that looked too big for him. He was in his twenties, I knew that, but he appeared much older. There was stubble on his face—I guess you didn't worry about shaving when you were in prison—dark circles under his eyes, and his hand trembled when I shook it to introduce myself.

But, despite all this, he seemed much more aware and alert than he had in court. I remembered his mother saying they had put him on some kind of new drug regimen, so I guess that had helped him get past whatever deranged state he'd been in when the police first picked him up on the street.

I decided to start with the incident in the park when he'd been arrested for attacking the woman.

"Why did you do that?" I asked him.

"I don't really remember anything until the arrest. Well, I do . . . but it was like a dream. I was back in Afghanistan. The bomb that was planted under the vehicle I was traveling in was put there by a woman. I saw her place the bomb in front of us, but it was too late for me to do anything. And then my friends were dead, and I was badly hurt in the hospital—and my life has never been the same. When I saw the woman in the park, she became the woman with the bomb for me. I had to stop her before she did it again. That's what I was doing—saving me and my buddies. But then I was suddenly back in this park in New York and the woman was screaming and the police arrested me. After that . . . well, everything else happened then."

Wartime flashback, I thought to myself. This was a clear-cut case of a soldier who should have received better medical treatment—and never got it. But what did that have to do with him murdering Riley Hunt earlier?

"Tell me about Riley Hunt," I said.

"Who?"

"The woman in the village that was killed."

He looked confused and seemed to be fading away more now. Almost like he was that first day in court. Like he was trying to be somewhere else—somewhere where he didn't have to deal with these kinds of questions.

I tried to bring him back to focus.

I took out a photo of Riley Hunt—one of her laughing at the basketball awards dinner the night before she died—and showed it to him.

"Why did you kill her?" I asked.

"I—I don't know."

"Did you kill her?"

"Yes."

"But you don't remember it?"

"Not really."

"Then how do you know you did it?"

"That's what everyone says. That I killed her. They must be right."

"But you don't have any recollection of that?"

"It's the same as with that woman in the park. I don't remember doing any of the things they say I did in Greenwich Village either. I was there. I know that. But all I remember is waking up and seeing the dead woman on the street next to me and realizing that I must have killed her. So that's what I told the police. I confessed. I must have done it. What other explanation is there? I'm a killer. I learned how to kill in Iraq and Afghanistan, and now I'm doing it here. That's why I ran from that dead woman's body. I would have kept running except they caught me."

The big break in the case had come when they found Riley Hunt's phone on him.

"Did you take her phone?"

"I guess so."

"Did you touch her body? Is that how her blood got on you?"

"I suppose . . . I wanted to see if she was maybe still alive."

"What were you doing in that neighborhood?"

"I lived there."

"On the street?"

"Yes."

"Near Washington Square Park?"

"That's right. I'd been living on the street there for . . . well, for a while."

"And that's where you saw her body?"

He nodded.

"And you took her phone?"

"I guess so. I remember the phone was lying next to her. I must have picked it up before I left her there."

"But you can't be sure you're the one who killed her?"

"No, no . . . Although, I must have."

He was shaking again now, and he had a vacant look on his face—I was afraid he might fade away from me very quickly. It was as if he only had enough strength or willpower to stay in the real world like this for a short time. I knew I was running out of time with Donnie Ray Bakely—at least for this interview—so I had to finish up quickly with everything I wanted to ask him.

"Did you ever meet Riley Hunt? Did you know her at all before that night she was murdered in Greenwich Village?"

He didn't answer me.

"Donnie?"

"I think so."

"What?"

"I think I might have known her. I thought I recognized her. When I saw her dead on the street, I realized that I'd seen her before. I'm not sure how. My memory is still very fuzzy when it comes to remembering things like that. But I felt like I'd seen her before. I'd been with her. Somewhere."

How in the world would someone like Donnie Ray Bakely ever have had any contact or connection with a woman like Riley Hunt?

"Think, Donnie. Think about how you might have known her before her death."

"I—I can't. I can't think about it anymore. If they say I killed her, I must have killed her. But I just don't remember what happened."

CHAPTER 35

I KNEW FOR sure now that I wanted to get Donnie Ray Bakely talking to me in an on-air interview about all this.

The question was how to get permission to bring a film crew into Rikers Island prison to talk to him.

I checked with my ex-husband Sam at the precinct who told me that was all being handled by the Manhattan district attorney's office. He said I would have to talk to someone there.

I only had one person I knew well in the DA's office. William Barrett, an assistant district attorney. I was going to have to put in a request through him to interview Bakely on air at the jail. The problem was I had personal baggage from the past with Barrett. He was known as William (Wild Bill) Barrett because of his sexual conquests over the years with women in the media and law enforcement. I'd been one of those conquests—and it ended badly between Billy and me. Still, I knew I had no choice except to talk to him again if I hoped to get the Rikers interview with Bakely.

So I asked him if he'd meet with me. I told him I needed a favor. I asked if I could come talk to him at the DA's office downtown to discuss it. But Barrett said he'd only meet up with me if I had a drink with him. We agreed on the location: an outside bar in Central Park near the boathouse and lake.

And so there I was waiting for him at 8 p.m. that night. It was a nice night, and the outdoor bar was packed. Everyone there looked very successful.

Upwardly mobile.

Just like me.

I took a seat that was empty, ordered a scotch and soda, and listened in on a heated discussion over the merits and minuses of the latest iPhone that had just come out. Nobody said hello to me. Nobody asked me for my autograph. Nobody asked me what I thought about the new iPhone. Maybe I should have brought along my Pulitzer.

I took a sip of my drink and looked at my watch. 8:15 p.m. No Barrett yet. I guess he was going to make me wait. I ordered a second drink and listened to segments of conversation from the people around me. The topic now was whether to buy gold or Bitcoin. I didn't know the answer to that one either.

Finally, William (Wild Bill) Barrett showed up. The last time I'd met up with him, he had gotten himself involved in a sex scandal with his secretary in the DA's office and some other women that nearly cost him his job—which put him on his best behavior for a while. I wondered if that good behavior had lasted. But—because he insisted on meeting me in a bar instead of his office—I doubted it.

Sure enough, on the way over to me at the bar, he stopped to whisper something into the ear of a mini-skirted blonde waitress. She giggled and playfully slapped him. Then he spotted me.

"Damn, you look great, Clare," he said. "No trouble picking you out. You're the prettiest woman in the bar."

"Oh yeah? What were you telling the waitress in the mini-skirt back there? That's she's the second prettiest?"

It was a variation of a line I'd used on Barrett before, but he never seemed to mind.

"Cute." He smiled. "You're a cute lady, Clare Carlson. What are you drinking? You want a refill?"

I looked down at the scotch and soda in front of me that I had just ordered. "I'm fine," I said.

He ordered a bourbon and water for himself, then turned to face me—looking closely into my eyes.

"Green, right?"

"Huh?"

"Your eyes. They're green, aren't they?"

"I call them turquoise."

"I call them bedroom eyes." He grinned.

I sighed.

"Maybe we can find out later," he said. "What do you think? Doesn't that sound good?"

"I'd rather be staked to an anthill."

He laughed. "Still quick with the tongue, aren't you, Clare?"

"In ways you can only imagine, but will never find out."

I took a big gulp of my drink. It was strong on scotch but not strong enough for me at this minute. I had a feeling I was going to need a lot more liquor to get through this conversation with Barrett.

"Let's talk about Donnie Ray Bakely and the Riley Hunt murder case," I said.

He took a drink of his bourbon. "Jesus, you don't fool around at all anymore, do you? All business, huh? Just remember, all work and no play can make you a dull girl, Clare."

I made a face and finished the last of my drink.

"Okay, you said you needed a favor from me, Clare. That's why you wanted to see me. What's the favor?"

"Get me permission to do an on-air interview with Bakely at Rikers. I've already been in there to talk with him but they wouldn't let me transcribe anything or shoot any video without approval from someone higher up. The District Attorney's Office could do that. You could reach out to the Corrections Department and get me in there to talk to Bakely with a Channel 10 video crew."

"That's a big favor to ask."

"I understand."

"What's in it for me?"

"My undying gratitude."

"An interesting proposal."

"Will you help me on this, Billy?"

He smiled. A big smile. I hated to owe Barrett a favor, especially a big favor like that, but it was the only way I was going to get a video crew into Rikers to interview Bakely.

"I'll see what I can do," Barrett told me. "I should be able to make this happen."

"Thank you."

"So now that we've got that out of the way," Barrett said, leaning toward me and touching my hand, "what do you say we change the topic of conversation? Let's talk about us."

"There is no *us*, Billy. That ship sailed a long time ago."

"C'mon, we're here right now so . . ."

"Actually, I've got to leave."

I got off the stool and picked up my handbag off the bar.

"Disappointed?" I said.

"You're damn right I'm disappointed. I'm crushed. And after all we've meant to each other."

"I'm sure you'll survive."

I headed for the exit. Before I left, I turned back toward Barrett. He was already making his way over toward the mini-skirted waitress.

Who said that only time can heal a broken heart?

CHAPTER 36

"WHAT IF HE didn't do it?" I said to Maggie.

"Bakely?"

"Yes. What if he didn't kill Riley Hunt? He was living on the street down there, maybe he just stumbled across the body after she died. He took her phone, he admits that. And it makes sense that he touched her body to see if she might still be alive. That's how her blood got on him. Then he gets arrested in Tompkins Square Park a few days later, they find Riley Hunt's phone on him, the blood and all the pieces fit together for the police. End of case, end of story. Except how can we be sure he really killed her?"

"He confessed it to the police, Clare."

"Okay. But that was at the beginning. He would have confessed to killing Nicole Brown Simpson, John Lennon, and Jon Benet Ramsey during the confused condition he was in then. He's better now—not a lot better, but some. And he doesn't remember actually killing Riley Hunt. He doesn't deny it. He just says now he doesn't know if he did it or not. If you take Bakely out of the equation, then we're back to square one on this story again. Maybe someone in Riley Hunt's life was the killer."

Maggie shook her head. "You're not going to let this one go, are you, Clare?"

"I've got a feeling—my news instinct as a journalist tells me—there's more to this story. A lot more."

"Your news instinct has been wrong before."

"It's been right too."

"Yes, it has. Hell, sometimes you've been right and wrong at the same time."

"Huh?"

"Laurie Bateman."

Laurie Bateman was a celebrity model/actress who was accused last year of murdering her billionaire husband for his money. At first, I believed she was innocent and my on-air coverage of the story helped her go free. But later my news instinct told me something was wrong about her account of what happened. I changed directions on the story and uncovered enough evidence to link her to the murder.

"I've learned not to bet against your news instincts, Clare," Maggie said now.

"I sure would like it if people remembered something else than #clarewereonlive when they hear my name."

*   *   *

After Maggie left my office, I started writing things down about the story on a long yellow legal pad. That always helps me organize my thoughts. When I was finished, I looked down at the list of angles I wanted to pursue.

Some of them involved people I'd already talked to in the past. Bruce Townsend, and his father the deputy police commissioner; Anthony Steffano and his son Johnny; Riley's roommate that I still thought might know more that she was telling me; and the mystery around the escort agency Orion that featured a picture of Riley Hunt on its site.

But there were other things I wanted to do on this story too.

I wanted to find out more about Riley Hunt too.

There was a lot about Riley that still didn't make sense to me.

Especially her relationship—or, more accurately, her non-relationship—with her mother, Elizabeth Hunt. That had bothered me from the very beginning. I had no idea if—or how—this had anything to do with her murder. But I was curious.

I decided to go back to Riley's hometown of Dayton—which was in my own home state of Ohio—to interview Elizabeth Hunt for the first time about her daughter's life and death.

Maybe she could give me some of the answers I was still seeking about Riley's all too brief life.

When I was finished writing, I looked down at everything I'd put down on the legal pad.

Bruce Townsend.

Deputy NYPD Commissioner Hugh Townsend.

Johnny Steffano.

Anthony Steffano.

Riley's roommate, Brianna Bentley—who was really Nancy Guntzler.

The escort service called Orion.

A jailhouse interview with Donnie Ray Bakely.

Go to Ohio to talk to Riley's mother.

Find out anything more I could about Riley's background in Ohio.

It was a daunting list, but that didn't bother me. In fact, I welcomed it.

I had been drifting for a while now—unsure what to do about my professional and my personal life and everything else.

I needed to find something to grab onto and give me purpose again.

A big story always did that.

I thought I had one in Riley Hunt's murder.

And it was over.

Or seemed to be over.

But now I believed—or at least I hoped—there was much more to the story.

And I was determined to find out the truth about Riley Hunt's murder.

For her sake.

For the people who loved her.

And for myself too.

Because right now I felt more alive than I had in a long time.

PART III

DOWN THE RABBIT HOLE

CHAPTER 37

THE NEXT DAY, I was flying at 30,000 feet aboard a Delta flight out of LaGuardia on my way to Dayton, Ohio—Riley Hunt's hometown and where her parents lived.

Ohio was also the state I came from.

And it was the first time I'd been back there in a long time.

The whole thing didn't seem real until we began our approach to the Dayton Airport, and I looked down at the ground below dotted with factories, little houses, and green lawns. It reminded me of where I grew up in a suburb of Cleveland. Of course, that was a few hundred miles away, in the northern part of the state. Dayton was in southwestern Ohio. But there was a certain sameness to the whole state of Ohio—a kind of Midwest, working-class feel—that was the same from town to town. The feeling made me uncomfortable. I wasn't sure coming here was such a good idea.

I had an editor once when I was a young reporter at a newspaper who warned me that you never knew where a big story might take you.

And that it could lead you to places you wished later that you had never gone.

"Sometimes, Clare, when a really big story comes along, it turns out to be more than you have bargained for. Sometimes chasing a big story is like going down a rabbit hole. You never know what you're going to find when you come out on the other side."

I remembered that editor's advice now as I thought about my own memories of being in Ohio.

My most vivid memory was when I came home to Cleveland during my freshman year in college and announced to my parents I was pregnant. My father ordered me to have an abortion. Maybe I would have under normal circumstances. But the more my father yelled at me to have the abortion, the more I became determined to have my baby. He threw me out of the house after that, and I had to work my way through college.

I eventually gave birth to a baby girl, and then I gave her up for adoption that first day at the hospital. It took me a long time to find her again, but she was now my daughter, Lucy, with a daughter of her own. I wasn't sure I had made the right decision back then when I was still a confused teenager, but I was glad now the way things had worked out.

The damage to the relationship with my parents was irreparable though. I had some contact with my mother, who felt badly about the situation. But she was an old-fashioned wife who never questioned her husband's authority. As for my father, he was too bullheaded and stubborn to ever apologize to me or try to make things right between us. So was I. I guess I inherited my own bullheaded and stubborn nature from my father.

He died a while ago, and I didn't go to the funeral. It seemed hypocritical for me to do that. My mother is gone now too. I feel some guilt about all of it, but I've always been able to sublimate that guilt by getting lost in New York City and my job in the media world there that made me forget about Ohio.

But now—as we came in for a landing and the houses and lawns and factories of Ohio came into closer focus—I felt all the emotions from when I was an unhappy teenaged girl coming back again.

And I wondered if Riley Hunt had felt that way growing up here too.

Maybe that's why she moved away to go to school in a place like New York City.

A person can lose themselves in a big city like New York.

Run away from their past.

Me, I'd run a long way for a long time to get away from my own memories of Ohio.

But not yet far enough.

No matter how far you run, you can't ever run far enough to escape the past.

*   *   *

The Hunt family lived in an old-fashioned, clapboard white house in the Dayton suburb of Oakmont. The street itself was lined with trees and shrubbery and well-manicured green front lawns. There was a station wagon with an "I Brake For Animals" sticker on the bumper in the driveway of the Hunt house. I could see another car inside the garage.

I thought again about how incongruous it seemed that a girl like Riley Hunt had grown up on a peaceful, quiet street like this and then wound up dying violently on the streets of New York.

I parked my rental car on the street, got out, and knocked on the front door.

The first thing I saw was a dog as soon as the door opened. It looked like a small black poodle, and it barked at me through the screen door. I wondered if it was the same dog that I saw in that picture of Riley Hunt as a little girl under a Christmas tree.

Probably not. This one looked very young. I figured it must be a new one. A family can replace a dog when it dies. You can't replace a daughter.

The woman who opened the door was Elizabeth Hunt, Riley's mother. I recognized her from the memorial service in New York and from pictures I'd seen of her. But this was the first time I'd met her up close. She looked to be in her 40s—but her face still held the same kind of classic youthful beauty that her daughter, Riley, had.

"My name is Clare Carlson," I said. "From Channel 10 News in New York City."

"I know who you are. I've seen you on TV when we were there. But what do you want?"

I hadn't called her in advance to tell her that I was coming or to formally request an interview.

I thought that might make it too easy for her to say no.

So I did what I do best—simply showed up at someone's door and hoped they talked to me. Even if it was only to get rid of me.

Now it was the moment of truth.

"I want to talk to you about your daughter," I said.

"There's nothing more to say."

"I want to make sure her killer is brought to justice."

"What are you talking about? The killer is already in jail. What else is there?"

I didn't tell her that I had doubts now about whether Bakely really was the one who murdered Riley Hunt. No sense in doing that yet—not until I had more evidence—and upsetting her. Instead, I said: "I want to find out everything I can about Riley. About her life—and her death. So that I can tell our viewers the full story about your daughter. Will you help me to do that?"

Elizabeth Hunt hesitated for a few seconds, and I could see—like the lawyer that she was—that she was going over all the facts in her mind. Finally, she nodded, reached for the door handle, and opened it up. The dog jumped on me and licked my hand as I started to pet it. Then I went inside.

CHAPTER 38

WE SAT IN the kitchen, drinking coffee and talking. It was a bright, cheery room—with a big picture window that looked out onto a backyard filled with trees, flowers, and even a large bird feeder. The dog sat on the kitchen floor, watching the birds intently.

"When is the last time you heard from your daughter?" I asked Elizabeth Hunt.

"She called here a few nights before . . ."

She couldn't finish the sentence.

"Before she died?" I asked.

"Yes."

"What did she say?"

"I'm not sure exactly. I didn't talk to her."

"Who did?"

"Her father."

"Were you home too?"

"I was."

"But you didn't get on the phone at all?"

"No."

That was strange. But then everything about this woman and her relationship with her daughter seemed strange. She went to work the day she found out her daughter was murdered. She didn't speak during the memorial service in New York, as her husband did. She collapsed afterward in an emotional breakdown that I assumed was due to grief. But now I wondered if there wasn't something more going on with this woman.

I asked her about that.

"Riley and I always had a really good relationship for most of the years that she was growing up here. And when she first went away to college too. But the last time she came home to Dayton, we had a big argument. I wanted to make up with her. I wanted to make things right—but it never happened. And so, when I found out she'd been murdered, it hurt even more because I never got the chance to do that. Never got the chance to tell her how much I loved her, despite all the bad feelings we'd had at the end. I never had any closure with my child. It's been incredibly traumatic for me. I've thrown myself back into my work, right from that first day, to try and forget the pain. But I never will. And I guess I will never forgive myself for not making things right between me and Riley while she was alive."

"What was the argument between you and your daughter about?" I asked.

"Oh, just mother and daughter stuff."

"Anything specific?"

"I don't want to talk about it. Not now. Not after she's gone. It hurts too much. I'm sure you can understand that."

I nodded, even though I didn't really understand.

"Did your husband tell you what he and Riley talked about in that telephone conversation?"

"He said it was about her normal school stuff. She'd found out she was going to make the dean's list again. She was also excited about participating in some political campaigns in the future—I think she planned to do that on her summer vacation. Riley was very interested in politics."

"Right."

This wasn't getting me any information that I didn't already know.

"Did she sound worried or upset about anything that was happening to her on campus, according to your husband?"

"Not that I'm aware of."

"She didn't mention any problems at all she might have been having?"

She shook her head no.

"What about money?"

I threw that question out there to see where it led.

"No, Riley never asked us for money."

"How did she live in New York?"

"Her father and I paid for her dorm and a meal ticket at the dorm on campus. We sent her an allowance for living purposes too. She always indicated to us that she had plenty of money to live on between that—and what she made on her own. Said her and that band cashed in on some big paydays playing off-campus events."

I didn't figure that band dates paid her and other members of the group all that much.

But working as a professional escort sure might.

I wondered if Elizabeth Hunt had any idea about that.

"What did you know about her love life?"

"Not much."

"She was engaged to be married."

"She never told me about that."

Not exactly a close mother-daughter relationship.

But then I never had one with my parents either.

I found myself relating to the dead Riley Hunt even more than I had before.

"You went to Easton College too, didn't you?"

"That was a long time ago."

"Is that why Riley wanted to go to Easton? Because you did?"

"I suppose that played a part in it."

"How did you feel about that?"

"I advised her against it. I wanted her to go to college someplace else, someplace closer to here. But the more I argued against going to New York City and to Easton, the more determined Riley became to do it. That was the way Riley was. Very stubborn sometimes. So I lost that argument. If I hadn't—if I'd just left well enough alone—maybe she would have gone somewhere else. And she might be alive today. That's something else I have to live with for the rest of my life, Ms. Carlson. That kind of guilt. Do you understand?"

I nodded.

There wasn't much else for me to do.

We talked a bit more, and then I had one more question for her.

"Did Riley have any close friends around here that I might talk with to find out more about her?"

"Well, there's her ex-boyfriend. Ray Bonner. She went out with him during her senior year in high school. He's still around. But I can't imagine Riley was still in contact with him. They had a pretty unpleasant breakup. Ray works at a garage not too far from here. I saw him there the other day."

She gave me the address of the garage.

"You might try Linda Cullers too. She goes to the University of Dayton and still lives in town. Linda and Riley were best friends in high school."

"Did they still talk?"

"If Riley was still in touch with anyone back here, it would have been Linda."

*　*　*

Riley's father, Dr. Robert Hunt, came home at one point.

He wasn't of much help in finding out any more about Riley.

But he did seem like a nice man who had loved his daughter very much. He wanted to talk about his grief over losing her. Most of it was the same kind of thing he had said in previous interviews, and I didn't really need to hear it again. But I sat there patiently while he poured his heart out to me.

He showed me family picture albums of happier times long ago. Riley as a little girl on a swing. Riley at her first Communion. Riley opening up gifts on her sixteenth birthday party. Riley as her high school homecoming queen. There were pictures of him and his wife too, including one from their wedding day.

"Elizabeth and I met in college," he said to me at one point.

"Oh, you went to Easton too?"

"No, Purdue. Elizabeth transferred there before her senior year, and that's where she graduated. She then went on to law school at Ohio State. We've had such a wonderful life; we had a wonderful daughter, and now..."

He looked down at the pictures and began to cry.

"You do everything you can to be a good father," he said. "You try to raise your daughter the right way, to give her love and everything she needs. And then something as horrible as this happens, and she's gone forever. It isn't fair."

He looked at me sadly.

"I'm sure your father would feel the same way."

"My father's dead."

"Oh, I'm sorry."

"It happened a long time ago."

I tried to change the subject.

"What was your reaction when you heard Riley's accused killer had been arrested and was in jail?"

I expected him to say he hoped Donnie Ray Bakely spent the rest of his miserable life in jail. Or that he wished New York would reinstitute the death penalty so that Bakely could suffer a painful and excruciatingly awful death. That's the way most families of crime victims feel. But Robert Hunt surprised me.

"It doesn't really matter," he said.

"Don't you want revenge?"

"Revenge won't bring Riley back to life. Revenge can't do that."

No, but it makes you feel a damn lot better, I thought.

CHAPTER 39

Ray Bonner was working under the hood of a car when I showed up at the garage and told him who I was.

"I don't talk to the media," Bonner said.

"Right. You and Kanye West."

"Huh?"

"Ray, has anyone in the media ever cared about anything you had to say until this very moment?"

That one stopped him. He pulled out a rag, wiped some grease off his hands, and walked over to a desk in the garage. He took out a pack of cigarettes, lit one, and sat down behind the desk.

"I want to ask you some questions about your relationship with Riley Hunt," I said.

"I don't have any relationship with her."

"But you did."

"Right. Until she ran off to New York and decided she was too good for someone like me."

Sitting there watching him clench and unclench his fists in memory of how Riley Hunt had left him, I wondered how a smart, talented girl like her could have ever been with a guy like Ray Bonner in the first place. He was kind of good looking, I guess. But not the kind of guy you want to fall in love with and spend the rest of your life married to.

Bruce Townsend fit that bill much more nicely. On the other hand, Riley Hunt had apparently been with Johnny Steffano too—who was basically a meaner, tougher version of Ray Bonner. It was frequently difficult to understand a person's choices when it came to romance. And I was the last person to second-guess anyone in that department, given my own history of bad choices.

"Were you upset when Riley broke it off with you?" I asked him.

"Of course I was."

"How upset?"

"What do you mean?"

"Did you argue with her?"

"I guess."

"Hit her?"

He didn't say anything.

"You did hit her, didn't you?"

"Okay, I did. Once or twice. She used to hit me too. It was a very volatile relationship. Especially at the end. Riley really did a number on me. I was plenty pissed off at her."

"Pissed off enough to maybe go to New York City and confront her?"

He looked at me now and suddenly realized what I was saying.

"Wait a minute! You don't think that I was mad enough at Riley to kill her?"

"The thought did cross my mind."

"I was 500 miles away."

"There's airplanes between here and New York."

There was a method to my madness. Bonner was clearly an angry, volatile guy. If I could get him rattled enough, he might say or do something stupid that could help me. There was a possibility in my mind too that he really could have killed her. So maybe he'd even break down and confess to me on the spot. But I wasn't counting on that happening.

"Oh, sure," he said sarcastically. "I went to the airport that night, caught a plane to New York, murdered Riley in Greenwich Village—and then flew back here in time to finish the lube job on Mrs. Fredericks' Chevy Impala."

"It's possible," I told him.

"Well, I've got an alibi for the time of the murder."

"That's interesting."

"What do you mean?"

"Just that Riley was murdered at around 2:30 in the morning. Most people don't have an alibi ready for 2:30 in the morning. At 2:30 p.m., they can say there were having lunch or something specific like that. But most people can't tell you exactly what they were doing at 2:30 in the morning. Except sleeping. But you say you have a specific alibi for that time. I find that interesting."

Bonner shrugged. "I don't care whether you believe me or not. I know I didn't kill her. I could never have killed her. And there's a very good reason for that."

"Which is?"

"I loved Riley."

Maybe he did love her. Maybe he'd gotten a raw deal from her. Maybe he'd make some other woman a good husband someday. But I didn't like him. I knew a lot of guys like Ray Bonner when I was growing up in Ohio—and I didn't like them any better now.

And I still couldn't put him and Riley Hunt together.

But it turned out there was more to his story.

He was too angry for all of this to have happened more than a year ago when they were both still in high school.

"You tried to get back together again with Riley, didn't you?" I asked.

"Yeah, that's right."

"How?"

"I went to New York. Not the night she was killed, like you said. A few weeks ago. Only it didn't turn out too well. She didn't want to talk to me or see me at all. And when I kept pushing, I got . . ."

His voice trailed off.

"You got what, Ray?"

"I got beat up."

Bonner winced at the memory. He probably figured he was a tough guy. He didn't like remembering this.

"Who did it?"

"I don't know his name. He was a big guy. Really muscular. He told me to stay away from Riley. That she complained I was harassing her. And that this beating that he gave me was a message for me to keep away from her for good."

Johnny Steffano, I thought to myself.

"Did he say he was going out with Riley himself?"

Bonner shook his head. "No, he said someone else was."

"Who?"

"Someone from a big shot family in the mob. It scared the hell out of me. I caught the next plane back to Dayton. I knew I was in over my head. I only hoped Riley wasn't too."

I described Johnny Steffano to him.

"No, that doesn't sound like the one who beat me up."

"Anything specific you can remember about him? Besides that he was big and muscular?"

"Just that he had a ponytail. His hair was long, but wrapped up in the back in a ponytail."

The guy from Steffano's restaurant.

The one I called Fettuccine Guy.

CHAPTER 40

LINDA CULLERS, RILEY'S best friend in high school, turned out to be easy to find. She had a big social media presence, so I was able to message her and arrange for a meeting. I went to see her at the off-campus house where she had a room at the University of Dayton.

She was tall, with straight dark hair, a nice figure, and dressed very fashionably. I could see why she and Riley would have been best friends. They both must have been among the most popular girls in the senior class in high school. Then Riley moved to New York, and Linda Cullers stayed here in Ohio.

Unlike Ray Bonner, she seemed very happy to talk to me. She loved it that I was a TV journalist.

"Riley would have loved meeting you too," she said. "She had some aspirations for maybe being a journalist too. Getting into politics one day was her big dream, of course. And she was really into the music she played too. But she still talked about getting journalism experience also, maybe at the Easton school paper. Riley had so many big dreams . . ."

She talked to me more about her and Riley. Things they did in high school. And how they wound up going in different directions after graduation.

"Riley always wanted to get out of this place and move to a big city like New York," she said. "Riley loved it in New York. Talked about it all the time to me whenever she came back to Dayton. Said she wanted to live there the rest of her life. Of course, no one knew her damn life would be so short."

"She didn't like being back in Dayton?"

"No, she always wanted to get back to New York. Especially at the end. I guess her and her mother weren't getting along too well."

That sure jibed with what the mother had told me.

But why?

What was going on between Riley and her mother?

"What about Riley's father?"

"She was okay with him. It was her mother she had a big problem with."

"Do you have any idea why she and her mother had such a bad relationship?"

Linda Cullers shook her head no.

"I asked her about that, but she never told me."

"How long had this been going on?"

"I don't remember it being that way when we were together in high school. Or even when she first went away to college. But, when she came home last time, she was very mad at her mother. I did ask her about it the last time we talked. But she got kind of defensive and angry when I did. So I stopped."

"And that was the last time you talked with her?"

"Yeah. Maybe she was mad at me for pushing her on it. But I stopped hearing from her after that. Of course, she was in New York and I was here. Riley and I just wound up going our separate ways, I guess."

I nodded.

"Did she ever tell you anything about her romantic life in New York at Easton?"

"Not in so many words. But I was pretty sure she was seeing someone."

"Who?"

She shrugged. "Don't know. Riley was secretive about that too the last time I talked with her. I wondered if that meant he was married. Or there was some other reason she didn't want to talk about him."

"She was engaged to someone. A guy named Bruce Townsend. Did she talk about him?"

"No, never heard the name."

"How about a student named Johnny Steffano?"

"Nope. Sorry."

I kept asking her questions, hoping there was something more she could tell me about Riley that would give me some kind of answers to the mysteries of her life.

"Do you want to see her letters?" she asked me at one point.

"Letters?"

"Well, email really." She laughed. "No one sends letters anymore, do they? There were a few postcards from Riley though. And some texts and emails that she sent me from New York."

She showed me, and I read through everything. They all seemed the typical kind of stuff a young girl on her own for the first time in New York City might send back to her best friend at home. Postcards. Emails about people she'd met and places she'd gone to. Pictures of her standing in front of tourist attractions.

"Hey, Linda," one of the messages read. "Here I am in the big city. Don't worry about me, everything's fine. I love it here. I don't know how you can stay in a place like Oakland or Dayton. Me, I want to spend the rest of my life in this big and wonderful city. I want to experience everything I can here. I want to live my life to the fullest. And New York City is the place where I can live that kind of life."

Live her life to the fullest?

Except now she was dead before she even made it past the age of twenty.

The irony and sadness of that was difficult to ignore.

One of the things Linda Cullers got from Riley was a picture from Radio City Music Hall. "Maybe someday you'll see me playing music on stage here," she said in the message she sent with it. "I've got so many things that I want to do. And I'm going to try and accomplish as many of them as I can, Linda. I'm having the time of my life!"

I was almost finished going through it all when I found an email with a picture of Riley in front of the Empire State Building. She was standing on the sidewalk in front of the main entrance, and she had her arm around the shoulder of someone else.

"Look at your BFF from Oakland here in the Big Apple," the message with it read. "We rode the elevator all the way to the top—all 102 stories—and my friend here pointed out all the neat parts of New York City for me. It was so cool looking down on it all. I felt like this whole town belonged to me. Maybe someday it really will."

I stared at the picture. Not just at Riley Hunt, but at the person next to her. It was a man. A man wearing an Army cap. The cap had writing on it that said: "Afghan Warrior: Operation Enduring Freedom."

I recognized the man right away.

I'd seen him twice before.

Once in a courtroom.

And again at Rikers Island Prison.

He looked more normal here—not like a crazy man when I'd seen him—but it was definitely the same man.

Donnie Ray Bakely.

CHAPTER 41

"WHERE WERE YOU all day yesterday?" Susan Endicott wanted to know.

"Working."

"Not here, you weren't."

"No, I went to Dayton."

"What's in Dayton?"

"I was there investigating a story."

"What story?"

"The Riley Hunt murder."

"That story is over."

"I'm not so sure about that."

"You're supposed to be my news director here, running the evening broadcast."

"You also told me you wanted me on the air breaking exclusives. To do that, I need to go out on the street—and sometimes out on the road—in order to work a story like a reporter does. That's what I was doing yesterday. Working the Riley Hunt story for an exclusive."

"Let me see if I understand this correctly," Endicott said. "Riley Hunt is dead. The man who killed her is in jail. So what's the big story you're still chasing on it?"

I sat there thinking about how much I should tell her. Or at least how much I wanted to tell her.

"Goddamit, Carlson! I asked you a question. I'm the executive producer here. I need to know what you're doing. That's my job."

She was right about that. So I told her. Well, I told her some of it. About how I was working with Barrett in the District Attorney's office to set up on-air interview at Rikers with Riley Hunt murder suspect Donnie Ray Bakely.

"He told me he would get approval from both the DA's office and the Department of Corrections for me to do it. Exclusive interview. Thirty minutes to an hour—depending on how long Bakely is able to talk coherently—with a camera crew there with me."

Endicott's eyes opened wide, and she nodded her approval.

Okay, she liked that.

"But what does this have to do with whatever you were doing out in Dayton?" Endicott wanted to know.

I told her I wanted to find out more about Riley Hunt before the jailhouse interview. How I'd talked with her mother for the first time. Also, Riley's ex-boyfriend and her best friend in high school. I didn't tell her about the picture I'd seen of Riley and Donnie Ray Bakely together at the Empire State Building. I didn't really know what that meant yet. And I didn't trust Endicott with that kind of information until I did know more. So I simply told her I had a lot of good profile stuff on Riley Hunt I could put on air along with the upcoming Bakely interview.

She liked that too.

At some point, she asked me again about the status of the personnel moves in the Channel 10 newsroom she'd talked about earlier.

I'd bluffed her once before by pretending I had Brendan Kaiser's support if it came head-to-head between us on this firing issue, and I did it again now.

"I don't want to fire anyone," I said. "Not Stratton. Not Brett or Dani. Not anyone."

"Even if I order you to do it?"

"No."

"I could fire you for that right now."

"Sure, you could. If Brendan Kaiser lets you, of course. But, if that did happen, then I'd just take my exclusive interview with accused Riley Hunt murderer Donnie Ray Bakely to another media outlet in town. You can watch it on Channels 2 or 4 or 7."

Endicott shook her head. "You're a real piece of work, Carlson."

"I take that as a compliment."

I looked around the office. All of Jack Faron's things were gone now. Framed pictures of his family; awards we'd won together as a station for news coverage; shots of people on the staff and friends and lots of other wonderful memorabilia he had that made him come alive as a person and as a warm, caring human being.

In their place were a lot of self-aggrandizing things about Susan Endicott. Pictures of her posing with celebrities and other famous people. Awards she'd won, framed articles about her from media publications, and lots of pictures of herself. This room was about Susan Endicott now, no one else.

God, I missed Jack Faron. Sure, Jack and I butted heads on more than one occasion in here. But I admired his judgement and his intelligence and his compassion, no matter how much I ever disagreed or got mad at the man.

"Let's talk about how we're going to handle this Bakely interview," she said before I left. "I'll do a big promotional campaign on all the shows during the day leading up to the newscast. 'A Monster Murderer Speaks: Exclusive Interview with the Man who Killed Riley Hunt.' That ought to really grab us some huge ratings for the show."

"What about the idea that he's going to tell us in the interview that he doesn't remember killing Riley? How there are new questions out there now suggesting maybe he didn't do it and—"

She shook her head no. "I like my idea better."

"But..."

"You just get the interview, Carlson, and I'll sell it to the audience. I know how to do that."

I smiled. "You furnish the pictures; I'll furnish the war," I said.

"What?"

"William Randolph Hearst said that."

She still didn't understand. I guess Susan Endicott wasn't as astute a student of journalistic history as I was.

"When it looked like the U.S. was about to go to war with Spain at the turn of the 20th century, William Randolph Hearst decided a war like that would be great for his newspaper's circulation. He sent some of his top writers and photographers to Cuba—which was then under Spanish control and a likely flashpoint for the war with the U.S.—to send him sensational pictures to put on Page One. Meanwhile, he was inflaming the American public with wartime rhetoric to encourage the U.S. entrance in a war there. Well, one of his photographers got to Cuba, saw nothing happening, and messages Hearst: 'There is no war here.' Hearst wrote back: 'You furnish the pictures; I'll furnish the war.'"

Susan Endicott laughed at this.

Really laughed.

"I like that. I like that a lot. Well, Carlson, you furnish the interview with Bakely, and I'll furnish the ratings."

CHAPTER 42

PETE BEVILACQUA AND I had dinner together at Tavern on the Green in Central Park. Yes, I finally gave in and agreed to see him again. Tavern on the Green is an elegant, historic restaurant where you can dine and look out at the rolling meadows and trees of the park. The scene there had a kind of stark beauty to it, if you cared about that sort of thing. But the truth is I was more interested in Pete Bevilacqua than the view or the food. This was the third time I'd seen him and he really came across as a nice, caring guy.

Afterward, we did something I had never done in New York. Took a ride on a horse and carriage through Central Park. It was his idea. It didn't seem that great a thing to do to me at first, but once the driver yelled giddy up to the horse and we began roll-ing . . . well, I got really into it. Traveling this way wasn't as fast as the subway, but it was a lot more fun.

It was almost midnight when he took me back to my place. He suggested coming up for a nightcap, and I said yes. Dazzle me with a horse and buggy ride, and I'll say yes to anything.

I brought out some coffee and bourbon, and we sat on the couch drinking it and talking. He asked me some questions about the Riley Hunt story he knew I was consumed by. I told him about going to Dayton and also about my plans for a big exclusive jail-house interview with Donnie Ray Bakely, the accused killer. He acted like he was interested, and maybe he really was.

But I knew where this was likely headed, and I was pretty sure he did too. Still, I figured I'd just let it play out and see what happened. Waiting for him to make his move. Which, of course, he eventually did.

"I had a nice time," he said.

"So did I."

"I'd like to see you again."

"Works for me."

I smiled.

We sat there staring at each other.

"Would it be too pushy for me to ask you for a good-night kiss?" he finally said.

I pretended to think about it for a minute.

"Okay. It has been a pleasant evening. I think a good-night kiss would be all right."

He leaned forward and kissed me on the lips. I kissed him back. We held onto each other for a long time. When I came up for air, he looked at me and grinned. His face was still close to mine.

"I don't suppose I could talk you into a second good-night kiss," he said.

"Sure, let's live dangerously."

We kissed again.

"You'll tell me if I'm being too pushy, right?"

"You'll be the first to know."

We were almost horizontal on the couch by now.

"Actually," I said, in between kisses, "we're running a house special tonight. All you can kiss."

"That's good. Real good."

His lips explored all the parts of my face and my neck and then touched down my chest, almost to my breasts. I felt a tingle of excitement through me now.

"Clare?" he murmured.

"Hmmm."

"Are we going to go to bed tonight?"

"I wouldn't be a bit surprised."

He took me by the hand and led me into the bedroom. Then he undressed me—first my skirt, then my blouse, followed by my bra and the rest of the clothes. I did the same thing to him. It all happened very slowly. Haste makes waste.

It was later—much later—when I looked over at him in bed and smiled.

"Well, well, well," I said.

"Interesting response to what we just did."

"I have a real way with words. It's my business, you know."

He got up and went into the bathroom. I heard him splash water on himself. When he came back, he started putting on his pants and shirt.

"Where are you going?" I asked.

"Home."

"Wham-bam, thank you, ma'am? You don't want to spend the night?"

"I can't. I've got an early class and I need to get back to Princeton for it tonight."

"Oh."

I was disappointed, but I tried not to let it show.

He was dressed now. He leaned over and kissed me. More shivers.

"I'll call you tomorrow," he said.

"Right. Tomorrow."

*   *   *

After he was gone, I had trouble falling asleep. I decided it was because I was hungry. Sex always makes me hungry. I put on my bathrobe and slippers and padded into the kitchen to check the refrigerator. There was a Sara Lee cheesecake in there and a half pint of chocolate marshmallow ice cream. Tough decision. I solved it by taking both out and putting them on a plate together. Resisting temptation is not my strong suit.

Even after I finished off all that cheesecake and ice cream though, I still wasn't sleepy. Too much was running through my mind.

I thought about Donnie Ray Bakely and my upcoming exclusive interview with him at Rikers. Would he be able to tell me what he was doing in a picture with Riley Hunt at the Empire State Building—looking like two tourists—before she was murdered and he supposedly stumbled on her body near Washington Square Park?

I thought about Ray Bonner, the angry ex-boyfriend back in Dayton who'd come to New York to confront her—only to get beaten up by Anthony Steffano's man from the restaurant and fleeing back home to Ohio.

I thought about Johnny Steffano and Riley Hunt, and how they still did not fit together in any logical way.

And I thought about Bruce Townsend, the deputy NYPD commissioner's son, who turned up on that security video I'd found on the same night and not long before Riley was murdered. I needed to find out more about that now. Did the police know yet that Townsend—and Townsend's father—had lied about his whereabouts that night? And, if they did, were they trying to cover it up?

Yep, I had a lot to think about.

But most of all, as I lay there in bed trying to finally get to sleep, I thought about Pete Bevilacqua and the perfect evening we'd shared together—culminating in some pretty great mind-blowing sex.

So much for Dear Abby's advice about saving myself until I was sure the right man had come along.

Forgive me, Abby, for I have sinned.

CHAPTER 43

THE NEXT NIGHT I had dinner with another of the men in my life. But this one was from my past. My ex-husband Sam Markham, the homicide cop.

Sam didn't seem too thrilled to hear from me when I called him. But then again, my ex-husbands never really did.

"You want to do what?" he asked.

"Have dinner with you and talk."

"Why?"

"I need your advice."

"Really? That's a shocker. I thought you always knew everything."

"C'mon, Sam, it's important."

There was a long pause at the other end.

"Who's buying?" he asked finally.

"I am."

"Hmmm." He thought about that for a minute. "Okay, where?"

"You like Italian?"

An hour later, we were standing at the counter of a pizza parlor near St. Mark's Place and First Avenue in the heart of the East Village. Outside the window, you could see punk rockers, aging hipsters, and assorted other Village types walking by.

Sam picked up a piece of sausage pizza and wrinkled his nose. "When I said I'd let you buy me an Italian dinner," he said, "this wasn't exactly what I had in mind."

"No?" I said, taking a big bite out of my slice. Some of the sauce dripped down my chin, and I wiped it off with a napkin.

"I was thinking of a normal Italian restaurant. You know . . . waiters, checkered tablecloths, stuff like that."

"Are you kidding? This is the best pizza in New York City. Besides, I'm on a very tight expense budget."

"Yeah." He sighed. "So's everybody in the media who ever bought me dinner."

A girl with purple hair walked by. She was wearing a pair of razor blades as earrings and a black T-shirt with the words "Born To Party" on the back. I wondered what someone like that thought about when she got dressed in front of a mirror in the morning.

"What did you want to talk about?" Sam asked.

"I've got a problem."

"I heard. You sure got your tit caught in the ringer with that open mic on the live newscast mistake that everyone's talking about."

"Actually, I don't think the term 'tit caught in the ringer' is acceptable language in this new enlightened era of male/female discourse."

"I'm your ex-husband. I can say anything I want to you."

"Interesting approach."

"So do you still have a job there or what?"

"At the moment . . ."

I took another bite of the pizza. Lots of cheese, tasty tomato sauce, not too doughy. I gave it my four-star seal of approval.

"I want to talk to you about a story I'm working on."

"What story?"

"Riley Hunt."

He gave me a quizzical look.

"That story is over. We got the guy who did it. He confessed. What else is there?"

"I talked to Bakely at Rikers."

I told Sam about Bakely saying now that he didn't remember killing the girl. That he was confused when he confessed. About his mother saying how he was such a good kid.

"What do you expect her to say? Or him? Some lawyer gets to him, tells him to recant the confession. But we know he was there. He had her phone. Her blood is all over him. Of course the mother thinks he's innocent. How could her little poor misunderstood boy be a killer? C'mon, Clare, anyone would have to pretty naive to buy that story."

"I believe him."

"That he didn't kill her?"

"That at least he doesn't think he killed her."

"Let's say—for argument's sake—that Bakely is telling the truth now. That he did just stumble on to the body that night on the street. And that he did just happen to take her phone. And just happened to get her blood on him because he was a good citizen trying to see if she was dead or not. Forget it. I won't even be hypothetical about this with you. There's no way anyone could buy that story of his."

"What did you find on her cell phone?" I asked. "The one you say he had on him when he was arrested."

"That's confidential."

"So you did find something on the phone?"

He sighed.

"You know something about that last phone call she got at the bar before she left?" I asked. "You know who it was from?"

"Yes. It doesn't make much sense, but I know who called her. It was Donnie Ray Bakely."

That was not the answer I was expecting.

"How would he even know how to reach her?"

"You tell me. But he knew her number. He had this burner phone we found out he'd bought a while back at some bodega. It still had minutes left on it. That's what he used to make the call to her. It was a very brief call. Only a minute or two. But long enough that there must have been some conversation. Although I have no idea why Riley Hunt might have taken a call out of the blue like that."

"Maybe it wasn't so out of the blue," I said.

I told him about the picture I'd seen of Riley Hunt and Donnie Ray Bakely together visiting the Empire State Building.

"How in the hell did Riley Hunt know someone like Bakely?"

"That's one of my questions too."

"Well, I don't think that picture of them together helps prove your theory he might be innocent. And this phone call makes it even worse. I think it makes him seem more likely to be guilty. He knew her. So maybe he had some kind of motive. Maybe he was stalking her that night..."

I'd thought about that possibility. Maybe Bakely was the person she thought was watching her or following her. But I had trouble believing that. It just didn't fit the picture I'd gotten of Donnie Ray Bakely—as troubled as he obviously was—from the time I spent talking with him about Riley at the prison. I told that to Sam.

"Okay, I have a question for you," he said.

"Go ahead."

"Can you imagine any better suspect than Bakely? He seems to hit all the marks to me."

"I know, but I have a feeling about this, Sam. If you take Donnie Ray Bakely out of the equation, then the killer could be—very likely might be—someone who has a personal motive to want Riley Hunt dead. That opens a lot of possibilities. Two people in particular."

I went through it with him.

First, there was Johnny Steffano. The son of Anthony Steffano. I said he'd been seen with her in a bar shortly before she wound up dead in another part of town. And that his father—as well as Johnny Steffano himself—had both made it clear to me that they didn't want him connected to this case in any way.

"You think Johnny Steffano killed her?"

"It's a possibility."

"The kid does have a hair-trigger temper."

"Yeah, me and his temper have met."

Sam chuckled. I think he was imagining what a confrontation between me and Johnny Steffano would have been like.

"Who's the other person you think could have done it?"

"Bruce Townsend."

I could see the look of shock on Sam's face. I'd wondered if he saw him at all on that security camera, like I did. Even though I'd dropped him a big hint to look closer at some of the unseen security video footage in the area, it was clear now that he hadn't. This was all new to him.

"Jesus," he said.

"Yeah."

"The deputy commissioner's son."

"And her fiancé."

I told him about the Townsend kid showing up on the security camera of the store several blocks away a few hours before Riley Hunt's body was found.

"That doesn't mean he killed her. Only that he was in the neighborhood that night. There's a lot of people walking the street in the neighborhood."

"Except he said he was at his parents' house on Long Island that night."

"Maybe he got confused about the timing. After all, his fiancée was dead and all."

"His father backed up his story."

I looked down at the pizza left in the box. It didn't look so appetizing anymore. Pizza is like that after you've eaten a few slices.

I'd printed out the picture of Bruce Townsend from the security camera video. The picture of Bruce Townsend walking the streets of Greenwich Village—not at his parents' house on Long Island— the night of his fiancée's murder. I took it out of my handbag now and laid it on the counter for Sam to see. He stared at it for a long time.

"What do you expect me to do, Clare?" he asked finally.

"Ask Bruce Townsend about his alibi for that night."

"Which means . . ."

"You have to ask his father too. The deputy commissioner. Ask him why he lied about his son's whereabouts on the night Riley was murdered."

Sam shook his head in frustration. "Do you understand the position you're putting me in?"

"Shoot the messenger, right?"

"Exactly."

"Hugh Townsend is going to blame you for opening this whole thing up."

"If you're wrong about the Townsend kid being involved, this could be the end of my career."

"But what if I'm right about it all?"

"I have to think about this . . ."

"I'm sure you'll do the right thing, Sam."

CHAPTER 44

DONNIE RAY BAKELY'S mother lived in a small town in central New Jersey called Springdale. I called to tell her I was coming out to talk to her, then rented a car for the hour and a half trip.

When I got there, Springdale looked like a different world from New York, not just a different state. Quiet streets with quaint shops and old houses with big porches and lawns in front. Many of the homes had American flags hanging in front of them. This was where Bakely had grown up. He was an All-American kid.

Then he'd gone off to war and come back as damaged goods. "He was never the same after Iraq and Afghanistan," his mother had said to me. But did Bakely—who grew up in this idyllic small town—really change enough to brutally murder Riley Hunt for no apparent reason?

We sat in Mrs. Bakely's living room and I showed her the picture I'd gotten from Linda Cullers of Riley Hunt and Donnie Ray Bakely together at the Empire State Building.

"Did you ever see this before?" I asked her.

"No, I don't think so."

She looked at the picture more closely now.

"Is that who I think it is with Donnie?"

I nodded.

"Riley Hunt."

"So he did know her."

"Yes. He told me he thought he recognized Riley Hunt when he saw her dead on the street, but he didn't know how. I've also learned from the police that your son made a call to Riley Hunt on the night she died. All this—the call and the picture—shows he was telling the truth about knowing her beforehand. Which maybe means he's telling the truth about the rest of it too. Including that he doesn't remember—he's not sure—that he killed her."

She stared at the picture in her hand. The picture of her son at the Empire State Building. Smiling with Riley Hunt. Maybe one of the few happy memories in his sad life.

"He looks so normal in this picture," she said.

"It was taken a few months ago. Mrs. Bakely, you told me that first day in my office that you thought Donnie had gotten better for a while. That you had noticed a marked upturn in him. But then he wound up back on the streets of New York and attacked the woman in Tompkins Square Park. Before that, he supposedly killed Riley Hunt too. I don't think he did kill Riley. I know you believe that too. But tell me more about his mood swings in the days before it happened."

"Yes, Donnie had seemed to be making constant improvement. Acting normally in most situations for a while. But then something happened a few weeks ago. He was confused and was having trouble telling reality from fantasy. He kept imagining he was back in the war. It was such a sudden change in his behavior."

"I noticed the same thing the two different times I saw him," I said. "In court that first day, he seemed totally gone—in a world of his own. Like he didn't understand what was happening to him. But later, when I talked to him in prison, he was much more aware.

He was scared too. I thought that was good. He understood the gravity of his situation."

"I saw that when I visited him in jail too," she said.

"The question is what changed. What changed to make him worse? There has to be something. The only thing I can think of is drugs. Was there any change in Donnie's drug usage during this time?"

"You think that maybe some drug he was taking made him the way he was?"

"How many drugs was he prescribed and taking? Was he taking any others? Did this change dramatically for some reason in those last weeks?"

She shook her head in frustration.

"I don't know. All I can tell you is he went into a veterans' facility in the city a few weeks earlier. We thought it might help him. He had been spending time working with some veterans' service groups. That really seemed to help him for a long time. He really was acting normally and engaging with people. I thought maybe he had turned a corner.

"He had made so much improvement, we were hoping for more. But, instead, he got worse. He stayed here a few days after he was released from the hospital, but he was a mess. Complaining about nightmares of the war and how he couldn't sleep and how he kept having flashbacks of being in Afghanistan. Then one day I came home, and he was gone. That was the last time I saw him until after he had been arrested for the girl's murder."

"Can you tell me more about this veterans' place where Donnie went?"

"Like what?"

"Well, let's start with the name . . ."

* * *

On my drive back to the city, I called Maggie from the car and asked her to check out the place more for me.

"It's called the Fremont Veterans Center, and it's located in the Lower East Side. Not far from Tompkins Square Park where Bakely was arrested."

I gave her the specific address and phone number I'd gotten from Mrs. Bakely.

"When do you need this?"

"By the time I get back."

"Good to know there's no pressure on me."

Maggie came through on it, as usual. When I got to the office, she had a list of facts about the place—history, numbers of patients, medical stats, etcetera. But that was just part of it. She'd also uncovered some much more interesting information about the Fremont Veterans Center.

"It doesn't have a very good reputation, Clare."

"How so?"

"Apparently federal funding for treating war veterans is big business. Especially veterans from recent wars like Afghanistan and Iraq where a lot of the people who come back are really messed up. Emotionally, as well as physically. So a lot of money is spent in Washington on treatment of these returning veterans. Some of it is helpful, and the veterans get good medical care. But other places seem to be in for a quick government handout, and don't care that much about the veterans they're supposed to be treating. They take shortcuts to maximize their profits from government funding. Fremont Veterans Center seems to be one of those."

She told me how Fremont had been cited several times by federal watchdog agencies for questionable practices and misuses of government funds—but was still operating.

"Why do people go to a place like that?"

"Because it can provide positive results for them—at least at first. I found a *New York Times* investigation which talked about a lot of places like Fremont. Most of the veterans who go to them are suffering post-war trauma—nightmares, insomnia, and a detached sense of reality over being home again after what they saw and did in the war. Fremont puts them on a heavy drug dosage, which seems to help immediately. But it's only masking the problem. And, in fact, it can make all the PTSD problems even worse for the patients once they're released, according to some studies. Some of them even totally lose touch with reality and imagine they're still back in the war. Sounds like Donnie Ray Bakely, huh?"

That explained a lot.

Like why Bakely had been acting more normally for a while, but then regressed so badly after leaving the center.

But how did Riley Hunt figure into this?

Well, Riley was very big into charity work—that's what her family and friends said—including working with homeless military veterans.

Maybe that's where she and Donnie Ray Bakely met—and how she wound up in that picture with him at the Empire State Building.

And maybe she even gave him her cell phone number if he ever needed help or someone to talk to.

From everything that people said about Riley—and her drive to try to help people—it seemed like a plausible scenario.

Maybe Bakely would be able to remember more when I asked him about all this again at Rikers.

I was really looking forward to this interview now.

I hoped Billy Barrett would make it happen soon.

CHAPTER 45

I'm a great believer in the journalistic technique known as the stakeout.

The stakeout is basically as simple as it sounds. You stay at one key location for as long as it takes until someone does something that makes news. Yep, that's all there is to it. All you need is plenty of time, patience, and a functioning bladder to pull it off.

When all else fails on a story, I turn to the stakeout.

The stakeout is definitely my go-to approach as a reporter.

I've gotten a lot of exclusives over the years as a journalist by spending time on stakeouts.

The only problem was that to do an effective stakeout, you need to figure out the target you're going to be staking out for a story.

I wasn't sure who—or what—to stake out this time.

I couldn't stake out Donnie Ray Bakely because he was in jail.

I couldn't stake out Deputy Police Commissioner Hugh Townsend because he worked at 1 Police Plaza, and it would be very difficult for me to fit in there.

I could stake out his son, I supposed—he'd be easy to spot because of the big hair and tall physique.

Or I could stake out Anthony Steffano and his son.

I went with that idea.

If I went to Steffano's restaurant—which he owned and where his son worked—I had a shot at getting at least one of them during my stakeout. Maybe even a double hit.

The restaurant opened for lunch at noon. I got there about eleven, found a seat on a park bench outside a bodega across the street where I could get a good view, and pretended to be reading a book or scanning my iPhone.

Sure, they'd seen me at the restaurant when I went in there—and later as I got thrown out when they found out I was a reporter. So I decided to make myself look different. I put on a New York Mets baseball cap, a big pair of sunglasses, and a baggy T-shirt and jeans. I either looked like a downtown hipster or a bag lady, I wasn't sure which. But I figured no one would recognize me.

Clare Carlson, Master of 1000 Disguises.

A lot of people started going in and out of the place. First people who worked there, then customers. But none of them seemed to be Steffano or his son.

I was close enough that some of the smells of the Italian food they were cooking came wafting across to me. That made me hungry. There was a Dunkin' Donuts on the street so I stopped in there and got a big coffee and a box of half a dozen donuts.

My plan was to ration them out carefully, maybe eating one every hour or so. But by the end of the first hour, my donuts were gone. I got a refill of the coffee and kept waiting.

Because the traffic in and out of the place had slowed by now, I tried to think of ways to amuse myself and pass the time.

I decided to rate all the men I'd ever had sex with for their desirability.

That gave me a lot of options. I'd been married three times. I also got pregnant from the first man I ever slept with—Doug Crowell in college who was the biological father of my daughter, Lucy. I'd also slept with the adoptive father of Lucy that I gave her up to when she was a baby. I didn't sleep with the adoptive father she had after that, but then I didn't know who he was until much later.

There were a lot of other men along the way, besides my three husbands. Like Scott Manning, who was married—but not to me. And, of course, my current romantic partner, Pete Bevilacqua. I decided to make Pete first, mostly because he was the man I was with now and he was the only one who still offered some exciting future opportunities.

But it was a real contest for second place.

By 5 or 6 p.m., the dinner crowd started to arrive. It made me realize I was going to have to explain to Susan Endicott why I was out of the office all day and what I was doing. I'd told Maggie about it, leaving her to run the newscasts tonight. I didn't want to deal with Endicott. Not yet. But I knew another confrontation with her was coming.

From what I could see, smell, and from people talking, the specials on the Steffano restaurant menu tonight were clams with linguini and a spicy meatball lasagna dish. Sure sounded good to me. I was hungry again, but couldn't handle any more donuts. There was a McDonald's nearby. I went there, got a Big Mac and a Coke, with fries, then returned to my spot outside Steffano's.

It was a little after 7:30 when something finally happened. Not at the front door, but at one of the side entrances I could see. A man came out that I recognized and got into a car. Anthony Steffano then came out the door and watched him go.

I'd brought a car of my own along with me for this kind of situation, leaving it parked down the street. I ran there now, started it up, and got back to the restaurant just in time to see the other car pulling away.

It made its way slowly through the streets of downtown Manhattan, but then it didn't have very far to go. It stopped several blocks away on Park Row. I knew that location well.

The address was 1 Police Plaza.

The man I'd seen leaving Steffano's parked the car now in a reserved NYPD space, got out, and walked through the front doors of Police Headquarters.

No one stopped him, and why would they?

Everyone there knew who he was.

Just like I knew who he was when I saw him come out of Steffano's Restaurant.

It was Deputy Police Commissioner Hugh Townsend.

Holy crap!

What in the hell was going on here?

CHAPTER 46

AT THE SAME time that I was trying to unravel the growing mysteries surrounding the death of Riley Hunt, I also had to deal with protecting my staff from Susan Endicott.

She wanted me to shake up my staff—particularly the on-air group—in order to give a boost to our ratings.

Which basically meant she wanted me to fire some of them.

She thought firing people like Brett or Dani or Steve Stratton was the solution.

I had another idea.

Actually, Jack Faron and I had come up with the idea together.

"You need to do something, Clare," Faron said to me when I went to him for his advice on dealing with Endicott. "You can't keep putting her off indefinitely. You need to do something proactive. Something that will make her think you're moving in the right direction she wants for shaking up the newscast and the people on it. Without having to get to the point of firing anyone. It's a compromise, Clare."

"I'm not good at compromising," I said.

"You get used to it in this TV business."

And so we came up with our plan.

"Will it work?" I asked him when we were done.

"Depends on how much Endicott is willing to compromise herself. How much she's willing to avoid a full-out confrontation with you. How much she wants to avoid having to keep battling with a pain in the ass like you."

"And you figure she'll go along to avoid dealing with me being such a pain in the ass?"

"I always did." He smiled.

*　　*　　*

I started with Dani and Brett.

First, I called Dani into my office.

"How are you and Brett getting along these days?" I asked.

"Fine."

"No, really, Dani? Married people don't usually get along 'fine.' Especially married people who work together in a high-pressure, high-visibility job like you and Brett."

"Okay, not so fine between us."

"Tell me the ways."

Dani then ran through a series of domestic issues ranging from childcare to housekeeping duties to sex that she and Brett were constantly arguing and fighting about at home.

"But we never bring it to the studio with us," she quickly pointed out. "We're always totally professional on the air."

"Don't do that anymore," I said.

"What?"

"Don't put on a phony front of marital bliss. I want you and Brett to be real on the air. If you're mad at him at home because he won't help do the dishes, stay mad at him on the air. If your sex life isn't going the way you want, throw a few disparaging comments at him in the banter you do at the anchor desk between stories."

"You want us to fight on the air?"

"I want you to act like a married couple. I think the audience—especially those with problems and issues in their own marriages—will relate to that very well. Tell him what you think on the air, just the same way as you do when you're home. What do you think?"

"I can do that," Dani said.

I ran through the same stuff later with Brett.

"It's simply not natural for a married couple to act lovingly and fondly to each other like you two try to do on the newscasts. Hey, we're the only newscast in New York City that has married co-anchors. Let's take advantage of that. Be real out there. Show people what marriage really is, warts and all—not some glorified fairy-tale version of it. Everyone who is married will totally relate to that so much better."

"So you're saying that no marriage—no matter how good it looks from the outside—is really that happy?"

"Not in my lifetime," I said.

*   *   *

Steve Stratton, the sportscaster, was tougher to deal with than Brett and Dani.

I told him how I was hiring a new sportscaster. Not getting rid of him. But adding another personality to the sportscast. Her name was Deandra Lyons, and she'd been an All-American women's basketball player with the University of Connecticut and later had a stint with the New York Liberty in the Women's Basketball Association.

"She'll be a big help to you on the sportscast," I said.

"I don't need anyone to help me do sports."

"Yes, you do."

Stratton clearly was not happy about this.

"We'll expand the sports segment time on the show. She'll start doing some of the sports and other things that you're not a fan of—soccer, women's basketball, gymnastics as well as focusing on politics and social justice issues in the sports world."

"She's black, right?"

"Deandra is a woman of color."

"What if I don't agree with her on some of these things? Like kneeling down at the national anthem and all that crap?"

"Then debate it with her on air. It would be must-watch TV."
Stratton sighed.

"What if I refuse to share the sports with her or anyone else?"

"Then Deandra will be doing the sports on her own."

"You'd fire me?"

"Work with me on this, Steve. That's what I'm trying to avoid."
He nodded. I was pretty sure he understood.

"Susan Endicott, right?"

"I think you and Deandra will make a great team," I said.

*   *   *

Wendy Jeffers was a lot easier. She wanted to do different things on air. And now I was going to let her.

"I want you to interact more with the audience," I said. "Maybe put you out on the street and have you mingle with people while you're on air doing the weather."

"Like Al Roker does on the *Today* show."

Yep, Wendy always wanted to be a female Al Roker on the show.

"Maybe we could have you take questions and comments about the weather—or other stuff too—while you're on air, instead of just standing and pointing at a weather map."

"That's good."

"I have another idea too. I hope you're okay with it. Run contests about the weather. Have viewers predict how much rain will fall. Or how strong the winds will get. Or the top temperature in a heat wave. The winner who guesses the forecast the most correctly will win a prize from Channel 10."

"What's the prize?"

"You."

"Huh?"

"We offer them time with you. Maybe lunch. Or a visit to the studio to hang out with you. A lot of your fans out there—especially the men fans—would love that."

"So you're going to use sex—my sexy looks, if we're going to be honest here—to try to get bigger ratings?"

"Are you okay with that?"

I knew the answer from the smile on her face before she even answered.

"I love it," Wendy said. "When do we start?"

By the time I was finished with Wendy, I was pretty proud of myself.

I'd somehow managed to convince my married co-anchors to fight on air, to diversify the sportscast, and to sex up the weather report.

All in all, a helluva day's work.

Now I had to hope it was enough to satisfy Susan Endicott.

CHAPTER 47

MY APARTMENT DOOR was open when I got home that night.

Since I lived alone, that wasn't good. The smart thing to do was go right back down the way I came and get help. Yep, that was the smart thing to do, all right. But, after long years of practice in hardly ever doing the smart thing, I pushed my apartment door all the way open and went inside.

There were two men sitting in my living room. I recognized them right away. One of them was the guy from Anthony Steffano's restaurant, the one with the ponytail I called Fettuccine Guy. The other one looked like the driver of Steffano's car the day that they stopped me on the street and told me to leave the Steffano kid alone. There were some empty beer bottles and a tin of peanuts from my kitchen scattered over the coffee table in front of them. They'd obviously been waiting for me for a while.

"Aha, the lady of the house is finally here," the driver said.

I did my best to try and stay calm.

"To what do I owe this unexpected pleasure?" I asked them.

"We have to talk to you," Fettuccine Guy said.

"About what?"

"You've been nosing around again, and Mr. Steffano doesn't like that."

Damn.

Maybe my undercover disguise hadn't worked as well as I hoped.

"What do you mean?"

I decided to play dumb. That shouldn't be very hard for me to do.

"We found out you're trying to set up an on-air interview with the Bakely guy."

I heaved a sigh of relief. These two apparently didn't know I'd been staking out the restaurant.

"You see, right now this case is over. The police investigation is over. That way no one bothers Mr. Steffano or his son anymore, and everyone's happy. But, if you put Bakely on the air, he's probably going to start talking about maybe he didn't do the girl's murder. That could create public pressure on the police to take a fresh look at the case. They won't find anything. But it's going to cause problems. Problems for Mr. Steffano's business, his family life, and—most of all—problems to his temperament. Which will be a problem for you, Carlson. You see, Mr. Steffano can be quite vindictive against people he's angry with."

"So I've heard," I said.

"Then why are you doing this?"

"I think Bakely might be innocent."

"The rest of the world thinks he's guilty."

"Yeah, well, I've never been one to go along with the crowd."

"And that's the only reason?"

"No. I think Donnie Ray Bakely has a right to be heard in public. He wasn't able to do that in court. So I'm going to give him the opportunity to plead his case on air. Maybe it will convince some of those people who've already convicted him enough to get this whole homicide case reopened. That's what I'm trying to do anyway."

"Who the hell are you? You're not a police officer. You're not a prosecutor or a defense lawyer. You're just a goddamned journalist. What gives you the right to act so high and mighty about this?"

"The First Amendment. It's called Freedom of the Press."

"Oh, yeah," he chuckled.

He looked down at the empty peanuts tin. "You got any more of these?"

"I'm all out. But there are some chocolate eclairs in the refrigerator if you're still hungry."

"We ate those fifteen minutes ago," the other guy said with a laugh.

"Sorry," I shrugged. "Next time I'll try to be a better hostess. Listen, do you guys want to discuss anything else with me tonight? If not, it's late and I've had a long day."

They both stood up.

"Just remember this, Carlson, you've been warned," Fettuccine Guy said.

"I've been warned," I repeated.

"Twice."

"Okay."

"Don't make us come see you a third time or ..."

The unspoken threat hung out there in the air between us.

"Or what? What happens if you or Steffano or his kid decide you have to deal with me again because I'm causing you problems?"

"Believe me, you don't want to know," he said.

The two of them then walked out, slamming the door behind them.

I locked the door once they were gone. The lock still worked, which was a relief. Then I tried to figure out what to do next.

I should call the police. Report that my apartment had been broken into and I found intruders inside. Tell this all to the police, let them handle it.

But I wasn't sure I could trust the police. At least not at the top. Not after seeing NYPD Deputy Commissioner Townsend leaving Steffano's restaurant so secretly while I was watching the place.

I was also concerned about how Steffano and his people had found out about my plan to do an on-air interview with Bakely.

The person I'd been arranging it with was Billy Barrett from the Manhattan District Attorney's office.

I didn't necessarily think Barrett would have given or sold the information to Steffano's mob people himself. But he would have had to deal with other people in his office to set it up. There might be a leak there. Someone in the DA's office who was secretly on Anthony Steffano's payroll.

So I wasn't sure if I could trust the Manhattan DA's office very much either.

The bottom line was I wasn't sure who I could trust.

I looked out the window and down at the street below my apartment. Then I watched the two of them come out the front door, walk to a car parked on the street, and get in. I decided to keep watching until they were gone.

Except they didn't do that.

They sat there in the parked car.

Presumably looking at my building.

I wondered if they might come back up.

Maybe they wanted to talk to me some more.

Maybe they were still hungry.

Maybe they wanted to tuck me in for the night.

Finally, the engine started up and the car drove away.

I sat there for a long time until I was convinced they weren't coming back.

CHAPTER 48

"YOU MEAN THEY actually broke into your apartment?" Pete asked me.

I could tell he was shocked when I told him about my visit from Steffano's two mob guys.

"I found them sitting there in my living room helping themselves to the contents of my refrigerator and cupboard when I got home."

"Did you call the police?"

"No."

"Why not?"

I told him how I wasn't sure I could trust anyone in the Police Department or the DA's office right now.

"Anyway, nothing really happened. It was all talk. Threats, yes, but still only talk. They didn't actually do anything to me."

"I know, but . . ."

"Look, I don't want to escalate this any more with Steffano. But, if they keep threatening me or do anything violent, I'll go to the authorities. I'll figure out some way to do it that I think is safe. Maybe through my ex-husband who's on the force. I know I can trust him. Don't worry, Pete. Believe me, I'm not going to put my life on the line for Channel 10 News."

"From what I've heard and read about him, Steffano can be a pretty dangerous person to people who do things he doesn't like," Pete said.

"So I'm told too."

"Word is he's even killed some people"

"Killed a LOT of people, according to the legends around him."

"Jeez, Clare . . ."

"Well, there's one good thing about all this," I said.

"What's that?"

"If Steffano does knock me off in a mob hit because I'm working this story on him, that will be great for our ratings! Even my new boss Susan Endicott will love me then. I'll go out in a blaze of glory."

"You're kidding, right?"

"I'm kidding."

We were eating dinner this time in the South Street Seaport in Lower Manhattan. The food was good, and the river view was even better. From the window next to our table, we could see the East River, the lights of the Brooklyn Bridge and Manhattan Bridge to the north, and the Brooklyn skyline across the water.

It was a nice late spring night out. So, after we left the restaurant, we decided to walk for a while instead of taking a cab, Uber, or subway. There were sections of the walkway that ran right along the river, and I never got tired of seeing and experiencing these scenes in New York City.

"You really love being here in the city, don't you?" Pete said when I told him that.

"New York, New York, my kind of town."

He smiled.

"If you can make it here, you can make it anywhere," I told him.

"Is that why you came to New York? To work in the media here? Because you knew it was the media capital of the world?"

"Absolutely. I wanted to work with the best. The top of the media business. And that's always been New York. Still is, as far as I'm concerned. I don't think I could ever work anywhere else. Even Los Angeles or Washington. New York City is where it all happens in my business."

"Not so much for me."

"What do you mean?"

"Princeton—well, Ivy League schools like Princeton—are at the top of the academic world. Outside of Columbia, there's not really much else in New York City that would work for me as a college."

"You don't aspire to teach one day at Easton?"

"Uh, no. It's a nice college. So is NYU and the rest here. But definitely not for me."

I wasn't sure what that meant for us if this relationship ever advanced to the stage of us wanting to live together. It seemed there'd be a lot of commuting involved between New York and Princeton. But I wasn't worried about that now. I was just enjoying the evening and the company I was with. We decided to walk all the way back to my place near Union Square. It was a couple of miles, but that gave us more time to talk.

Eventually the conversation, as it always does with me, came back to the story I was working on.

The Riley Hunt murder.

"Anthony Steffano is involved somehow, although I can't figure out exactly how. Probably because of his son, who apparently had a romantic relationship with Riley Hunt. Does this mean Steffano killed her for some reason? And his father's trying to cover it up, like he covered up the business of his kid threatening the professor at Easton? I'm not sure. But it must be important to Steffano for him to meet me himself on the street to warn me off the story—and then send his goons to my house to deliver the message even more forcefully."

"That really sounds like it could be dangerous for you, Clare—if you don't do what this Steffano guy wants."

I shrugged.

"It's part of the job. I don't let anyone intimidate me."

"Even Anthony Steffano?"

"Especially Anthony Steffano."

I told him about the other things that bothered me about the case: the whereabouts of Riley's fiancé on the night of the murder; the fact that Bruce Townsend's father was also in charge of the murder investigation; the strange relationship between Riley and her mother; the links to the escort service and the drug dealer in Washington Square Park.

"I don't understand though," Pete said when I finished. "The police have the ex-soldier in jail for the murder. They say it's an open and shut case that he did it. He was the one who murdered Riley Hunt. But you don't agree?"

"I like to make my own judgements on a story—not go along with what everyone else thinks or tells me is true."

I told him how I was really looking forward to the on-air interview I was about to get as a big exclusive with Donnie Ray Bakely at Rikers.

"I'm hoping to get some of the answers I'm looking for in that interview."

"Isn't he pretty much out of it and delusional though?"

"He was when I saw him in court. Not so much when I talked to him the first time at Rikers. It's like he was coming out of whatever weird trip he was on. Maybe some kind of drugs—or else a lack of drugs—at Rikers was helping him become more cognizant. He told me at Rikers that day he didn't remember killing Riley Hunt. But he didn't know why he was there with her body or exactly what he did. I'm hoping he can tell me more in this interview."

"But, even if he denies killing her, how can you believe him?"

"That's not all I'm looking for."

"What else?"

"There are too many moving parts to this story that don't make sense. Steffano. The Townsend kid. The mother-daughter relationship. Plus all the rest. But the biggest thing that still doesn't make sense to me is Bakely himself. He doesn't seem to belong with all the other people and things in Riley Hunt's life. Why did he call her that night? Why was he there on the street with her? What's his role in all this? If I can find out some answers about that when I talk to him, maybe I can figure out the other answers too."

Pete shook his head.

"It sounds to me like Bakely probably just killed the girl for no reason. He was crazy, Clare, and crazy people do crazy things. Maybe all the rest of it—strange as it seems—really has nothing to do with her murder. And that's the final answer in all of this. Doesn't that make a lot of sense?"

"It is the obvious conclusion," I said.

"But you don't like the obvious answer, do you?"

"Never have."

"Well, be careful," he said. "I don't want anything to happen to you, Clare."

We had made it all the way back to my apartment house by now. The night was still as beautiful as it had been earlier. The stars twinkled clearly in the sky. A big, almost full, moon was above us. Even the sound of traffic from the street seemed to have died down a bit. A beautiful spring night in New York City. What more could I ask for?

Pete walked me to the front door of my building.

Then he kissed me.

I kissed him back.

"This was a nice night," I said.

"Night isn't necessarily over yet."

"It is late."

"Not that late."

"Do you want to come upstairs with me?"

"I thought you'd never ask."

He kissed me again, and we went inside.

CHAPTER 49

AND THEN SOON after that—without warning—everything changed on this story.

I got a wake-up call from the office telling me Donnie Ray Bakely was dead.

Bakely had been found unconscious and unresponsive in his cell at Rikers when a guard went there shortly before 7 a.m. to give him his breakfast. Medical personnel were called who gave him CPR and tried to revive him. But he was declared dead shortly afterward. There was a piece of bedsheet wrapped around his neck, and the sheet was tied to a light fixture in the cell.

The official ruling was suicide by hanging.

It made sense for a lot of reasons.

Department of Corrections officials released medical records from Bakely's military service showing he suffered from PTSD and was mentally unstable and guilt ridden because of things he had done and experienced in Afghanistan and Iraq as a soldier. Despite efforts to provide him treatment as a veteran, he had disappeared from the system until he showed up as a homeless person living on the streets of New York.

The prison psychiatrists who examined him told a similar story. They said he was paranoid and schizophrenic and consumed by guilt for the things he had done.

This guilt became overwhelming for him when he realized he had killed an innocent woman on the street in Riley Hunt—and he simply couldn't deal with that guilt anymore, they theorized.

Bakely's death was officially ruled a suicide by hanging.

I wasn't so sure though.

There were a lot of questions I still had about Bakely's death—I wasn't convinced it was a suicide.

For one thing, they had found several broken bones in Bakely's neck. This was explained by medical people and prison officials as common in suicide by hanging cases. Bones were simply damaged during the constriction around the neck prior to or during death by suicide. Maybe so. But there was also a very real possibility in my mind that he might have been strangled in his cell—and then someone wrapped the bedsheet around his neck after death to make it look like a suicide.

The timeline was strange too. An autopsy showed that he died sometime around midnight. But his body hadn't been discovered until several hours later by the guard with Bakely's breakfast. Was it really possible or believable that a high-profile prisoner like Donnie Ray Bakely could have been lying dead in his cell for that amount of time without someone checking on his status?

But the biggest thing—the real reason I wasn't buying the suicide story—was the set of circumstances surrounding Bakely's death. The fact that I was about to interview him on air in prison to find out what he really knew about Riley Hunt's death. And that he might implicate other people in the case. But now he'd been silenced. And those other people, if they were still out there, were safe.

Who might they be?

Obviously, the name that jumped out most for me was Anthony Steffano.

Steffano seemed the most eager to make the case go away, and he was the one with the means and ability to take Bakely out of the picture. I had no doubt that Anthony Steffano could have someone killed in prison and cover it up by making it look like an accident or a suicide.

Is that what happened here?

If so, I had played a part of my own in Bakely's death. I was the one who pushed for the jailhouse interview. Steffano had found out about that upcoming interview, and sent his men to my apartment to try to convince me to call it off. When I refused, that might have been the impetus for him having Bakely killed before he could talk to me on air about what he might or might not know.

It was a disturbing thought.

* * *

Despite all that, the death of Donnie Ray Bakely was a big news story. "Riley Hunt's Accused Murderer Kills Himself in Jail" led both our 6 p.m. and 11 p.m. newscasts that night.

I did the on-air report myself. I was able to talk about my meeting earlier with Bakely in prison too—which gave it a personal touch the other news outlets in town didn't have. Plus, I was able to set up another interview with Bakely's mother. She was devastated, of course, but I had the feeling that she knew her son's story was going to end tragically.

"He was my son, no matter what he did or didn't do," she said in a dramatic on-air appearance with us. "And he'll always be my son.

He was a good boy. But those wars, they changed him. He was never the same when he came back. He gave his life for his country. Not the way some people do it, I guess. But that's what happened to my Donnie."

I asked her at one point if she believed the official story that her son had committed suicide.

I was hoping she'd say no.

But instead, she responded: "It doesn't matter. He's dead. What did he have to live for? I don't care how he died. Just that he's dead. Whatever happened, my son is still dead."

The whole thing turned into a ratings blockbuster for us, and Susan Endicott was ecstatic.

"This is the story that never stops giving for us," she chortled jubilantly as she looked at the ratings numbers. "First the murder, then the investigation and arrest, now this! Thanks to Donnie Ray Bakely for making my job so much easier. Oh, we didn't get the interview we wanted. But even so, this story has produced the best ratings numbers since I got here."

Me, I wasn't so happy about the way things had worked out.

I felt badly for Bakely, who I'd gotten to know a bit during our meeting in jail and I felt compassion for him. No matter what he had done or not done, he was a tragic person to me, not an evil one.

I felt badly too for his mother, who had come to me with a plea to help her son. Instead of helping him, he was now dead. And that might have been partly my fault.

But maybe the person I felt most badly for right now was myself.

I had been counting on my upcoming interview with Bakely as an opportunity to break this case wide open.

I really believed that he held secrets—whether he realized it or not—that could help me answer many of the questions I had about Riley Hunt's murder.

But now he was dead.

And those secrets had died with him.

Which meant that I was back at Square One on this story . . .

CHAPTER 50

"How's your love life going these days, Clare?" Janet Wood wanted to know.

"Sensational! And I have you to thank for it."

"You and the guy from Princeton?"

I nodded enthusiastically.

"Really?" Janet said.

"Why so surprised?"

"I generally don't get an answer like that from you when I ask a question about some man I fixed you up with. Most of the time you just complain about how boring they are."

"Well, I guess you had to get one right, sooner or later."

We were walking down Madison Avenue, not far from Janet's law office, eating ice cream cones we'd bought from a vendor in Madison Square Park.

Ice cream cones are messy and tough to handle under any circumstances, but especially walking on a busy New York City street. Janet didn't seem to be having any trouble. She held her cone daintily in her hand and took small, careful bites from the pistachio ice cream. But I was making a mess with my chocolate marshmallow cone. Fortunately, I'd grabbed a big wad of napkins from the vendor to help deal with the collateral damage to me from the dripping cone.

"So where is this relationship going?" Janet asked me.

"Why does it have to be going anywhere?"

"All relationships are going somewhere, Clare."

"Maybe Pete and I can keep going the way we are for the time being—without making any decisions about what the damn relationship is or where it is headed."

"Relationships don't work that way," Janet said. "They don't stand still. Even if you want them to."

"Yeah, I know." I sighed.

I took a big bite of my ice cream. I figured the more of it I ate quickly, the less would be left to drip out over my face and clothes. It was a good plan, I decided. So I kept taking as many big bites as quickly as I could.

"Any big problems between you and Pete so far?" Janet asked.

"Just the logistics."

"What do you mean?"

"He's in Princeton, and I live in New York City. That works out to about 50 miles of distance between us a lot of the time. Most of the time. He does come into the city, of course. But I have my job here, and he has his teaching and other faculty duties down at Princeton. So we only have had a limited amount of time together."

"Well, they always say that absence makes the heart grow fonder."

"You better believe it."

She asked me more about the Riley Hunt story. And, of course, about the death in prison of Donnie Ray Bakely. I told her about how I'd been counting on the prison interview with Bakely to give me some kind of a break in the case. And about my own guilt that I might somehow have caused his death by setting up the interview where he might say some things on air that certain people—like Steffano—didn't want to make public.

"You can't blame yourself," Janet said when I was finished. "Bakely might really have killed himself. It makes sense. He was unstable and confused and depressed. He very well could have hanged himself in his cell just like they say he did. He didn't want to go on living anymore with all his guilt and the rest.

"But, even if Steffano did have him killed in prison to keep Bakely quiet, that's not on you. You were only doing your job. Trying to get the story like any good journalist would do. You have to be professional about your job. You know that as well as I do. You can't make things personal."

"Is that the way you handle it, Janet? Do you never feel guilt or regret if something happens to one of your clients because of what you did representing them?"

She shook her head.

"I don't let myself get personally involved in my cases like you do with a big story. I do my job. Most of the time I'm successful at it. But, if I'm not, I don't let the job get to me. I don't let it eat me up inside like your job does with you."

I tried to bite another big chunk off of my ice cream cone, but I missed. The ice cream fell out and onto the sidewalk. I finished off the rest of the cone, then wiped leftover chocolate from my mouth and cheek.

"I guess I don't have the same kind of self-control as you do," I said.

"You mean for eating ice cream?" She laughed.

"For everything."

She finished her ice cream and threw the napkin in a waste can.

"I wanted to find justice for Riley Hunt. Maybe for Donnie Ray Bakely too, if he really was innocent. I can't stop thinking about that. Do you understand?"

"I do. That's the reason I love you, Clare. Your passion."

She put her arms around me and gave me a big hug.

"But it's time for you to move on from this story now."

"I realize that."

"Just put it behind you."

"Yep."

"So is that what you're going to do?"

"Have we met?"

"Right."

She sighed.

"So what *are* you going to do now?"

CHAPTER 51

THERE WERE A lot of loose ends still bothering me about this story. But one of them jumped out at me now as I went back over my notes on Riley Hunt, looking for some sort of new angle. Brianna Bentley. Whose real name was Nancy Guntzler. Riley's strange egocentric roommate. She had been a loose end from the very beginning. A piece of the puzzle that didn't fit. I didn't like her, I didn't trust her, and I was pretty sure that first time we met she wasn't telling me everything she knew about Riley.

I tracked her down at a class on campus, waited for her to come out, and then began walking along with her.

Her face brightened when she saw me. More publicity for her acting aspirations, I guess.

"I want to you ask some more questions about Riley," I said to her.

"Sure, whatever you want."

She looked around behind me.

"Is there a video crew with you?"

"No cameras, Brianna. Only you and me right now."

"Will you quote me on the air then?"

"Depends on what you say."

"What's this all about?"

"Tell me again about Riley's missing computer."

That seemed to startle her. She didn't look so happy to see me anymore.

"I told you everything I knew."

"Tell me again."

"Riley told me she had lost her computer. That's all."

"Have you looked everywhere in your dorm room for it? I mean, it still could be found along with whatever files of Riley's are on it."

"Uh, I think it was stolen so . . ."

"Wait a minute, do you know if Riley's computer was lost—or was it stolen?"

She was getting flustered now.

"I'm sorry. I get confused. Look, this all happened before she died and I guess the shock of that shook me up more than I realized. Riley did say it was stolen. Someone grabbed the computer from her—she had it in a bag over her shoulder—while she was walking on 8th Street a few days earlier. Yes, that's what happened."

"Wow, that must have been pretty traumatic for her."

"Oh, it was."

"Do you think there might have been something on her computer that the person who took it was specifically looking for?"

"No, I can't imagine why. I think it was merely a coincidence that the computer theft happened and then she was murdered."

Just a few days apart, I thought.

Quite a coincidence.

"And so whatever was on Riley's computer disappeared—like the computer itself?"

"I—I guess so."

I didn't say anything for a few seconds. Brianna was clearly getting more and more uncomfortable.

"What happened then after the theft? Did she report it to campus police?"

"I suppose so."

"I checked. They said there was no record of any complaint from her."

"Maybe she called the NYC police instead."

I shook my head no. "Not any record of anything from them either."

"I guess she didn't report it to anyone then. I'm not sure."

"So let me get this straight," I said. "Someone approached her on the street, snatched the computer away from her—and Riley never bothered to report it to any authorities? Never did anything about it? Never told anyone it was stolen except you?"

"I—I guess . . ."

Brianna Bentley turned around nervously now, like she was trying to find a place to get away from me. I think she had changed her mind about me making her famous. The last thing in the world she wanted now was for me to keep interviewing her about this.

"There was no stolen computer, was there, Brianna?"

She stood there with a shocked look on her face. Shock, plus nervousness and fear. She opened her mouth to start to say something, but then closed it again. I guess she realized she couldn't pull this lie off with me anymore. Even she knew she wasn't that good of an actress.

"Where's the computer?" I asked her.

"Back in my room at the dorm. I hid it there."

"What's on it?"

"Nothing."

"What do you mean *nothing*?"

"I deleted it all. I deleted everything on the computer."

"Why?"

"Because I didn't want anyone to see it. Not the police. Not you. Not anyone."

"What is it you didn't want anyone to see?"

She sighed. "There were pictures of me on her computer. Pictures I sent to Riley. Pictures of me in various—well, X-rated poses. Pictures of me naked. Pictures of me doing sexual things for the camera."

"Were these pictures for some kind of role in a movie or anything?"

She shook her head.

"No. These were for Riley. She was the only one who was supposed to see them. I sent them to her on an impulse one day. Then—when she didn't react the way I hoped she would—I regretted it. She was really freaked out about it, and I just wanted those pictures to go away now. And so, one day when she was out of the room, I stole her laptop with the pictures on it. She thought she had lost it—left it somewhere. That's why she never reported it to the police. And then, after she died, I deleted the pictures and everything else on it. I didn't want any mention of me in those pictures or anything she might have written about sending them to her for anyone to see. That way, even if someone found the computer, there would be nothing about Riley and me on it."

"Did you and Riley have a sexual relationship?"

"No. I wanted one. I was in love with her. Passionate, crazy love. But she was only interested sexually in men, not women. And definitely not interested in me. Do you know how frustrating that is to be living every day with a person you're hot for and know there's no chance for you? Anyway, I deleted everything. But, even after that, I wasn't sure they were really gone. There are people who know how to recover lost stuff on a computer. I was afraid of someone doing that if they found it."

"But you kept the computer?"

"Yes."

"After you deleted the files, why didn't you just throw it in the Hudson River or somewhere?"

"Because that computer was so important to her. It was like a part of her that I still had left. I couldn't bring myself to throw it away."

She began to cry now. Real tears. She wasn't putting on a performance anymore.

"I loved Riley. I really loved her. You have to believe that."

I did believe her.

Believed she did love Riley Hunt.

Just like Bruce Townsend loved her.

And maybe Johnny Steffano loved her too.

Everyone loved Riley Hunt.

Except the person who killed her.

* * *

I convinced Brianna to give me the computer. That was the good news. The bad news was that Todd Schacter told me after examining it that she had apparently done a really good job of deleting the material on it.

"No way I can access those pictures of her. She made them disappear."

"Not what I was looking for, believe me. What about Riley Hunt's files?"

"No. The best I can do is see some of the names the files had been given. But there's nothing there in the file for me to access."

"I thought you were a genius at stuff like this."

"There's limits to what even us geniuses can do."

It was one of the first times he'd attempted to say anything at least remotely humorous like that. Maybe I was having some effect on his personality. But I still had my problem.

"The file names," I said. "Can you tell me what any of those said?"

Many of them turned out to be from classes or activities she was doing on campus. There was a bunch of others that didn't really mean anything to me. I made Todd run through them all for me.

"There's one that keeps coming up in a bunch of the files," he said. "Something—or someone—that Riley Hunt seemed very interested in. The title on these files is 'Betty Jenkins—Easton.' Does that mean anything to you?"

At first, the name didn't.

But then it hit me.

Betty Jenkins.

Betty was a version of the name Elizabeth.

I told Schacter to do a quick background check for me on Elizabeth Hunt. It didn't take long to find out what I was looking for. Her maiden name was Jenkins.

Riley's mother had gone to Easton twenty years before Riley.

And so these deleted files on Riley's computer were about her.

CHAPTER 52

THE PRESIDENT OF Easton College was a man named Vernon Adcock.

Adcock was distinguished looking, with silver hair and a silver-gray goatee and sideburns that stretched almost all the way down the side of his face. He was wearing a black pinstriped suit with an expensive looking paisley shirt and a red tie. The shirt couldn't conceal the ample size of his stomach though—it looked like Adcock had spent a lot of time at the buffet table while attending alumni and faculty functions.

He sure looked a lot different than the other academic man I knew: Pete Bevilacqua.

Looking at Adcock now, I sure was glad I was sleeping with Pete and not Vernon Adcock.

I had been sitting there for more than fifteen minutes listening to him tell me all the achievements and attributes of Easton College. The list of academic awards, the faculty members who were renowned in their fields, and all of the wonderful cultural opportunists on the campus. By the time he got to the school library, I was afraid he was going to start listing it all book by book for me.

I was so bored I wanted to jump out the window to get away from the sound of his voice as he droned on, but his office was only on the third floor. I figured if I did jump, I wouldn't even be hurt, just mess up my hair and get grass stains on my clothes. So I waited for him to take a breath, and then I jumped in with a question.

"Can you tell me about Riley Hunt as a student here?"

He smiled. A big smile. He looked like the kind of guy who smiled a lot. His description about Riley Hunt at Easton sounded as rehearsed as the speech about the school. Outstanding student, wonderful person, a credit to the school, blah, blah, blah. When he finished, I asked him another question.

"Can we talk a bit now about Anthony Steffano?"

"Why do you want to know about him?"

"You're answering a question with a question," I pointed out.

He wasn't smiling anymore.

"Mr. Steffano has served on the Easton Board for several years. As well as being a major financial contributor to the school. He's a man dedicated to improving educational opportunities for the people of this younger generation, and he has been a major factor in our efforts to provide academic excellence to them at Easton."

I waved my hand in the air for him to stop. He looked at me quizzically.

"Do you practice that speech in the mirror before you deliver it at academic functions or anywhere else anyone asks you about Anthony Steffano? You must—you can't make that kind of BS up on the spot. And that's all it is, BS. You know that as well as I do."

"What are you talking about?"

"Steffano is a bad guy. An underworld boss. He's one of the top crime leaders in New York. He is also a violent man who is probably responsible for the deaths of many people who got in his way. I'll bet you don't include that bit of biographical information when you tell alumni or faculty groups what a swell guy Steffano is."

"I don't know anything about that," he said stiffly.

"Of course you do. Steffano donated millions of dollars to the renovation of the Easton Library and other buildings on campus. Not long after that, his son, Johnny Steffano, was reinstated as a student. He'd been expelled for threatening the life of a teacher. I'll bet the teacher wasn't too happy with that. But then I guess a few million dollars makes up a lot for unhappy faculty members. Unless you're living in a total academic ivory tower, you must be aware of all this. So I'm sure you understand why it's clear to me that there was a quid pro quo here to get the Steffano kid back into Easton."

"I don't know what any of this has to do with Riley Hunt or her death. I thought that's what you were interested in."

"Johnny Steffano was involved romantically with Riley Hunt."

Adcock stared at me. That last statement from me had shaken him up. I knew now he wasn't aware of it.

"And you think he could be implicated in her murder?"

"He's on my list of suspects."

"But what about the man the police put in jail? The one who killed himself? They said he was Riley's killer."

"I'm pursuing some alternative theories in the case."

He didn't look happy. The smile was long gone now. It was replaced by a frown on his face. It was an even worse look for him than the fake smile had been.

"I still don't see what I can do to help you, Ms. Carlson. What do you want from me?"

"In covering this story, I have uncovered a lot of information that makes Easton . . . well, let's just say it would be embarrassing to the school and to you if it became widely known. Like the details of the Steffano business. There's also some stuff about drug deals in Washington Square Park and an escort service that might have utilized students like Riley Hunt and . . . do you want me to keep going?"

Adcock looked pale. He looked like he wanted to jump out the window now.

"None of this has been put on the air by us at Channel 10 yet. I'm not sure if any of it is directly connected to Riley Hunt's murder. I want to investigate more. I need your cooperation to do that. If you help me, that would make it easier. If you don't, there could be consequences for you and the school by exposing some of this information about the school."

"That sounds like a threat."

"Like I said, I'm looking for a favor from you."

"What's the favor?"

"I need someone to get me all the information in your school files—confidential as well as public—on someone who was a student here."

"Riley Hunt?"

"No."

"Johnny Steffano?"

"Nope, this is someone who attended Easton a long time ago."

"Who?"

"Betty Jenkins. Who now is Elizabeth Hunt. Riley's mother. Can you do it?"

"What does she have to do with this?"

"You're answering a question with a question again, President Adcock."

"I'm not sure I can do this."

"Why not?"

"There's confidentiality issues . . ."

"I'm trying to work with you here, Adcock."

He thought about it some more.

"If I help you with this, you'll leave all that other stuff you mentioned about Easton out of the story you put on air?" he asked me finally.

"I promise."

"Really?"

"Cross my heart and hope to die."

I made an elaborate cross on my chest to emphasize the promise.

"Okay," he said finally. "Let me get you the information you want..."

CHAPTER 53

THE CASE FILE from Easton campus security on Betty Jenkins was bigger than I expected. Adcock handed the file to me without comment. Then he led me into a small room away from his office, pointed to a table and a chair, and said only: "You have thirty minutes to look through this. Afterward, it will be returned to Easton confidential files."

He turned away and walked out of the room. I guess he wanted to put as much distance between himself and what I was doing as he could. Plausible deniability in case it blew up in his face.

I started reading through the file and making notes on what I found as soon as he was gone. The first entry was dated October 29, 2002. On that day Betty Jenkins—now known as Elizabeth Hunt—was arrested by campus police.

According to the documents in the file, she was picked up at 8:09 that night in Washington Square Park and charged with possession of drugs. The drug was marijuana. Which certainly didn't seem like such a big deal on a college campus.

But then, once she was in custody, the charges were upped to selling of drugs, obviously a more serious offense. And, on top of that, the list of drugs she was accused of selling now included cocaine, heroin, crack, and all sorts of upper and downer pills.

Christ, I thought to myself, this very quickly exploded from a minor pot arrest to a massive drug dealing operation she was accused of being involved in.

But that wasn't the end of it.

There was more.

A lot more.

As the investigation continued, she was subsequently charged with prostitution. Being part of a ring of college girls selling sex in return for money and drugs.

It certainly could have resulted in a lengthy prison sentence if she was convicted on the charges.

I assumed at the very least that she would be immediately suspended from Easton College. Which she was, according to the documents in the file. Expelled and banned from campus—at least pending the outcome of the charges against her.

But then a very strange thing happened.

At some point early on, the case had been turned over to the NYPD by campus police. It was the NYPD—not Easton security—who lodged all the additional charges against Betty Jenkins.

I guess that made sense.

Sort of.

But what didn't make much sense was what happened after that.

A week later, all the charges against Betty Jenkins were abruptly dropped by the NYPD. And subsequently by campus police. According to NYPD documents quoted in the file, she was cleared of all charges, because of what police described as an "unfortunate error in judgement by the original arresting officers."

"It appears that Ms. Jenkins inadvertently was in the park that night and got caught up in a dragnet seeking drug and prostitution arrests. Upon further investigation, it has been determined that no charges of any kind will be filed against her."

Amazingly enough, it ended that quickly.

She was then reinstated to Easton College and continued to attend classes for most of the rest of the school year.

So why did she later leave Easton in New York—and wind up graduating from Purdue?

The answer to that was in the file too.

Which meant that campus police were still interested in her and her activities, despite the dismissal of the charges against her.

Maybe they didn't buy the NYPD story of complete innocence on her part. In any case, her departure from Easton was documented in the file.

It also gave the reason she left Easton.

She told school officials she was dropping out of school because she was pregnant—and intended to have the baby.

It didn't take a whole lot of investigative skills for me to figure out that her baby had grown up to be Riley Hunt.

Robert Hunt told me he and his wife met when she went to Purdue.

That was after she'd left Easton.

So that raised a real question.

Who got her pregnant at Easton?

At the end of the report, there was a list of law enforcement people who had been involved in the case—from the original arrest of Betty Jenkins for pot possession, the filing of subsequent more serious charges, and later the dropping of all the charges against her.

The names of several campus security officers were included.

And members of the NYPD who quickly took over the investigation.

Most of the names didn't mean anything to me.

But one name did.

This name practically jumped off the page at me.

The name of an NYPD cop—a police lieutenant who ran the drug and prostitution investigation—before unexpectedly dropping the charges against Betty Jenkins.

It was Hugh Townsend.

CHAPTER 54

I NEEDED TO talk to Townsend again. Not Hugh Townsend. Not yet. First, I wanted to go back to Bruce. I figured it would be easier to confront him again about everything than his father. But I had to do it without his father being present too.

I'd seen the dynamics of their relationship during the interview I had with the two of them—father and son—at the beginning of this story. The father ran the interview; the kid was careful to say only what the father wanted him to say. Probably even coached him beforehand on what not to talk about with me.

I didn't know much about the two of them at the time of that interview.

Now I knew a lot more.

I found out Bruce Townsend lived in a dormitory building on East 23rd Street, not far from Baruch College where he was taking courses in criminal justice. I went over there and asked a few students in the dorm which room he was in. I was surprised that anyone would give up information like that to a strange woman. But one of the students recognized me from TV, and was clearly impressed that I was visiting there. Being a TV newswoman sure opens doors, lots of doors, for me. And one of those was the door of Bruce Townsend.

He was surprised to see me. He could have shut the door in my face, I suppose. But I didn't think he would do that. He wasn't an aggressive or forceful person. His father pushed him around. Probably Riley did too. Maybe I could do the same. I walked through the door into his room, and he didn't stop me.

"What are you doing here?" he asked.

"I need to ask you some questions."

"My father told me not to talk to you anymore."

"You're in some trouble here, Bruce. I'm trying to help you."

"What kind of trouble?"

"The kind of trouble even your father can't protect you from."

I took out a printout of the picture I'd made from the security camera showing him walking near Washington Square Park on the night Riley Hunt was murdered there.

"Look at the time stamp and location printed on the bottom of that photo of you," I said. "That's you there in that place at that time. The same time you and your father told everyone you were spending the night at your family's house on Long Island. As you can imagine, that raises some real questions for me."

Townsend's face turned pasty white and he slumped down in a chair. He was alone now here with me, no father to help him. I was counting on that being enough to get him to come clean with me.

"Who else knows about this?"

"The police do. Even if they haven't done anything about it yet. For obvious reasons. I imagine your father has put a lot of effort and influence into keeping this covered up."

"Are you going to put it on the air?"

"That depends."

"On what?"

"I'm not looking to destroy you, Bruce. I'm trying to find out what happened that night. If you help me by telling me the truth, I'll do my best to help you."

"I didn't kill Riley," he blurted out.

"I didn't think you did."

"Then why are you doing this to me?"

"Because you're a big piece of this puzzle I'm trying to solve. Now who put you up to lying about being on Long Island that night? Your father?"

He nodded.

"It was my father's idea. It's always my father's idea. Everything I do. When I told him I was in Greenwich Village that night, near where she was killed, he came up with the Long Island story and told me to tell that to anyone who asked. That I was at my parents' house all that night. And he said he'd back up my story."

"Did he think maybe you murdered her?"

"I can't imagine so."

"Then why was he so worried?"

"All I know is that he said neither of us—me or him—could be connected in any way to what happened to Riley. He told me to trust him on this. He said that he was doing it for my own good."

Or maybe more for his own good, I thought to myself.

"What happened between you and Riley that night?"

"She broke off our engagement. Earlier in the evening. Called me from some bar where she was at and said we weren't going to get married. I thought she might be drunk, but she was very serious. She said she'd found out some things about me, and that now it was over between us. Then she hung up. I wanted to talk to her in person; I wanted to confront her face-to-face—I admit that. I went down to Greenwich Village looking for her around the campus and the area, but I couldn't find her. So I went home. I figured we'd talk it through the next day. That's all that happened. That's all I did that night in the Village. You have to believe me."

I did believe him.

It was too strange a story for him to have made it up.

Besides, I didn't think he had the ability to lie about it.

I had one more question for him now.

"Why did Riley so suddenly decide to call off the engagement to you? Did she give you a reason?"

"Yes. She said that she had found out something that made it impossible for her to marry me."

"Which was?"

"I . . . I . . ." he stammered. "I really shouldn't tell you this. You are a reporter, right?"

Oh, please do, I thought to myself.

"And I still don't understand it."

"What was it, Bruce? Why did Riley say she didn't want to marry you anymore? What did she find out that made her call off the marriage?"

"She told me that she was my sister," Bruce Townsend said.

PART IV

IT'S NEWS TO ME

CHAPTER 55

ON MY WAY back to the office at Channel 10, I tried to make some sense out of all this.

Okay, Deputy NYPD Commissioner Hugh Townsend knew Riley Hunt's mother twenty years earlier when he was a street detective in the Greenwich Village area and she was a student at Easton College.

Townsend helped Riley's mother—who was then Betty Jenkins—by dropping charges against her of drug dealing and prostitution, which allowed her to stay in school at Easton and out of jail.

And now Townsend's son says that Riley Hunt told him in their last phone conversation before she died that she couldn't marry him because she had recently found out that she "was his sister."

Ergo, Hugh Townsend must have been Riley Hunt's biological father.

Simple, right?

Except it wasn't so simple

Because, if that were true, it raised a lot more questions.

Did Hugh Townsend know that Riley Hunt was his daughter?

Did Townsend even know that Riley was the daughter of a woman named Betty Jenkins that he'd had a relationship with—presumably both a professional and a sexual one—some twenty years earlier?

Did he realize his son, Bruce, was dating, and even engaged to marry, his own biological daughter—and, if so, why would he have allowed that to happen?

And, most importantly of all, what did any of this have to do with Riley Hunt's murder?

I thought about what to do next. I pondered this for quite a while on the subway ride back from Townsend's dormitory on 23rd Street. Then I made a decision. I would have lunch. That's been one of my mottos in life for a long time: When the going gets tough, the tough go eat.

After I left the subway, I stopped at one of those overpriced coffee shops you find on Park Avenue. I took a seat at the counter and ordered the Cheeseburger Special.

While I waited for my food, I checked the time. I still had an hour or so before the afternoon news meeting. So I took out my cell phone and made some calls.

First, to Elizabeth Hunt—aka Betty Jenkins—in Dayton. I tried both her home and law office numbers, but only got voice mail at each one. I left a message on both phones. It said: "I know what happened to you at Easton twenty years ago. And I know about your connection to Hugh Townsend, Bruce's father and the top police official investigating your daughter's death. We need to talk about Riley's real biological father. Call me back . . ."

Then I did the same thing with Townsend. Asked for his private voice mail, then left a message that laid out the same basic facts. Except I added one more thing. "Your son just told me Riley claimed she was his sister. Can you explain that?"

I figured that should get both of their attentions.

Although I wasn't very confident either one would call me back.

I probably was going to have to confront both of them again face-to-face to find out the real truth.

I thought about calling Susan Endicott too, and telling her everything I knew. But I decided against it. No, I would keep working this on my own to the end, then tell her later. Things worked better for me that way without getting caught up in another power struggle drama with Endicott.

I sat there at the counter and kept thinking about it all—everything that I knew, and what I didn't know, about Riley Hunt.

What about Anthony Steffano and his son Johnny? How did the Steffano family fit in with all this? I had absolutely no idea.

And then there was Donnie Ray Bakely. If he really was murdered, presumably by Steffano to prevent him from talking to me on air, then Steffano must have feared Bakely knew something pretty important. Maybe Riley confided something in him on that trip to the Empire State Building while she was working with troubled veterans like Bakely. But what was it? And was it important enough that this confused, sick guy had to be killed? Unless he actually did commit suicide. But I was operating on the theory that he didn't kill himself.

I continued to feel pangs of guilt, too, over Bakely's death because I might well have set it in motion by going to Billy Barrett and asking him to get the DA's office to set up the on-air jailhouse interview for me.

Steffano's men knew about this planned interview when they came to my apartment, so someone—Barrett or another person or persons in the Manhattan DA's office—had let that information get out and it presumably led to Donnie Ray Bakely's death.

I needed to find out more about how that could have happened.

And, to do that, I knew I had to go back for another face-to-face meeting with William (Wild Bill) Barrett.

I sighed. God, that was going to be uncomfortable for me to see Barrett again.

Almost as comfortable as the face-to-face meetings I needed to have with Hugh Townsend and Riley Hunt's mother.

But I was going to have to do it all.

Barrett.

Hugh Townsend.

And Elizabeth Hunt/aka Betty Jenkins—Riley's mother.

I kept going through all this over and over again until my food arrived. That cheered me up. But not for long. The Cheeseburger Special turned out to be a mistake. My cheeseburger was stringy, the French fries soggy, the Coke watery, and the service surly. But I got even. I stiffed the waiter on the tip. Then I left.

It was time to go back to work . . .

CHAPTER 56

JUST WHEN I thought this story couldn't get any crazier and more confusing, something totally unexpected happened.

Anthony Steffano was arrested.

But not for anything related to the murder of Riley Hunt.

At least nothing that was obvious.

Federal agents from the Treasury Department swooped down on his restaurant a little before 8 p.m.—right during the middle of the dinner hour—and took Steffano into custody with several of his people.

It was quite a scene, almost like something out of a movie. The feds burst in with guns drawn just as people were eating their meals. A lot of the customers said afterward they'd feared it might be a mob hit attempt. That's the thing about going to a mob restaurant in Little Italy—the food is usually good, but not necessarily good enough to risk your life for.

It took a while to get everyone out. But eventually Steffano and his cohorts were carted off to jail in Foley Square. The restaurant was closed and the people who had been there were left scared, confused, and hungry. No one knew if the place would ever open up again. But I figured it would.

An incident like this at a New York City restaurant can make it famous in a way no other advertising or publicity can.

Like Sparks Steakhouse, for instance.

That's still remembered nearly 40 years later as the place where crime boss Paul Castellano was gunned down by John Gotti's men in one of the most infamous underworld killings in New York history. For years afterward, the joke went: "Every time someone ordered 'duck,' customers dived under their tables."

The official charge against Steffano was tax fraud, both in his legitimate business dealings and his underworld operations. They said Steffano owed millions and millions of dollars in unpaid taxes. They couldn't nail Steffano for murder or extortion or all the other things that he had done over the years.

So they got him on taxes.

I found all this out from Nick Pollock, a Treasury agent who helped organize the raid and arrests.

I'd met Pollock on another story I was doing a year or so ago, and we'd become friends. I'd been hoping it might be more than friends. He was a really good-looking guy. Reminded me a bit of Brad Pitt. I definitely would have been interested in establishing a romantic relationship with Pollock back then.

Except for one big problem. He was married to someone else. And that someone else was a man. I might have had a shot at getting a married man away from his wife. But not from another man. So we'd become friends. Good friends. I talked with him about my professional problems, my personal problems, and all sorts of stuff.

He was kind of a male version of my best friend, Janet Wood. He was a nice guy, he listened to everything I said, he laughed at my jokes.

All in all, Nick Pollock and I had an almost perfect relationship.

Except for the sex thing.

He gave me an exclusive heads-up on everything that was going on with Steffano and the raid. So I was able to break the story with a news bulletin during our evening Channel 10 programming. Then we had a complete report on the 11 p.m. newscast, along with video as Steffano and his people were being led into the courthouse for arraignment.

Afterward, Pollock told me more about it at his office.

"Some of this is because of you, Clare," he said.

"What do I have to do with Steffano's tax problems?"

"We were able to infiltrate someone into his organization that gave us an inside look at his state of mind. The informant told us that Steffano was very upset at you. About you pushing him and his son on the Riley Hunt murder. He was talking about a lot of crazy stuff behind closed doors about it, and we weren't sure what he might do next. So we decided to take him in on the tax charges."

"Nothing about Riley Hunt?"

"We don't have any evidence on that."

"What about all the other terrible, violent things he's done to people?"

"Hey, we took what we could get. The tax stuff."

"Like Elliot Ness took down Al Capone, huh?"

"Yeah, like Ness and Capone." He grinned.

There was more though. I could tell it from the look on his face.

"Look, Clare, we might not be able to hold Steffano in custody for very long. A day or two tops, before he gets bailed out. And— well, according to our informant—he's very likely going to blame you for a lot of his troubles."

"I didn't have anything to do with his arrest."

"Steffano thinks it all came about because of the Riley Hunt business and you asking questions about him."

"You think the mob might come after me?"

"We have to consider that possibility."

I thought about that. I'd been threatened before on stories I'd worked. Threats had never worked on me. But that didn't mean that I liked them. And these were potential threats from a pretty scary guy in Anthony Steffano, if the threats were true.

"This isn't a joke, Clare," Pollock said. "According to the informant, you could be in some real danger from Steffano. I'll try to have someone keep an eye on you as best I can, but I'm limited in what I can do here to help at Treasury. Maybe you should take some time off and leave town for a while until this is all over."

"I can't do that, Nick."

"Yeah, I know." He sighed.

"Do you really think Steffano might try something with me?"

"He doesn't like you, Clare. And when Steffano doesn't like someone . . ."

He didn't have to finish the thought.

"So what should do I do if I want to stay on this story?"

"Maybe get Channel 10 to hire a private security team to guard you."

"Oh boy, I'd love to see my boss's face when she sees that on my expense account."

"She wouldn't pay to protect you?"

"No, but I think she might pay to have me rubbed out. She doesn't like me any more than Steffano does."

"What about going to the police?"

I thought about Deputy Commissioner Townsend and his secret meeting with Steffano at the restaurant that I had witnessed. About the message on Riley Hunt I'd left for Townsend. And how I'd put my ex-husband on the force, Detective Sam Markham, in a really uncomfortable situation by telling him about the security video from the night of the murder with Townsend's son near the crime scene.

"I'm pretty sure the police don't like me much either," I told Nick Pollock.

CHAPTER 57

EVEN THOUGH STEFFANO was in jail now, I still needed to know how he found out about my plans to do an on-air interview from Rikers with Donnie Ray Bakely. And if he had been the one who had Bakely killed in jail to make sure he couldn't talk. The leak about the interview must have come from the DA's office, which meant another uncomfortable conversation with my old pal William (Wild Bill) Barrett to ask him about it.

I went looking for Barrett that night at the bar where I'd met up with him to set up the Bakely interview. I knew it was one of his favorite hangouts after work, and I hoped I could find him there again. I could have called him at the DA's office, but the question I had for him—the big question—was the kind I needed to discuss in person to see his reaction. It would be tougher for Barrett to lie to me face-to-face that way, without me picking up on it. Tougher than on a telephone call.

Sure enough, Barrett was there, along with a pair of young women. They were hanging off each of his arms. One blonde, one brunette. All Barrett needed now was a redhead to complete the package.

But the presence of the other two women didn't stop him from coming over to give me a big greeting: "Clare, Clare, it's so good to see you."

"We have to talk, Billy."

"You bet we do."

He moved closer to me. I stepped back.

"Is this about my offer to take you to drinks, dinner, and then back to my place for whatever might happen after that? You've reconsidered, right?"

"Actually . . ."

"C'mon, Clare. After what we've meant to each other. Let's make a night of it."

"What about your friends over there? Are they going to join us?"

He smiled.

"That's Gloria and Elaine."

"Okay, but I'm going to just call them Bambi and Thumper."

"Huh?"

"From a James Bond movie."

"I must have missed that one. But they won't complain. We could all join in. A little *ménage à trois*."

"I think a *ménage à trois* usually has two women and a man. Not three."

"So we break the rules. What do you say?"

"I hope Bambi or Thumper remembered to bring a pair of handcuffs along for your fun tonight."

Several years ago, when I had really been going out with Barrett, the relationship ended badly when I walked in on him handcuffed to a bed by a pretty young policewoman, who'd been working with the DA's office. She was "interrogating" him by using her hands on several of his body parts. Well, especially one body part. Needless to say, finding your partner handcuffed to the bed and engaging in sex acts with another woman is pretty much a deal breaker in any relationship. I'd never stopped letting Billy Barrett forget about that embarrassing moment after our breakup, even though it didn't seem to bother him very much. That was the kind of guy Barrett was.

"Do you want a drink?" he asked me now.

"I want some answers."

I told him about my suspicion that Donnie Ray Bakely didn't really kill himself. That maybe someone murdered him in prison and made it look like suicide. And that maybe they'd done that because they found out I was going to do an on-air prison interview with him that might reveal secrets they didn't want made public. Which meant that I—and he, Barrett—could have indirectly led to Bakely's death.

"How many people did you speak to when you were trying to set the interview up for me?"

"I didn't talk to anyone about it."

"C'mon, someone in law enforcement or the prison system or other people in your office had to be in the loop."

"I'm telling you I never mentioned a word to anyone about it."

"Then how were you going to set up my interview with Bakely?"

He reached over for a drink he'd laid down on the bar and took a big gulp. He looked uncomfortable. And I soon found out why.

"Clare, I never did anything about that interview like I promised you I would. I just hoped by stringing you along I'd get you to . . . well, you know, be with me. I was never going to put myself on the line in the DA's office by going to bat for you like that. My position there is still pretty tenuous because of the sex allegation stuff against me in the past. So I left here that night we talked about it, and never did a damn thing. I simply told you I was working on it. That's the truth."

"Then how did someone find out about the interview I wanted to do?"

He shrugged. "Maybe it wasn't that at all. Maybe Bakely really was a suicide."

"But if not?"

"Then someone else leaked the word out. It wasn't me."

*   *   *

When I got home, I sat there for a long time alone in my apartment trying to put it all together.

If I believed Barrett—and for some reason I did believe Barrett—then he had not been the source of the information about the interview.

Bringing my keen investigative skills to bear on this, that left me with two alternatives:

A) Bakely's death was not caused by someone who feared he would reveal damaging information in an interview. It might indeed be suicide. Or even a prison killing for some other reason or an imagined slight to another inmate.

Or:

B) Someone else besides Barrett told the information about my planned interview to a person like Steffano who would go to any lengths—including murder—to keep him quiet.

But who could that be?

I'd only talked with one person about the Bakely interview: and that was Barrett.

Except Susan Endicott. Could she have been the one who let the word get out? But why would she?

It had to be Endicott—there was no one else I'd told about the Bakely interview.

Wait a minute: there was someone else.

I talked about it with Pete Bevilacqua when we had dinner.

I didn't think that Pete would deliberately do anything with the information, of course. But what if he told someone else about it? And that someone told someone else, etcetera, etcetera. I couldn't imagine there were many people at Princeton who had connections with anyone who might be responsible for something like having Donnie Ray Bakely killed in prison. It sounded like a long shot. But I needed to check with him to make sure he had never mentioned it to anyone after our conversation.

I called his number. I got his voice mail.

"Pete, it's Clare. I need to talk to you about something. Remember that jailhouse interview with the accused murderer of Riley Hunt I told you I was trying to arrange? I need to find out if you talked about that interview to anyone else afterward. This is really important, Pete. Call me back as soon as you can. I'm home."

I hoped, half expected actually, that he might call me back right away. That he'd missed the call, but saw the voice mail afterward. That happens a lot. Except Pete didn't call me back right away. He didn't call at all.

I sat up for another hour and a half, replaying all the events that I'd just gone through.

It wasn't any help.

I couldn't figure any of it out.

Maybe I should have taken up Billy's offer for the *ménage à trois*.

Bambi, Thumper, and Clare.

And Billy, of course.

Maybe we could even make a sex tape and become famous.

I looked down at my phone. Still no calls from Pete. No voice mail. I left him a new message, then gave up and went to bed.

I didn't sleep very well that night.

CHAPTER 58

THE FIRST THING I did when I woke up in the morning was check my phone to see if there were any messages from Pete. Nothing. I tried his number again, and I got the voice mail. I left another message telling him it was important that he call me.

I called his number numerous times after this—when I was getting ready for work, on my way to the office, and much of the morning from my office in the Channel 10 newsroom.

All I got was the same voice mail message:

"Hi. This is Pete Bevilacqua. I'm not here right now to answer the phone. But leave me a message, and I'll get back to you very soon."

Except he hadn't gotten back to me very soon.

All I kept getting was the damn voice mail message.

Until I tried it for maybe the 100th time around midday, and suddenly there was a different message from his voice mail.

This was an automated message from an operator, which said: "The number you are trying to reach is no longer in service."

I tried it again, figuring that somehow I might have dialed it wrong, but the operator's message was the only thing I got again. Pete Bevilacqua's voice mail message was gone. His phone was gone. And he was gone too. But where? And why?

The only thing I was sure of was that whatever was going on here couldn't be good.

And I needed to find out what it was as soon as possible.

I called Janet and asked her again how she found out about Pete Bevilacqua. She repeated what she told me before. She never knew him herself, but one of her ex-clients contacted her and asked if she could arrange a meeting between him and me.

"All I know is that he'd seen you on TV, and he really wanted to meet you."

"Right."

"Is there a problem with him, Clare?"

"I hope not."

*   *   *

I told Maggie that I was leaving for the day and she should run the 6 p.m. and 11 p.m. newscasts.

"Where are you going?"

"Princeton."

"Why?"

"Chasing a story."

Maggie gave me a funny look. She knew Pete was from Princeton. But she didn't ask me any more about what I was doing.

"What if Endicott asks about you?"

"Say I'm out running down a big exclusive. A very big exclusive. That ought to make her happy."

Then I went to Penn Station to catch a train to Princeton. The ride on New Jersey Transit took only about an hour. Then there was a small shuttle train that took me from the Princeton station to the actual Princeton campus.

When I got there, I figured the best place for me to start was the Department of Spanish and Portuguese. Well, it wasn't just the best place for me to start searching for Pete. It was the only place I knew that might have any information about him. I had no address or idea where he even lived down here. Which maybe should have served as some kind of a red flag to me, but didn't seem that important at the time since he always came to see me in New York. But I should have asked him more questions along the way. I realized that now.

At this point, nothing about Pete Bevilacqua made sense to me anymore.

I wasn't sure how to find him. It was a huge campus. And I didn't necessarily know that the people there were going to give up information about a faculty member to some strange woman. Even if I was carrying press credentials.

But I met a nice administrator woman in the Department of Spanish and Portuguese. She seemed to understand my urgency when I said I needed to talk to him right away. She said she'd try to find out how to locate him.

I fully expected her to come back to me after checking and say Professor Pete Bevilacqua was on an extended sabbatical to South America or something like that—but instead she said he was teaching a class at the moment in a nearby building.

Well, that was a relief.

At least Pete Bevilacqua did exist at Princeton.

He wasn't simply a figment of my imagination.

We walked over to the building, then up to a third-floor classroom. She knocked on the door and announced there was a visitor that needed to see Professor Bevilacqua right now, even though it was the middle of his class.

I was running through in my head the things I was going to say to Pete when he came out of the classroom. Would I be mad at him? Would I be relieved to see him? Probably a bit of both.

A few minutes later, the door opened again and the administrator came out with the class instructor behind her. "Professor Pete Bevilacqua, this is Clare Carlson who says she needs to talk to you."

Bevilacqua stared at me.

And I stared at him.

He was about 5 foot 9, a bit overweight, with thinning blond hair and a goatee.

"I'm Professor Bevilacqua," he said. "What can I do for you?"

I had never seen this man before in my life.

*   *   *

"A while back, I was the victim of identity theft," Bevilacqua told me later back in his office.

"I had a lot of trouble for a while—money being taken out of my bank accounts, credit cards being opened in my name, purchases made of expensive items. Whoever was doing it had an ID forged that convinced everyone he was really me. This person literally stole my whole identity. It was a terrible and scary experience. But I was able to get it all straightened out in the end. And no money has been taken from me anymore. The person that did it presumably still has my ID. But if he's still using it, why would he do that if not for money?"

Because he could order a phone in your name, I thought to myself.

And he could be you in other ways and places too.

Like wooing a woman as the fake Pete Bevilacqua, then disappearing when she started asking questions.

But what was the reason?

Why did he do it?

And for who?

The obvious answer was to get information out of me about the Riley Hunt story—including the fact that I planned to interview her accused killer.

"Did you ever find out the identity of the man who took your identity?"

"No. I always wondered who he was. I'm afraid that never came out in all the checks we did. I have no idea who he is."

"I do," I said.

CHAPTER 59

Two days after Anthony Steffano was arrested, there was an even more shocking development: Deputy Police Commissioner Hugh Townsend was found dead. I'd been trying to reach Townsend ever since I found out about the connection between him and Riley Hunt's mother. And also his relationship, whatever it was, with Steffano. I'd made at least a half dozen calls to his number just that morning, but he never answered. Now I knew why.

Townsend's body had been found slumped over the steering wheel of his car, a single gunshot to the side of his head. The gun lay on the front seat next to him.

The car was parked on a Lower Manhattan street a few blocks from 1 Police Plaza, the NYPD headquarters building where he'd checked out after leaving his office a little after 8:30 p.m. The time of death from the shooting was estimated by the Medical Examiner's office to have occurred shortly after that.

Townsend normally would have driven home to his house on Long Island, arriving there around 10 p.m. When he didn't show up, his wife called 1 Police Plaza to check on his whereabouts. No one there knew anything, which made both his wife and police extremely concerned. Townsend was known to be a rigid, by-the-book man who kept to a tight schedule. Not the type who would impulsively stop off for a night of drinking or whatever on his way home.

By daylight, they were about to organize a search for him when an early morning jogger passed by the car and saw the body of Townsend inside.

On the face of it, Townsend's death appeared to be a suicide. Or at least it was supposed to look that way. It wasn't hard to imagine— especially after the last message I left him—that he felt things were closing in on him and took the suicide route out. Finish your day's work, get in the car like you normally do—but instead eat your pistol. Well, the gunshot wasn't in his mouth, it was on the side of his head. Still, it all made sense.

Except for one thing.

"Hugh Townsend wasn't the type to commit suicide," my ex-husband homicide detective Sam Markham said to me. "The guy loved himself too much to blow his own brains out like that."

I agreed.

"Besides, what problems would Hugh Townsend have bad enough to push him into killing himself? I can't think of anything."

"I can," I said.

I told him what I'd found out. About Townsend's strange meeting with Steffano at the restaurant. About him being the same NYPD detective who investigated the case of Riley Hunt's mother twenty years earlier. Plus, of course, I reminded Sam of the fact that Townsend had lied about the whereabouts of his son at the time of Riley's murder. I didn't say anything about how I thought Townsend might be Riley's biological father. Not yet. But what I did tell Sam was pretty shocking to him.

"Jesus," he said when I was finished. "Are you going to put all this on the air?"

"Not yet. Not until I know the full story. I need to find out more about what Townsend was involved in before I go public with this. But, when I do, people are going to question the idea of suicide. They're going to think there's something more suspicious about all of this. Like we both do."

"Look, if it's not suicide—and, like I said, I'm pretty sure it's not—then whoever pulled the trigger on Hugh Townsend was not any amateur. No suicide note, but everything else fits in with the suicide angle. This would have to have been set up to look like a suicide by a professional killer."

"Someone like Anthony Steffano."

"Or one of his people."

I thought about Fettuccine Guy, the big brute of a mobster I'd encountered a couple of times already—at the restaurant, in the car on the street, and in my own apartment. I could see him pulling a gun on Townsend, shooting him in the head from close range—and being expert enough in killing to make it appear like a possible suicide.

"Of course, it might be beneficial for the NYPD to leave it as a suicide," I said. "If Townsend really was messed up in dirty stuff, a connection with someone like Steffano might be embarrassing for a lot of people in the department. That could come out in a murder investigation. A suicide would be simpler to deal with. Do you think the NYPD might cover it all up like that?"

I thought he might get mad at me for the question. I pretty much expected him to when I did it. Asking an inflammatory question like that was a trick I sometimes used in interviews to get people emotional enough to open up to me. But he laughed. He knew me

too well. That's the problem of dealing with ex-husbands. They
know all your tricks.

"Give me a break, Clare. You know the answer to that as well as
I do. The police department investigates every murder based on the
evidence and the facts. We don't cover up anything no matter how
important someone might be. We do everything we can to solve all
murders and bring all killers to justice. That's a fact. Except there's
one exception. When the victim is one of our own, another cop.
Like Deputy Commissioner Townsend. Then we multiply that
effort by a hundred or a thousand times. That's how I feel about it
too. If someone murdered Townsend, I'm going to catch the killer.
Whether that's Anthony Steffano or one of his men or someone
else."

*   *   *

My phone rang after I left Sam. I looked down at the screen and saw
the name Pete Bevilacqua. Must be the guy from Princeton I'd
tracked down as the real one. I wondered what he wanted. Maybe
he remembered something else about his identity theft. I answered
the call.

"Hello, Clare," a familiar voice on the other end said.

It wasn't the real Pete Bevilacqua.

This was the fake one I'd known and I'd slept with and maybe
even fallen in love with.

"I know, you probably don't ever want to talk to me again after
everything that happened, right?"

"I thought your phone was out of order now," I said. "I tried your
phone constantly when you disappeared. Then I went looking for
you. Guess what I found out about you at Princeton?"

"This is another phone I used with the Pete Bevilacqua name."

"Wow, you are clever. You can do a lot of things, can't you. Except tell the truth."

"I'm sorry. I never meant for it to turn out this way."

"Really? How did you think it was going to turn out? You and I were going to live happily ever after as Mr. and Mrs. Pete Bevilacqua? That would be difficult to pull off. Since you're not really Pete Bevilacqua."

"Look, it was never supposed to get so involved between you and me. I was only trying to get close to you, trying to find out what you knew. That's what they asked me to do. But then something I didn't expect happened. I fell in love with you. And then . . . then things fell apart. So I knew I had to go."

"Who were you working for? Who wanted to get information about what I was doing on the story?"

There was silence on the other end.

"Let me guess. Anthony Steffano." Still no answer. "Is that what you really are? A mobbed-up guy? Do you work for organized crime?"

"I got in way over my head in debt to some people. Bad people like Steffano. And I couldn't pay them what I owed. They gave me an out. Use the stolen ID they had on this Bevilacqua guy and use it to get information out of you. It didn't seem like that big a deal at the time."

"You were the one who told Steffano about my upcoming interview with Bakely. And then Bakely wound up dead. That's because of you."

"Don't you think I know that? It's why I disappeared. When I heard he died, I understood exactly what happened. Steffano had used my information to have him knocked off in prison, even though it was supposed to be a suicide. I couldn't live with that. I couldn't keep working for Steffano, no matter how much money I still owed him. And then when I found out Steffano got arrested . . . I was afraid they'd come after me next. So I left. I didn't know what else to do. I wanted to talk to you. I wanted to tell you all about it. But I couldn't. I just couldn't do that, Clare."

"So this is your explanation?"

"And my apology."

"Why now?"

"I'm hoping maybe we can still see each other again."

"You're kidding, right?"

"What we had was very real, Clare."

"What I had was a relationship with Pete Bevilacqua. That guy doesn't really exist anymore. He's gone. Just like whatever we once shared between us is now gone. You should know that as well as me."

"Is there anything at all I can do to try to make things right with you? Even a little bit right?"

I thought about that.

"Well, there is one thing."

"What is it?"

"Tell me your real name."

"I—I can't do that."

"Just your first name then."

"Why?"

"So I don't have to think of you as Pete anymore."

There was a long silence, and then he said: "It's Dan."

"Dan."

"Yes, my first name is Dan."

"Thanks," I said. "You owed me at least that much."

Then I hung up.

CHAPTER 60

"HUGH TOWNSEND IS dead," I said to the woman who now called herself Elizabeth Hunt instead of Betty Jenkins. "Anthony Steffano is in jail. Don't you think it's finally time to tell the truth about everything?"

We were sitting in the kitchen of her house in Dayton again. I flew there to confront her once and for all about what she knew. Her husband was not there. I wondered if he had left on his own when she told him that I was coming, or she had devised some reason to get him out of the house. Not that it really mattered. This wasn't about her husband. It was about her. About her and her past.

"I suppose I should say I'm sorry about Townsend," she said to me now. "That's what people do when someone has died, isn't it?"

"That's usually considered appropriate."

"Well, I'm not sorry. I'm happy he died."

"I can understand why."

"Do you know what he did?"

"I have a pretty good idea."

I went through with her what I knew. Some of it was speculation, but even that was based on facts I'd uncovered in recent days.

"Here's what I think happened. You were a student at Easton who got busted for smoking pot on campus. No big deal, lots of kids do it. You probably figured you'd get some kind of a summons or reprimand, and that would be it. But then everything suddenly began to escalate.

"First, the campus police who arrested you turned the case over to the NYPD. Not exactly sure why they did that, but I assume they were in cahoots with the police somehow. Not all the police, but one cop in particular. A dirty cop. The detective who was assigned then to the precinct in the Washington Square neighborhood. Hugh Townsend.

"Townsend ups the charges by saying you also had cocaine and crack and all sorts of pills, which he no doubt planted on you. Then he gets someone to say you were trying to sell drugs. And it gets even worse. He gets someone else—probably a stoolie or informant for him—to claim you were selling your body as a prostitute, as well as selling drugs. Suddenly, you are looking at serious jail time.

"Except Townsend has a way out for you. You can work for him. And then he'll make sure the charges disappear. Which is what happened. How am I doing so far? Is that pretty much the way it all went down?"

Elizabeth Hunt had a haunted look on her face. Like she'd seen a ghost. In a sense she had. The ghost of her own past had come back to haunt her long after she thought she had run away from it.

"That's pretty close," she said. "Not all of it, but close."

"Fill in the missing pieces for me."

And that's what she did.

"He made me work undercover for him on campus," she said. "Telling him about students I knew who were doing drugs. Then he'd arrest them with the goods on them after I told him who and where to go after. It helped him build up an impressive record of arrests, and I guess that's why he rose so high in the police department. Which was fine for him. But I felt terrible about doing what he was making me do.

"Then it got worse. I found out Townsend was also using his badge to make money on the side too. Not just with payoffs and shakedowns, but also with a prostitution ring run by Steffano that he provided police protection for. They had some kind of relationship, Townsend and Steffano. I'm not sure what the relationship was, but my assumption was that Steffano had blackmail information on Townsend, something he knew about Townsend's illegal activities that he could use to get him to do what he wanted. Just like Townsend was doing with me. Ironic, huh?

"Anyway, Townsend put me to work for the prostitution outfit too. No, I didn't sleep with men. I wouldn't do that. But he forced me to recruit women on campus I thought might be good targets—attractive, desperate for money, personality issues like daddy hang-ups or whatever—that he could turn into prostitutes. Either voluntarily or the same way he turned me into a snitch. God, I felt guilty about doing that. But I had no choice, or so I thought at the time. And I was just glad he didn't force me to have sex with the men who were clients.

"But I did have to sleep with Townsend. He began using me for sex regularly. And then, a few months later, I got pregnant. It was Townsend's baby. I knew that for sure. When I told him I was pregnant, he laughed and said he would make sure I got a quick abortion. Then everything between us would continue on the same way.

"That's when I ran away. I just disappeared. I moved to the Midwest, I had my baby, I enrolled at Purdue to finish college, I met Robert Hunt, and I changed my name. I thought Townsend might come after me, but he never did. I suppose he found some other woman to use for his needs, I wasn't worth the trouble. Anyway, I finished college out here, then went to law school and became an attorney. I was afraid for a while that my police record might show up when I applied to law school and then took the bar. But it never did. I guess because Townsend had erased all the charges—at least officially—once I started cooperating with him. After that, I thought all of it was in my past. Until now."

"What about you and Riley?"

"For most of her life, Riley assumed my husband was her father. Then she did some kind of family tree project and figured out the numbers didn't work out right. She'd been conceived while I was still at Easton, and I didn't meet Robert until later. So she got very angry and demanded to know who her biological father was."

"But you didn't want to tell her that, did you?"

"No. So I made up a story. I said that I'd been with a man at Easton who went into the Army, then died fighting in Afghanistan. Afterward, I said, I met Robert Hunt and married him. She believed that, at least for a while. That's when she became very active in working with veterans' groups, helping the soldiers who came back from places like Afghanistan to adjust to life back here in the U.S. Trying to help them in memory of the man she now thought was her father."

Which explained her connection to Donnie Ray Bakely, I thought to myself. She wanted to help Bakely adjust to life back in the U.S. She wanted to make him feel better. She wanted to give him the homecoming the man she believed was her real father never had. She became his friend. Or at least the closest thing to a friend he had. And, when the drugs he'd been given at the hospital began to make him lose touch with reality, he reached out to Riley for help. She must have given him her number when they knew each other from the veterans group. So he called her that night when he was desperate for help, and she probably agreed to meet him later in Greenwich Village. But, by the time Bakely got to her, she was dead. That sent him completely over the edge into a full-scale breakdown.

"Eventually Riley found out the real truth. That there was no father who died fighting in Afghanistan. I'm not sure how she knew. But Riley was relentless. I guess she'd gone to try and find out more about her hero military father while she was at Easton. That's when she discovered there was no such person.

"She confronted me. It happened the last time she came back home to Dayton. I had no choice. I had to tell her again that I had lied. I told her everything then. About Townsend and Steffano and the rest. Well, not everything. I never said how Hugh Townsend was her father. I said I didn't know who her father was. But I did tell her about the prostitution ring, and I sort of implied that he had been one of the men who were clients there. Even though in reality I had never had sex with any of them.

"I thought that telling her the story—or at least most of it— might make things better between us. But it didn't. She got even more furious at me for all the lies she had been told. We had another huge fight and she stopped speaking to me. So I had no idea what she was doing until . . ."

She looked at a picture of her daughter on the wall of the room where we were sitting—Riley all dressed up in her cap and gown for her high school graduation as valedictorian—and began to cry. I just sat there and let her do it. I didn't know what else to do. Finally, she pulled herself together enough for me to ask her a question that had bothered me since my last visit here.

"That last night, when she called and spoke to your husband, why didn't you talk to her?"

"She didn't want to talk with me."

"How much did your husband know about all this?"

"Nothing."

"Nothing at all?"

"No. I lied to him just like I had lied to Riley in the beginning. I told him the same story about being in love and getting pregnant with a soldier who died in Afghanistan. Except he believed me. I begged Riley not to ever bring up the things she'd found out—and how painful it would be for him. Even though she was mad at me, she agreed to that. She never discussed any of it with her father. Even on that last phone call she had with him. That's what he told me. He never knew."

"What about now?"

"I told him. I told him everything after Riley died. I thought he had a right to know the truth. He's been very understanding about it, very loving . . . which is so important to me right now. I've lost my daughter over this; I couldn't stand losing my husband too."

There was something else about that last phone call bothering me. The one between her husband and Riley. The one when she said that she never talked to Riley.

"When is the last time you did speak with Riley?" I asked her.

She hesitated.

That's when I knew.

I was pretty sure what her answer was going to be even before she told me.

"The next day. The day before . . ."

"She died?"

Elizabeth Hunt nodded.

"I called her at the school. I felt so badly about the way things had been between us. I begged her to forgive me. I promised her I never would lie to her again. That's when she told me what she had been doing . . ."

"Which was?"

"Trying to make Townsend and Steffano pay for what they had done all those years ago. It was like she was on some kind of mission. Which was very much like Riley. She always wanted to make the world a better place, a just place—and that's what she was trying to do here because of what happened to me.

"She said she had started a relationship with Townsend's son to try to get more information from him about his father. And then, when she found out Steffano's son was also at Easton like her, she started spending time with him too. She said they were both in love with her, and I think she took some delight in that. But she said she was just doing it to find out more about their fathers.

"She also told me she had made friends with a drug dealer in Washington Square Park who had been there for years and knew about Townsend and the drug busts he'd made there in the past.

"She said she had even signed up under an assumed name for an escort service called Orion—which was really a front for prostitution. She said she never had sex with anyone there. But she was just trying to find out more information about the Orion operation because she had discovered the owner of the site was . . ."

"Anthony Steffano," I said.

"That's right. Steffano was still running a prostitution business, but he'd gotten more sophisticated and up-to-date with the time over the years. I was horrified when Riley told me this, as you might imagine. I said she had to stop doing all this. That Townsend and Steffano were evil men, and she was putting herself in terrible danger. And then I told her the whole truth. I finally told her that Hugh Townsend was her father."

"And later that night she was murdered?"

"I was devastated when I found out the news. Overwhelmed with grief, of course. But I also blamed myself for what had happened to Riley. I figured there had to be some connection between what I told her—and her murder hours later. That's why I couldn't deal with any of it on that first day. I just had to go to work. To try to forget by burying myself in my work."

I thought about how much this woman and I were alike.

I did the same thing when I was upset.

Turned to my work for solace.

I felt badly for her. Yes, she had made mistakes. But a lot of it wasn't her fault. And she had loved her daughter and tried to build a good life for her. Until that life was taken away one New York City night. And now she had to face the awful truth that her actions long ago might have been the cause of Riley's death now.

It was a helluva story. And it would make a helluva story for Channel 10 News. It was clear to me now what had happened. Riley had gone on some kind of crazy, bizarre mission to get revenge against Townsend and Steffano after she found out what they did to her mother. She'd sought out the Townsend kid because he was Hugh Townsend's son. The same with Johnny Steffano. And all the rest—the Orion escort agency run by the Steffano family, the connections to the drug dealer in Washington Square Park, possibly still connected to Anthony Steffano and Hugh Townsend.

Everyone said she was a dedicated, decent person who wanted to do the right thing. She wanted to get into politics to help make the world a better place. To right wrongs that had been done. And she'd started by trying to right the wrong that had been done to her mother twenty years earlier at Easton College. Even though she was mad at the mother too for lying to her about it all these years.

Of course, she didn't know until the end that Townsend had gotten her mother pregnant. That he was her biological father.

"When she first told me she wanted to go to Easton, I begged her not to go," Elizabeth Hunt said. "She said I had gone there, why couldn't she? I wanted to tell her the real story then, but I didn't. If I had, Riley might be alive today."

"We don't know that for sure," I said. "We still don't know for sure if this was why she was killed. We won't know that until we find the person who did it."

"Who is that? Who killed my daughter?"

It was a good question.

Townsend?

Steffano?"

Or someone else?

I'd uncovered a lot of answers so far.

But I still didn't know the answer to that one.

CHAPTER 61

THERE WAS A message for me from Susan Endicott when I got back to Channel 10 the next morning. It said: "Carlson, I want to see you in my office right NOW!" Yes, she had capitalized and underlined "NOW." She had also marked the message "Urgent" and "Priority." I figured it must be important.

I hadn't told Endicott I was going to Dayton or what I was doing there or what I had found out. I'd instructed Maggie to run the news meeting and manage the broadcasts until I got back, as I had a few times earlier since Endicott had arrived. It seemed to work better if I kept Endicott out of the loop so she didn't get in my way or mess anything up. That approach had worked pretty well for me so far. But now I knew I was going to have to pay the price.

It got worse when I walked into Endicott's office.

Brendan Kaiser was there.

I think it's safe to say being summoned like that to the executive producer's office with the owner of the station in there too was not likely to be a pleasant experience.

"Where were you all day yesterday?" Endicott asked me as soon as I came into the room.

"Dayton, Ohio."

That answer seemed to surprise her.

"What were you doing in Dayton?"

"Working on the Riley Hunt story."

"Without telling me?"

"I figured you would have been too busy working on some of your great new ideas like 'Take Back New York' to care."

Endicott glared at me, then turned to Kaiser—who hadn't said anything yet.

"Good morning," I said to him.

"Morning, Clare."

"What are you doing here at Channel 10?"

"Susan asked me to come to deal with a problem."

"And that problem is . . ."

"You."

"Right."

Endicott said to me now, although I knew she was really talking to Kaiser: "You don't tell me anything you're doing. You defy my authority. You ridicule my ideas publicly. Any explanation for that?"

"Which one do you want me to start with?"

"Any of them."

"Okay, let's talk about your ideas. Like Take Back New York. Want to know why I ridicule it?"

"Yes, I do."

"Simple answer. It's stupid."

That did it. Endicott exploded. First at me, then to Kaiser.

"See, this is what I've been talking about. Total insubordination. What are we—what are you—going to do about her?"

Kaiser sat there looking uncomfortable. I'm sure he dealt with a lot of big problems and confrontations in his business at his far-flung companies around the world that were bigger than this problem at Channel 10. But right now, he looked like he'd rather be at any of those other places instead of in this room trying to deal with me and Endicott.

I wasn't sure exactly how this was going to play out. I knew that Kaiser liked me. And I knew he was grateful for a lot of the scoops and notoriety I'd brought to Channel 10 in the past. But that kind of gratitude and support can be fleeting in the TV business. He was a businessman, that was the bottom line. And, in the end, he was going to decide who to back—either Endicott or me—based on what was best for his business.

"I know Clare's methods are often unorthodox," Kaiser said to Endicott now. "And she can act inappropriately at times. Okay, let's face it, she can be a real pain in the ass. But she's also done a lot of great things for the station and for me. She's a winner. I like winners. And so I stretch the rules a bit—I make allowances, if necessary—when it comes to them."

Then he turned to me.

"Now, Clare, I admire your energy and enterprise in chasing down a big story the way you think you can get the best results. You've certainly been very successful at that. But there is a chain of command. Susan Endicott reports to me, and you report to her. When that chain of command breaks down, it's bad for everyone. Do you understand what I'm saying?"

"I should have told Endicott I was going to Dayton."

"Yes, you should have."

"You're right. I'm sorry about that."

Kaiser relaxed a little. I guess he thought he might have gotten through the crisis. But Endicott wasn't buying any of it.

"I want her gone," Endicott said to Kaiser. "I can't work under this arrangement. You brought me here to accomplish certain goals. I'm trying hard to do that. I want someone else as news director. And I want someone else to work the Riley Hunt story as a reporter too. We don't need Clare Carlson. She's not worth the trouble. Don't worry, we'll be fine at Channel 10 without her."

"Maybe if the two of you tried just a little harder to get along," Kaiser said.

"No," Endicott told him. "You have to make a decision here right now. Its either her or me. You can't have both of us."

She sat back and looked at Kaiser.

Kaiser looked at me.

I looked at both of them.

"Aren't you going to ask me what I was doing yesterday in Dayton, Ohio?" I finally asked Endicott.

"I don't care what you were doing in Dayton."

"You should."

"Why?"

"I got a big story."

"Okay, what were you doing in Dayton?"

I told her and Kaiser about my interview with Riley Hunt's mother. About the connection between her and Deputy Commissioner Townsend twenty years earlier. About the links with mobster Anthony Steffano. About how Riley Hunt had been looking into this when she died. And about how Townsend was Riley Hunt's biological father. And about how all of this was what could have led to Riley Hunt's murder.

"It's a helluva story," I said. "I've got Riley Hunt's mother on video telling it all. I hired a local video crew to get her on camera while I was in Dayton. I was planning to air it all on our newscast tonight as a big Channel 10 exclusive. But if Endicott here somehow manages to convince you to fire me, I'll take it to one of the other stations in town. I'm sure they'd be glad to run it."

I smiled at Endicott when I was finished.

"Still want to stick with that 'her or me' ultimatum?" I asked.

CHAPTER 62

This is the News at Six with the Channel 10 news team. Brett Wolff and Dani Blaine at the anchor desk. Steve Stratton with sports; and Wendy Jeffers with your up-to-date weather forecast. Remember, Channel 10 is with you . . . let's all get together and Take Back New York!

And now, here's Brett and Dani:

BRETT: We have a major exclusive breaking on Channel 10 News tonight.

DANI: There have been shocking new developments in the case of Riley Hunt, the Easton college woman found murdered in Greenwich Village.

BRETT: Here with the story is our Pulitzer Prize–winning News Director at Channel 10, Clare Carlson.

ME: Earlier this month, Easton College student Riley Hunt was murdered on the street a short distance away from the school's Washington Square Park campus. Since then, there have been many questions about who killed Riley Hunt and why. Tonight, we finally have some of the answers. This is a story that began twenty years ago on the Easton campus. It involves a corrupt top police official, a mob boss, and—most astonishing of all—Riley Hunt's own mother.

I went through everything on the opening segment of the 6 p.m. newscast. About Townsend. About Steffano. And how Anthony Steffano had warned me—and later threatened me—not to air his involvement in this story.

Then I did it all again for the 11 p.m. program.

In between both newscasts, the story blew up on social media—on our Channel 10 Twitter, Facebook, and Instagram accounts first, and then it went viral in a ton of other places online too.

It was a good night.

I had broken a big story that everyone else was now chasing.

And I had won my office power struggle with Susan Endicott, at least for now.

But I still had one big problem: Despite everything that I had uncovered, I didn't know yet who actually killed Riley Hunt.

And why?

*　*　*

I guess I was still thinking about that when I left the Channel 10 office and headed home, a little after midnight. But I didn't go directly to my place near Union Square. Instead, I kept going downtown to Washington Square Park, the neighborhood where Riley Hunt had died.

I sometimes do this on a story. Go back to the scene of the crime. Try to put myself into the victim's place in hopes of finding some sort of inspiration. It was the middle of the night—close to the time when Riley Hunt had been murdered—and I went to the spot on Sullivan Street where her body had been found. I tried to imagine I was Riley and feel what she might have been experiencing in those last minutes of her life. But there was nothing.

Finally, I started walking north toward Washington Square Park. Which is the same direction Riley Hunt had been heading. That's when I thought I heard something. Like someone was behind me. Watching me. I whirled around, but I didn't see anyone.

Weird thing was I'd felt like someone was watching me or following me when I left the Channel 10 offices too and got into a cab for the ride downtown. Crazy, huh? I guess I was just being paranoid. Maybe it was because I'd spent too much time imagining I really was Riley Hunt on these streets.

I started walking faster. Ahead of me, I could see the park and the lights of buildings around it. Once I got there, I'd be okay. There was no reason to worry. No one was stalking me. Just my imagination running wild.

That's when I suddenly saw him.

Standing on the sidewalk ahead of me.

Holding a gun in his hand.

It was Johnny Steffano.

A car squealed up alongside then, and a door opened.

"Get in," he said.

"I don't think so."

"Get in the goddamned car!" he said, pointing the gun directly at me.

I got in.

The driver was the same guy who had been in the car the first time his father met me on the street and also shown up later in my apartment.

"What's this all about?" I asked.

"Shut up," Steffano said.

There didn't seem to be much point in continuing the conversation. Whatever was going to happen was happening, whether I liked it or not. The driver pulled away from the curb and then headed south. I tried to figure out what was next. But that soon became clear. It was a very short ride to Little Italy and the Steffano restaurant. The restaurant was still closed. I remembered hearing it had been closed ever since Anthony Steffano was arrested. They took me out of the car, led me to a back door of the restaurant and down some steps into a basement. I sure didn't like the feel of this, but I had no choice.

When we got there, we went into a small room—and Steffano pushed me down into a chair.

"My father warned you," he said. "I warned you. Everyone warned you. But you never listened. Instead, you go on the air tonight and tell the world all those things you weren't supposed to. It's too late to stop you from doing that anymore. The damage is done. But I'm going to make you pay for it."

"Pay how?"

Even though I was pretty certain I knew the answer to that.

"With your life, Carlson."

I tried to stay as calm as I could. Which wasn't easy under the circumstances. I tried to stay focused, like a reporter covering a story. Not like a reporter who might be the victim of their own story.

"Did you kill Hugh Townsend too?" I asked.

"No, that was my father. Townsend had to go. He'd been involved with my father's operations for a long time. He knew too much. Too much that could hurt my father if he talked. And my father figured he'd try to cut some kind of a deal for himself. He knew how the legal system worked. Townsend was a loose end. He had to be eliminated."

"And me?"

"My father gave me the job of taking care of you. I'm happy about that."

I looked over at the driver. He was watching it all with a bored expression on his face, like he was watching an old rerun of a TV show he'd seen before. He probably had seen this play out a lot of times before too.

"And Riley Hunt? Was she a loose end too, like me and Hugh Towsend? Did she know too much?"

"I didn't kill Riley."

"Why should I believe you?"

"I was in love with her. I told you that before. And I meant it. I would never have hurt Riley. I loved her too much."

Jesus, I thought to myself.

Him and the damn Townsend kid both.

Yep, everyone sure loved Riley.

It would have been funny except there was nothing funny about what was happening with me.

"You don't have to do this," I said, pointing to the gun in his hand.

"Yes, I do. My father wants me to get rid of you. To make you go away. And that's what I'm going to do."

"Killing a member of the media is going to bring an awful lot of heat on you. You were able to convince most people that Townsend—and Bakely before him—committed suicide. But no one who knows me is going to believe I killed myself. When they find my body . . ."

"No one is going to find your body. You're going to disappear after we're done here. No body. No evidence. No nothing. You'll just be missing. Forever. It will be a mystery to everyone, but there won't be anything of you left to provide any answers. My father knows how to get rid of bodies, and he taught me. You'll become a journalism legend. The mystery of what happened to Clare Carlson. You'll be famous once you're dead, Carlson."

I needed a miracle to escape now.

And then, just for a second or two, I thought I might have one.

The door to the room opened.

Maybe this was Sam and the police or the feds with my friend Nick Pollock who had somehow found out what was going on and were here now to save me.

But it wasn't any of them.

It was the big man I knew only as Fettuccine Guy.

The Steffano mobster from the restaurant and my apartment and who had been with Anthony Steffano that first day he stopped me on the street in his car to warn me off the Riley Hunt story.

"What's going on here?" he asked Steffano.

"I'm just about to finish up here and get rid of her for good."

I sat there listening to this all like it was about somebody else. Not me. I mean, it couldn't be me.

Fettuccine Guy nodded, turned to the driver, and told him to go upstairs to watch the front door to make sure there was no interruption.

"Right," the driver said and left the room to do that.

Fettuccine Guy walked over to me then, took out his own gun, and pointed it at me from point blank range.

"You just had to do it, didn't you, Carlson?"

"I'm a reporter," I said defiantly. "That's my job."

"Well, this is my job."

He pressed the barrel of the gun against the side of my head, then suddenly whirled around and shot Johnny Steffano.

I looked over at him in shock. Steffano was still alive, but he was bleeding badly. The gun was on the floor next to him. Fettuccine

Guy picked up the gun, put it in his own pocket, and then took out a phone.

"I need a team of agents at Steffano's restaurant right now. Watch out for one of his men who's outside by the front door. I got the Steffano kid in here. He's wounded, but he'll live. And Carlson"— he looked over at me and smiled—"Carlson is all right."

I stared at him.

Then I understood.

Nick Pollock had told me they had gotten someone in to infiltrate Steffano's underworld organization.

"You're the feds' undercover person . . ."

"Stan Lowell," he said. "Glad to meet you."

"Not half as glad as I am to see you, Stan," I said.

CHAPTER 63

JOHNNY STEFFANO TURNED out to not be as tough a guy as we all thought. He survived the shooting, but he caved and gave up everything under questioning afterward. He told authorities how his father had Deputy Commissioner Townsend shot to death and made it look like a suicide. How his father had ordered him to kill me and make me simply disappear once I went on air during the 6 p.m. newscast with the story. And even how his father was responsible for Donnie Ray Bakely's death in prison too.

The Steffano driver—who had been taken into custody outside the restaurant by the first federal officers and police to arrive at the scene—was talking too. He'd been around, he knew how the system worked, and he realized his best chance at this point was to roll over on Steffano and make a deal with authorities.

And then there was Stan Lowell himself, who had been working undercover in the Steffano crime organization for quite a while gathering information about him. His cover was blown now, but he told me that would have happened anyway soon—with or without me. His testimony would put Steffano and many of his people away in prison for the rest of their lives.

I told Lowell at one point how I'd been calling him Fettuccine Guy.

He laughed.

I liked Stan Lowell.

He seemed like a nice guy.

Of course, I do tend to feel more kindly to people when they've saved my life like Stan Lowell did.

So there is that.

As for me, my on-air account of my brush with death—along with the arrest of Johnny Steffano and the busting up of the Steffano crime organization—made me a big media star once again.

Bigger than I'd ever been before.

I was interviewed on NBC News; on MSNBC, CNN, and Fox News; featured on a few of those true crime cable channels; and written up in every newspaper in town—plus various publications around the country. And, at least for a while, #ClareCarlson was one of the top trending topics on Twitter. I wasn't exactly sure how I felt about that. But it sure was better than trending with #clarewereonlive!

All of this publicity gave us a big boost in the ratings too, which made Susan Endicott happy. Oh, I knew the battle wasn't over between us. There'd be a lot more skirmishes to come. But, for the time being, we had a kind of truce. She was letting me do my job, and I was letting her do hers. All we had to do was keep the ratings up to make this work!

So I should have been happy.

And I was.

Sort of.

Except—despite all this—there was something missing.

I still didn't know who killed Riley Hunt.

Johnny Steffano insisted he didn't do it, and I believed him. He'd confessed to pretty much everything else, so why not that if he was the killer? His father denied any involvement too. I wouldn't have necessarily believed anything Anthony Steffano said, but I did this time. Riley Hunt's murder didn't fit the style of a mob hit. What about the late Hugh Townsend? Could he have done it? Killed his own daughter because he realized who she was and he was afraid she might blow the whistle on him and his corrupt activities over the years? Maybe, but like with Steffano, this didn't seem like the way he would have committed such a murder.

No, this was a crime of passion.

Riley Hunt had been beaten to death.

Her killer was angry at her.

Which brought me back to a suspect I'd discounted in the beginning—but now I decided to take a fresh look.

* * *

Bruce Townsend seemed to be the ideal suspect in the beginning. He was her fiancé. She had broken off the engagement with him. And I knew from the security video I'd watched that he'd been in the same Greenwich Village neighborhood as her that night—and later lied about it by saying he was at his parents' house on Long Island.

But once I'd talked with Bruce Townsend, I pretty much eliminated him as a possibility. He seemed so weak, so shy, so incapable of doing anything on his own without his father there. I couldn't see him as a murderer.

And he insisted that he never met up with Riley that night.

But then Townsend also claimed that he'd been at his parents' house on Long Island too, so . . .

I remembered how much he'd depended on his father for advice and guidance. And strength too. But now his father was dead. That meant he needed to handle things on his own, which was a whole different ball game for me to interview him again. He would be much more unsure of himself, much more nervous and uncertain about what to do, without his father around anymore.

I decided to use that as a weakness against him.

I was going to come on strong with Townsend and see what happened.

To do that, I needed to run a bluff.

"I found another security video," I told him when I did confront him again.

"What do you mean?"

"Like the one I told you about earlier. Showing you in the same area Riley Hunt was, on the night Riley was murdered."

"I admitted to you I was there that night looking for her."

"But you said you never found her?"

"That's right."

"And I believed you. Before I saw the new video."

He looked shocked. That's when I knew I had him. Sure, there was no new video, but he didn't know that. My bluff was going to work.

"Does it . . . ?"

"Yes, it does, Bruce. It shows you a short time later, a few blocks away—not far from where Riley was murdered. You are talking to Riley on the street in this video. You look angry. The two of you are arguing. She starts to walk away. And then . . ."

"I . . . I hit her . . ." he said.

"Right," I answered, playing along with whatever he said at this point. "You hit her."

"I told her I loved her and I wanted to marry her," he said slowly now. "That's when she said that stuff about being my sister. I lied to you before. I didn't know it until that night on the street. She didn't tell me that on the phone when she broke off the engagement. But now she said she had gotten close to me just to get information about my father—and what he did to her mother at Easton twenty years ago. How she had discovered just now that he was her real biological father.

"She was very upset and she started crying. At first, I tried to comfort her. I put my arm around her and tried to kiss her. I told her I still loved her. But she pushed me away. She told me not to touch her like that. Then she talked again about how she now knew we were really brother and sister, and how crazy it was that I would fall in love with her. I guess I must have snapped at that point. I got angry. I started yelling at her and she began to walk away.

"I chased after her. I grabbed her. She pulled away, I grabbed again. And then I slapped her. I'm not sure why. I was so upset over everything falling apart between us—and here she was walking away from me. I'd loved her, but I realized at that minute she never took me seriously. No one ever took me seriously. Not my father. Not anyone. And so when she began walking away from that night I just . . ."

Jesus, I thought to myself, Bruce Townsend was confessing to me.

This was the answer I'd been looking for.

"You killed her," I said. "You didn't mean to kill her . . ."

"No!" Bruce Townsend shouted. "I didn't do it. I didn't hit her again after that. And I only slapped her, and the slap wasn't really that hard. Riley was still fine when she left me on the street. She wasn't hurt at all when she walked away. I followed her afterward for a block or two, saw her heading for the campus on Washington Square Park, and eventually decided to get out of there."

"You left her alone on Sullivan Street—where someone else killed her?"

"She was only a minute or so away from her dorm. I thought she was fine."

I was starting to believe him. His story was so crazy I didn't think he was a good enough liar to make it up.

"And then, Riley," Townsend said, "well, Riley met up with someone so she wasn't alone."

"That could have been her killer."

"I know that now."

"Why didn't you tell anyone?"

"Because I would have to admit that I was there and what I did. That's why I made up the story about being on Long Island. My father backed me up, but I never told him what really happened. I was too afraid. I didn't want anyone to ever know about me slapping Riley like that right before she died. I know how it looks—it makes me the obvious suspect. But I didn't do it. No matter what you think about me hitting her on that security video you found, I didn't kill her. I just left that night."

I let him go on like that for a while, emotionally professing his innocence—before I asked him the obvious question.

"Do you know who she met on the street after she left you?"

"No, I couldn't see her well enough in the dark."

"Her? It was a woman?"

"That's right."

"Do you remember anything at all about her?"

"Just that she had red hair. Does that help?"

It sure did. I knew one woman in Riley Hunt's life who had red hair. I went to see her again . . .

*   *   *

It didn't take long to get the whole story from Brianna Bentley aka Nancy Guntzler. I think she wanted to tell it all along. She was just waiting for the right moment to deliver her final lines. Like any actress would.

"Riley called me that night," she said. "I was so happy to hear from her, even if it was the middle of the night. I'd been lying in bed thinking about her. She said Bruce Townsend had been acting crazy and slapped her. She was afraid he was still following her, and she called me to meet her outside and walk back to the dorm with her. I ran out and did that right away.

"She was upset about the thing with Bruce, and I tried to comfort her. I put my arm around her. She didn't stop me so I tried to kiss her. That's when she went ballistic. Started screaming at me. Said she wasn't interested in me like that any more than she was interested in Townsend. She said she just wanted to be left alone. Then she said . . . she said she was going to request a new roommate because she didn't want to be around me anymore.

"I couldn't take it. I was angry. I guess I wanted to hurt her the same way she'd just hurt me. She had this metal trophy that she was carrying with her."

Of course, the trophy she'd been given earlier that night at the awards dinner.

"I grabbed it out of her hand, and I swung it at her in a rage. It hit her in the head. Hit her so hard that blood came spurting out and she fell to the sidewalk, hitting her head on the wall of a building as she fell. She just lay there, not moving. I suddenly realized she was dead. But I kept hitting her. Over and over. I was mad at her for the way she rejected me. I was mad at her for living such a perfect life, and now I was mad at her for dying on me. I don't remember everything else that happened after that. Except I knew I had to get out of there. So I ran back to the dormitory."

"What happened to the trophy you used to hit her with?"

"I threw that away later. Into the Hudson River. Like you said I should have done with the computer."

She began to cry. "I wish I could take it back. I wish it had never happened. I wish . . ."

We were sitting in her dorm room. I looked around and saw pictures of Riley all around. Riley playing with her band. On the basketball court. Hanging out on campus. I thought about her sitting here and looking at all these pictures day after day. She'd kept them all here. Just like she kept Riley's computer. She didn't want to part with whatever was left of the woman she loved.

She told me too that she had been Riley's unknown stalker—the one Riley had talked about with people in her band. She said she sometimes followed her around campus, to classes, to the band rehearsals, and everything else because she was so obsessed with Riley. She said she never wanted to scare Riley or harm her in any way. She just enjoyed being close to Riley like that. Because she loved her. Loved her so badly that—in the end, in a moment of passionate insanity—she killed her.

I called my ex-husband Sam at his precinct and told him everything.

"What happens now?" she asked when I hung up with Sam.

"The police will be coming."

"And then what?"

"I'm not sure. They'll take you into custody. Then they'll examine you. Maybe you'll be able to get a plea of temporary insanity. Because I think that's what it was. You're not really a killer."

"Will you talk about all this—about me—on the air?"

"Yes, you'll be our lead story tonight."

"So I will be famous."

"I guess so."

"At least for a little while."

I nodded.

"But Riley will still be dead."

She began to cry then. Quietly at first, then huge, heavy sobs of tears.

I reached over and took her hand. I squeezed it tightly, trying to comfort her.

Outside, I heard a siren.

Then more sirens as police headed to the Easton campus.

Just like they did on the night Riley Hunt died.

The sound of the sirens was getting closer now.

I held onto her hand until the first police arrived at the scene and took her away.

EPILOGUE

He still calls me.

Not as often anymore, but every once in a while, my phone will ring—and I can see it's him.

Pete Bevilacqua.

Or at least the man I once thought was Pete Bevilacqua.

I never answer his calls. I just let the phone ring and go to voice mail. At first, he left messages. But not anymore. Now there's only silence on the voice mail until he hangs up. It's like he knows I'm there listening, but I won't pick up. Or maybe that's just my imagination.

There's a part of me—the reporter part—that is curious to find out more about him. Who he really is. Why he did what he did. Where he is and what he's doing now. I could pick up the phone and find out. But I never do.

And so on this night when he calls after I go to bed, I let the phone ring again.

It rings—over and over—for a long time.

Finally, the ringing stops.

And it is silent again in my apartment.

I lie there awake in bed trying to forget about him. Instead, I think about happier things. Like going to work at Channel 10 News in the morning and maybe finding another big story to chase.

Yep, that's all I need right now—a big story.
A big story will make me feel better.
A big story always makes everything better.

AUTHOR'S NOTE

This is my fifth Clare Carlson mystery, and—as with the earlier books—I've tried to make the world Clare lives in as real as possible to the reader.

*   *   *

Starting with New York City.

I write about what I know, and that's definitely true when it come to New York. I've lived and worked as a journalist (*New York Post*, *New York Daily News*, *Star* magazine, NBC News) in this city for most of my adult life—and the locations in *It's News to Me* are very familiar to me.

I worked at 30 Rock (for NBC News) where Clare likes to go for drinks; same with the area around the South Street Seaport (for the *New York Post*) where she goes for dinner; and I have lived for many years in the Union Square neighborhood of Manhattan just as Clare does.

The crime scene in this book—and much of the action—takes place around Washington Square Park in Greenwich Village on the campus of a school called Easton College. Yes, I know it sounds

like NYU, which is in the same area, but Easton is a totally ficti-
tious place. What is real is the neighborhood around Easton with
familiar spots like Bleecker Street and MacDougal and other
Village locations. It's a beautiful part of New York, which is why I
thought it was the ideal place for the brutal, horrible, senseless
murder of Riley Hunt.

The main trip Clare takes outside New York is to Ohio, and I'm
pretty damn familiar with Ohio too. It's my own home state. I come
from Cleveland (the same place as Clare in the books), but I worked
at a newspaper in Dayton—which I made Riley Hunt's hometown
and where I set major scenes between Clare and Riley's mother,
family, and friends.

*   *   *

But the biggest element of authenticity I believe that I bring to the
Clare Carlson books is my description of what it's like to work in a
New York City newsroom.

Some people have asked me if there could really be a boss as crazy
and clueless and cutthroat as Susan Endicott.

Or feuding news stars who take out their bedroom frustrations
in front of the whole office like Brett and Dani.

Or reporters like Janelle Wright or Cassie O'Neal or Wendy
Jeffers or Steve Stratton with all their issues and problems and
insecurities.

My answer is yes.

I've worked in a lot of crazy newsrooms with people like that.

And sometimes even crazier.

*   *   *

But the most realistic thing to me about *It's News to Me*—and the other books in the series—is Clare Carlson herself.

Clare is a terrific journalist. A great boss. A brilliant, savvy woman who is at the top of her career. But at the same time the rest of her life is a disaster. Because she makes a lot of bad personal decisions; because she constantly puts her job as a priority over everything else; and because she . . . well, she can't keep her mouth shut sometimes when she needs to.

Readers always want to know if Clare Carlson is based on any real woman I worked with in the New York City media. And my answer is always the same. Yes. She's based on many of the fascinating women journalists from newsrooms where I have been over the years. Believe me, I've known a lot of Clare Carlsons in my life.

Terrific in many ways, but flawed too.

I think that's the reason—she's a fun, interesting character, but definitely not perfect—so many readers can relate to Clare.

And why they like her.

Hey, I like Clare too.

And, most of all, I like writing about her.

I hope to keep writing about Clare Carlson chasing after more big stories for a long time.

PUBLISHER'S NOTE

WE HOPE THAT you enjoyed *It's News to Me,* the fifth novel in R. G. Belsky's Clare Carlson Mystery Series. Clare is a smart, feisty, and certainly tenacious reporter who has tackled more than her fair share of formidable challenges in her career as a journalist and the manager of a NYC TV news channel. And R. G. Belsky has been chronicling them in this series.

While all five novels stand on their own and can be read in any order, the publication sequence of the first four is as follows:

Yesterday's News

"Tell me what happened to my daughter?" For fifteen years this anguished plea has haunted reporter Clare Carlson

"Belsky's *Yesterday's News* elicits all parents' deepest fear—the disappearance of a child. But this intelligent, gripping novel is about so much more: ambition, secrets, and, most shocking of all, truth."

—REED FARREL COLEMAN,
New York Times best-selling author

Below the Fold

"Murdered on the streets of New York: a homeless woman who called herself Cinderella—and how quickly the tragic murder of a 'nobody' falls *below the fold*

"In an era of 'fake news' and political attacks on the free press, reporter-turned-TV news director Clare Carlson personifies the best in journalism—tenacious, honest, and relentless in her pursuit of the truth and to giving a voice to those who can't speak for themselves."

—LEE GOLDBERG,
New York Times best-selling author

The Last Scoop

"News director Clare Carlson stumbles onto a serial killer no one knew was there— and no one can stop her from pursing the killer, exposing the truth, and finding justice for her beloved mentor

"Clare, the news director of a New York City TV station, looks into the death of retired journalist Marty Barlow, her friend and mentor when she was a cub reporter. Marty stopped by her office one day recently to tell her he was working on the biggest story of his life. Before they could meet up to discuss it in depth, Marty was killed in an apparent random mugging. Clare, however, believes his death is the result of his research into a possible serial killer, and she soon realizes that this could be the biggest story of her career as well."

—Publishers Weekly

Beyond the Headlines

"She was a mega-celebrity—he was a billionaire businessman—now he's dead—she's in jail.

"In *Beyond the Headlines*, Laurie Bateman, supermodel, actress, and the wife of an incredibly wealthy businessman, finds herself arrested for his murder. Television reporter Clare Carlson arrives at the jail to do an emotional and exclusive interview and instead finds herself caught up in proving Laurie's innocence."   *—Partners in Crime*

Thanks for reading *It's News to Me*. We hope that you will read all the Clare Carlson Mysteries and enjoy Clare's heroics as a journalist and news manager as well as her quirky, effervescent humor, and of course, her signature tenacity and integrity.

For more information, please visit the author's website: www.rgbelsky.com.

Happy Reading

Oceanview Publishing